THE CRAWLING DARKNESS

ELLIE JORDAN, GHOST TRAPPER, BOOK THREE

by

J.L. Bryan

Published 2015
JLBryanbooks.com

ISBN-10: 1505959713
ISBN-13: 978-1505959710

Acknowledgments

I appreciate everyone who has helped with this book. My beta readers include authors Daniel Arenson and Robert Duperre, as well as Isalys Blackwell from the blog Book Soulmates. The final proofing was done by Thelia Kelly. The cover is by PhatPuppy Art. Most of all, I appreciate the book bloggers and readers who keep coming back for more! The book bloggers who've supported me over the years include Danny, Heather, and Heather from Bewitched Bookworks; Mandy from I Read Indie; Michelle from Much Loved Books; Shirley from Creative Deeds; Katie and Krisha from Inkk Reviews; Lori from Contagious Reads; Heather from Buried in Books; Kristina from Ladybug Storytime; Chandra from Unabridged Bookshelf; Kelly from Reading the Paranormal; AimeeKay from Reviews from My First Reads Shelf and Melissa from Books and Things; Kristin from Blood, Sweat, and Books; Aeicha from Word Spelunking; Lauren from Lose Time Reading; Kat from Aussie Zombie; Andra from Unabridged Andralyn; Jennifer from A Tale of Many Reviews; Giselle from Xpresso Reads; Ash from Smash Attack Reads; Ashley from Bookish Brunette; Loretta from Between the Pages; Ashley from Bibliophile's Corner; Lili from Lili Lost in a Book; Line from Moonstar's Fantasy World; Lindsay from The Violet Hour; Rebecca from Bending the Spine; Holly from Geek Glitter; Louise from Nerdette Reviews; Isalys from Book Soulmates; Jennifer from The Feminist Fairy; Heidi from Rainy Day Ramblings; Kristilyn from Reading in Winter; Kelsey from Kelsey's Cluttered Bookshelf; Lizzy from Lizzy's Dark Fiction; Shanon from Escaping with Fiction; Savannah from Books with Bite; Tara from Basically Books; Toni from My Book Addiction; Abbi from Book Obsession; Laura from FUONLYKNEW; Lake from Lake's Reads; Jenny from Jenny on the Book; and anyone else I missed!

Also by J.L. Bryan:

For Christina

Chapter One

"So, spill already," I told Stacey. We had an appointment with a possible client in fifteen minutes, and we'd just stopped for fair-trade, organic, cruelty-free, artisan-brewed, Third-World-enriching coffee at The Sentient Bean by Forsyth Park. Since I hadn't brought my own mug, I'd paid the environmental surcharge for a biodegradable to-go cup.

"Spill what?" Stacey asked, sipping her iced chai concoction. Summer was in full bloom in Savannah, and we'd all be roasted alive if not for the towering trees, the live oak trunks lining the streets like thick columns, supporting the cooling canopy of leaf and moss that blocks out the searing sky above.

Of course, there's also the humidity, which just makes the heat sizzle, my mom used to say.

"Come on, Stacey," I said. "Last time I saw you, you were getting ready for your date with Jacob. I haven't heard from you all weekend. So...nothing to talk about?"

"I didn't think you'd want to hear me gab about my dates," Stacey said.

"After I spent fifteen entire seconds giving you advice about what to wear? I'm invested now."

Stacey leaned back in her seat, smiling. She's a pretty girl, with her blond pixie-cut hair and a body that's about what you'd expect from a girl who somehow believes that hiking and kayaking are fun weekend leisure activities, rather than the sweaty mosquito-filled nightmares they truly are. It hadn't taken a massive amount of flirting for her to grab the attention of Jacob Weiss, our new psychic consultant, a young accountant who happened to speak to the dead, but only reluctantly.

"It was fun," she said. "Blues concert in the park, dinner..."

"The two exact things I already knew..."

"He's funny," Stacey said. "I mean on the surface. He's smart. But you can tell there's a lot of stuff under there. When he doesn't know you're looking at him, his face is almost grim."

"He's been through a lot," I said. "The plane crash." Jacob had been one of a handful of survivors and awoken to find himself surrounded by the confused ghosts of dead airline passengers who'd been on the plane with him. That event had awoken his abilities to see and hear the dead.

"Did you know he lived in New York?" she asked. "He's from here, I mean his parents live in Savannah, but he went to school at NYU. He was working at a big firm up there, but he moved back home after the crash."

"Is he planning to move back?"

"I don't think he knows. He's kind of lost right now, I think. Who wouldn't be, after what he's been through? I asked him what it was like, hearing all those voices. He took me on a walk downtown, toward Colonial Park Cemetery, and he'd kind of trail his fingers along the outside of a house and tell me things about its history. Just glimpses. 'There was a girl here, she liked to whistle while she picked flowers, her mom would yell at her to stay out of the garden...' Things like that. Could you imagine going through life like that, seeing and hearing all those leftover memories of the dead?"

"It sounds distracting," I said. "How does he drive? Half these streets are built on top of old graves."

"I didn't ask." Stacey snickered. "It does sound crazy."

"So you had a nice dinner and talked about dead people," I

said. "And then?"

"And then?" Stacey raised her eyebrows. "Who says there's an 'and then'? Or that it would be any of your business?"

"So there *was* an 'and then'?"

Stacey blushed. "Okay...maybe he kissed me. That's it. He was a total gentleman, too, with opening doors and stuff. He even pulled out my chair at supper. Who does that anymore?"

"Sounds like he was well-trained by his mom. So are you going out again?"

"I think so. Whoa, check out the giant evil dollhouse." Stacey pointed.

I parked our detective agency's blue cargo van on the street near the new client's house. Stacey's description was apt. We were looking at a towering three-story Victorian, mostly in the style they call Queen Anne—living in Savannah and investigating lots of old haunted houses, you start to learn a few things about architectural style.

The house was stone at the foundations, solid brick on the first floor, and mostly wood by the time you reached the third floor. It had that crazy Queen Anne shape, with bay windows and gables jutting out on every side, and sunken porches like dark caves fronted with ornate wrought-iron railings—you almost thought a bear or a wolf would stalk forward and peer out through the railing like a zoo animal in a cage. A window-lined turret jutted skyward at one corner, and a matching turret roof capped the corner of the enormous wraparound porch, which ran across the front of the house and out of sight down one side.

Elaborately lathed gingerbread-style balusters, spindling, and overhang lay everywhere, and these would have lent the house a charming look if they hadn't been painted dark red, barely visible against the dark earth tones of the house and trim.

"Needs more pink," Stacey said. "And yellow. If you just painted it in cheerful colors, it would be so much prettier. Why spend a billion dollars on a house like this and then make it ugly?"

I didn't reply. My eyes had fallen on another house, visible over brick walls and high wrought-iron fences. It sat on the next street over, behind and one house down from our potential clients. Moss and ivy had nearly swallowed the massive old trees on the lot, making them look like giant monsters wrapped in shrouds.

That other house was tall and narrow, four stories of white

brick gone dingy and yellow with age. All the windows and doors were boarded up, giving it the blind look of a mausoleum.

I knew that house. Calvin and I had been hired to remove a very nasty sort of ghost from it about eighteen months earlier.

We'd failed miserably.

Now I saw the fate of that house—sealed up, bank-owned, dead to the world. I thought about the family who'd lived there. The Wilsons. Nice family, husband and wife, four young kids. Driven to insanity and grief.

"What's up?" Stacey followed my look. "Creepy place. Been there?"

"Yes."

"Not for a pleasant Christmas party, I'm guessing?"

"No."

"Feel like offering multiple syllables at once?" Stacey asked.

"Not really. Let's get to work." I climbed out of the van, grabbing my black toolbox while Stacey shouldered her camera bag.

Happily, Stacey didn't press me about the Wilson house. There was hardly time to fill her in on that old case before we spoke with our new client. It gave me the chills, though, visiting a house so close to that one. The back corners of their lots actually touched.

I was suddenly extremely interested to hear what our prospective client had to say. And I was worried for our safety.

We passed a cluster of four mailboxes, labeled A through D. The old Queen Anne mansion had been subdivided into apartments. Judging by the mailbox clusters up and down the street, so had a few others in the neighborhood.

The front steps led us up about half a story to the front porch itself, which was wide enough to host a large crowd, provided they didn't mind sitting in rickety old rocking chairs. A porch swing hung at the flared round corner of the wraparound porch, under the conical turret roof, its chains flaky with rust.

A brass letter "A" was nailed to the front door, which was inset with panes of colored glass and flanked by more colored-glass panes on either side. I rang the bell, half-expecting it to sound like the Addams family door chime.

The woman who opened the door was about my age or a little

older—early thirties, tops. She was an attractive African-American woman, her hair done in a hundred tiny braids and pulled back into a ponytail. She wore scorching-weather-appropriate denim shorts and a tank top.

"Are you..." She looked us over in our unseasonably heavy clothes. I've been scratched, bitten, burned, and thrown down enough stairs that I wear turtlenecks and my leather jacket when entering a new haunted house, regardless of the heat. Survival before comfort. And let's just forget altogether about fashion.

"I'm Ellie Jordan, lead investigator with Eckhart Investigations," I said. "This is Stacey Ray Tolbert, my tech manager."

"Just call me Stacey!" Stacey smiled.

"Are you Alicia Rogers?" I asked. "We spoke on the phone."

"Come on in," she said, but she sounded guarded and gave us a suspicious look. Perfectly normal. Clients spend our first meeting trying to assess whether we're scam artists or real ghost-removal experts. I spend the first meeting trying to assess whether the client seems sane or not, so that's fair. A number of people who call us have mental disorders, not ghosts—it's their neurons rather than their houses that are haunted.

Of course, living with a troublesome ghost can also *make* you crazy, so I have to judge carefully.

Alicia led us into a grand foyer, dominated on one side by a long staircase running straight up to the second floor without making a turn. The staircase was solid dark mahogany, the railing as ornately lathed as the gingerbread spindling outside the house. The ceiling, two stories above us, was patterned in alternating dark and blond wood, with a red geometrical shape suggesting a rose at the center. A four-level antique chandelier hung from the center of the rose design.

The colored-glass windows flooded the front room with light. While it had been built as an impressive entrance to the enormous house, it looked like Alicia used it as a living room. A sectional couch faced a TV screen hung on the wall next to the large, ornate fireplace, which had been constructed with three different colors of brick in an alternating pattern.

"Gorgeous place!" Stacey said.

"It's just a rental. So, y'all really do this?" Alicia looked at me, crossing her arms. "You can take ghosts out of people's homes?"

"In most cases," I said. "You didn't give me a lot of details on the phone." Like, zero details. "What kind of disturbance have you had?"

"Disturbance," she nodded. "That's a good word for it. My kids saw it first." She pointed upstairs. "Up in their rooms. First Mia, then Kalil. Then me." She added the last in a soft, troubled voice.

"How old are your kids?" I asked.

"Kalil's eleven, Mia's nine."

"How long have you lived here?"

"About six or seven months. We moved here a few months after my husband died. I couldn't afford the old place anymore."

"I'm sorry," I said.

"Drunk driver," she said. "We had to move to a smaller place. I know this room doesn't look small, but it's really most of the apartment. My room's through there." She nodded at a closed door near the foot of the stairs. "Kitchen's back there, kids are upstairs...and that's all there is to the apartment. We were lucky we could afford anything, and the rent was so low. I thought it would be a new start for us. Listen to me ramble on. So how does this work?"

"We can start by looking at the places where paranormal activities have been witnessed," I said.

"The hauntspots," Stacey said, and I wanted to give her an annoyed scowl. She'd made up that word and was trying to make it stick.

"Yes...where should we start?" I asked. "Where was the activity first witnessed?"

"Mia's room. Come on." Alicia led us up the stairs. Along the way, I noticed pictures on the wall—a young girl in a ballerina costume, a boy with strap-on glasses wearing a karate outfit. A family portrait showed Alicia next to a broad-shouldered, smiling man I assumed to be her deceased husband.

The family photos were interspersed with paintings—brightly colored swamps at sunset, jazz men on distinctly French Quarter street corners.

"Are these from New Orleans?" I asked.

"Oh, yes." Alicia smiled a little, looking back over her shoulder. "Gerard was from Louisiana, and we used to go to New Orleans for

Jazz Fest every year, before the kids were born." She smiled, very slightly, and continued up to the top of the stairs.

The upstairs hallway was as luxurious in construction as the rest of the house—high molding engraved with intricate little leaves, paneled walls alternating between dark and light wood, polished hardwood floors.

The hallway had clearly been truncated when the house was divided into apartments. It was short, with just a few doors.

"I told you there wasn't much to the apartment," Alicia said. "Up here, it's just the two kids' rooms, a bath, a linen closet. Apartment B has the rest of the second floor. They've got half the first floor, too. Hard to imagine one family needing this whole house for themselves back in the day."

She led us into a room that clearly belonged to a young girl, the pink bedspread fluffy and lacy and home to a nest of plush giraffes and pigs. Like the rest of the home, it was spotless and tidy, the toys, books, and dolls stacked away in cubbyhole shelving, organized by type. A big mirror, its frame pink and engraved with flowers, reflected the tall arched window, which was trimmed in smaller panes of colored glass. Cheerful Disney-animal prints hung on the bright yellow walls.

"This is Mia's room," Alicia said. "She saw it first."

"What did she see?" I asked.

"The Closet Man. That's what she called him." Alicia approached the closet, which had a pair of narrow double doors that slid aside into wall pockets.

The closet was deep and narrow, like a short hallway. The walls were rough brick instead of the smooth yellow-painted surfaces of the bed room, the floor sunken so I had to step down as I entered it. Old houses are full of weird, unexpected features like that.

Dresses and jeans were arrayed neatly down one side of the closet, completely sorted and separated by type, and I'm pretty sure the blouses and dresses were in ROYGBV rainbow order by color, too.

My Mel Meter spiked up to six milligaus as I passed through the door—a very high reading, especially on a bright summer day.

"Your daughter certainly keeps things organized," I said. "You said she was nine?"

"Mia?" Alicia laughed. "That girl will have this room trashed in three minutes after she gets home from her friend's house. Kalil's the neat one. This is my work, thank you."

I laughed. "Of course, it's normal for kids to be afraid of the closet, but this closet is particularly unusual. I could see it stirring anyone's imagination."

"That's what I thought," Alicia said. "That's what any parent would think. Closet Monster Syndrome, my mother called it. She would prescribe 200 cc's of hot chocolate, followed by bed rest." Alicia smiled. "She was a nurse, too."

"Is that what you do?" I asked.

"Over at St. Joseph's." Alicia nodded. "They've been putting me on afternoon shifts, so I come home late and don't get to see my kids much, which makes all this even harder on everybody..."

"What exactly did your daughter see? How does she describe the Closet Man?" I asked.

"She said he was a man with no face. He'd watch her from the closet while she was in bed. She always wants the closet doors pulled tight, with no gap in between. But she says he opens the doors sometimes—just a little bit, just enough to watch her."

"Creepy," Stacey said, shivering.

"Have you ever seen that happen?" I asked.

"No, but I've had a few nights where I closed the doors for her, then later she screams," Alicia said. "I'll come in and the doors will be open just a little bit. She always swore she hadn't done it herself, but of course I didn't believe her, or I thought her brother must have done it. I don't believe in ghosts. Well, I *didn't* before all this."

"When did Mia start seeing him?" I asked.

"A few months after we moved in. I understood she was scared —she'd just lost her father. We were all having nightmares. I thought that was all..." She shook her head. "For a long time, all he did was open the closet and look at her. Then it changed. She started saying he'd open the doors all the way and stare at her. Then he started coming into her room—by then, he wasn't Closet Man anymore. He was Fleshface."

"Like the horror movies?" Stacey asked.

"Just like those," Alicia said. "One night, Kalil smuggled home his friend's DVD of *Fleshface II: Flesh and Bones*. Kalil's not allowed to watch scary movies, he gets enough bad dreams as it is. And he's one hundred percent not allowed to show anything scary to his little sister. And don't you know that boy not only watched the movie in his room, but he let his sister see it, too? My aunt was in town watching them, and she'd fallen asleep downstairs. I was ready to smack that boy when I found out." Alicia shook her head. "Since then, it hasn't been Closet Man, it's been Fleshface. And Fleshface comes all the way into her room, sometimes. She's even woken up with him standing by her bed."

"And he looks just like the movie monster?" I asked. I had serious crawling-flesh feelings now. Was the old monster finally back? I tried to push aside thoughts of that old case, but I couldn't help it. The house was right next door—well, catty-corner, anyway, the back corners of the two lots just touching each other.

"That's what she says," Alicia told me. "Just like Fleshface."

"That must be scary." I hadn't seen *Fleshface II* (or *Fleshface I*, for that matter) but I'd seen the movie poster at the theater. It looked like your basic knock-off of *Friday the 13th* or *Texas Chainsaw Massacre*, a serial killer guy in front of an old cabin in the woods. He wore a mask that was apparently made of strips of skin glued together mummy-fashion, leaving only his eyes bare, and he wielded a chainsaw, in a clear stroke of complete unoriginality by the filmmakers. "Has he ever hurt Mia? Ever touched her?"

"He's pulled the blankets off her," Alicia said. "Just one more thing I didn't believe was supernatural. She screams, I run upstairs to check on her, and she says Fleshface pulled the blankets and sheets and threw them on the floor. Of course, when that started, I still didn't believe her. I thought she just had a nightmare and kicked off her own blankets."

"Of course," I said. "How often does she see him? How many times a month?"

"It was only every once in a while, at first," Alicia said. She hugged herself as if cold. "Gotten a lot worse lately."

"And he always comes out of this closet?" I asked.

Alicia nodded. "That's what Mia says. Kalil has seen it from his closet and from his bathroom door, too. One time he saw it looking in his window." Alicia opened another door, opposite from Mia's closet, and led us into a connecting bathroom. Again, it was spotless and gleaming. Even the toothbrushes, Aquafresh Kids pump, floss, and so on were arranged in a perfectly straight row on the marble counter. I wondered whether Alicia kept the house this immaculate every day. It seemed like a ton of work.

The bathroom led into the boy's room, decorated with posters of the solar system and the Milky Way. An autographed photo of Neil DeGrasse Tyson hung in a frame on the wall, next to family photos, and a few math and science trophies adorned the dresser. A model space shuttle was partially constructed on the desk. She told me the boy was away at some kind of math day camp.

"You said Kalil sees Fleshface watching him from this door, too?" I asked, swinging the bathroom door open and closed, as if that were going to tell me something.

"That door and the closet," Alicia said, and Stacey panned her camera around toward the closet door. Unlike the one in Mia's room, this seemed like a normal hinged door. Alicia opened it, showing us a phone-booth-sized closet crammed full of winter clothes.

"Boys don't need as much closet space," Stacey said, and Alicia nodded.

"How long has he been seeing the monster?" I asked. My Mel Meter again showed a spike of activity right at the closet door.

"I don't know. For months," Alicia said. She took a breath, hesitated, then let out a sigh, as if coming to a decision. "Kalil doesn't see Fleshface, though."

"What does he see?"

"He sees...little men. With big black eyes." She shook her head. "Aliens. He sees aliens in his closet."

"Whoa, like little gray guys?" Stacey asked.

"Those. I told him to stop watching those alien-abduction shows on the History Channel, because I thought they were giving him nightmares. I know it doesn't make any sense. I believe in aliens even less than I believe in ghosts, but he's terrified of them." She shook her head. "I'm not saying they're really Martians or anything. That's just what he sees."

"So he sees his own fears personified," I said, feeling myself tremble. This was sounding more and more like the Wilson case. "It certainly fits with his interest in outer space."

"Oh, he loves astronomy. I'm hoping to save up and get him a good telescope for Christmas, but..." Alicia shrugged. "We'll see how that one crumbles."

"What do the aliens do?" I asked.

"He says they usually just watch him from the closet, or they crack open the bathroom door and watch through there. Or he wakes up and one is standing over his bed, like it's studying him. It sounds like all those alien-abduction stories, which is why I thought he was just watching too much TV..."

"What changed your mind?"

"He woke up with scratches on his arm," Alicia said. "I still thought he'd done it in his sleep, but he kept talking about the gray aliens. Now I thought it was something serious, you know, a mental health issue. I had him evaluated, and they diagnosed him with ADHD and sleep disorder. He's on Ritalin and melatonin, but it hasn't helped with the monsters. Now I understand why."

Alicia led us out into the short hallway and fell silent, staring at another door near the end. It was round at the top, set into a decorative archway trimmed in tiny engraved geometric patterns.

"What's through there?" I asked.

"Nothing," she said, hugging her arms close against her again.

"An empty room?" Stacey asked.

"Not even that. That's where I've seen him come and go. Three times, now." Alicia shivered. The hallway did feel a bit colder now, despite the light from the tall windows trimmed in smaller colored-glass panes. "The first time, I was downstairs in my room, sleeping, and I heard Mia scream. I thought, 'Oh, Lord, here goes another nightmare.' It was late—one-thirty-seven in the morning, I remember looking at my clock. So I went upstairs to check on her.

"The house felt so cold that night. I thought I'd check the thermostat once I got Mia settled, make sure we weren't blowing up the electric bill. This was just a couple of months ago, near the end of May.

"So I'm barefoot and wearing my summer nightdress, and I'm freezing by the time I get to the top of the stairs. That's when I saw him. He came out through Mia's door." Alicia pointed to the girl's room.

"Was the door open or closed?" I asked.

"Open a little bit. Kalil, he won't sleep with any doors open—the closet, bathroom, and hallway door all have to be shut tight. Mia likes to keep her hallway door open so she can yell for me. Sleeps with a nightlight, but it burns out or just goes off for no reason, almost every night. It's not natural."

"Ghosts don't like too much light," I said. "A surge of photons messes with their electromagnetic fields. That's why they mostly come out at night."

Alicia nodded. "If you say so. It was dark that night, the hall lights were off, and I don't even think there was much moonlight. I couldn't see him very well, and he was like a heavy dark shadow, with no face, just like Mia used to say. The Closet Man." She looked up at the crown molding and light-and-dark patterned wood ceiling over the girl's door.

"What did he do?" I asked.

"He climbed up out the top of Mia's door." Alicia pointed to the top of the door frame. "He scrambled up the wall and along the ceiling. He was shaped like a man, I mean two arms, two legs, but he didn't *move* like any man. He crawled like a spider. His arms and legs kind of bent the wrong way. He was upside down, moving fast, and of course he gave me a bad feeling. I was horrified and felt sick all through my body. I knew I was looking at something evil, something that shouldn't be in this world." She wiped sweat from her forehead with trembling fingers.

"It sounds disturbing," I said.

"It was a long way beyond *disturbing*," she said. "He climbed on down the hall, and then he slipped into that door." She again nodded at the mysterious closed door nested in its ornate archway.

"Do you mind if I open it?" I asked. I still wasn't clear what she meant when she said there was *nothing* beyond the door.

"Go ahead." She backed away toward the steps, arms crossed. "It doesn't usually come out during the day."

"That's reassuring," I said. The door handle was a curved brass lever placed high on the door, about shoulder-height to me. I gripped it and turned, trying to prepare myself for the nameless cosmic horrors that lay beyond.

The door opened onto nothing. By that, I mean a smooth, flat piece of wall, painted a stark white, with none of the paneled wainscoting that adorned the rest of the hallway.

I blinked at it. The sheer blankness of it made me stupid, somehow, like my brain stopped functioning for a few seconds to focus its entire attention on processing what I was seeing.

"Yeah," I finally said. "Nothing."

"They must have left it here when they split the house into apartments," Alicia said. "I don't know why they would just leave a useless door like that."

"Maybe because of this sweet arch around it." Stacey pointed to the intricate hardwood trim. "They left it for decoration."

"Maybe," Alicia said. "I sure wish they hadn't. Would you mind closing that when you're done?"

"Sure." I shut the door. "Was it open or shut when he crawled inside it?"

"Shut."

"What did you do next?"

"I ran to check on Mia. My baby was so scared. Talking about Fleshface again."

"Did you come back and check the door?" I asked.

"After I got her calmed down, I made myself come out here and open it. There wasn't anything to see. I took Mia downstairs to sleep with me that night. By the morning, I told myself I'd just let my imagination get away with me. I was probably still half-dreaming when I went up those stairs."

"Do you have any idea what's on the other side of this wall?"

"Apartment B. The Fieldings. That's all I know."

"You said you encountered the entity again?" I asked.

"Come on downstairs," Alicia said, wasting no time descending the steps. "I'll show you."

Stacey and I shared a worried look. This was no simple nuisance ghost or residual haunting. The entire household was living in fear of a very creepy-sounding entity.

I couldn't wait to find it and eliminate it. Ghosts who threaten children have a special place in my heart—a place filled with malice and hate.

We followed Alicia down the stairs.

Chapter Two

"The second time, I saw him right here. Another late night."
Alicia pointed over the railing as we descended. "He crawled
alongside the bannister. He looked the same way. No face, shaped
like the shadow of a man. His arms and limbs bending strangely. He
climbed about halfway down the stairs, then he turned and went
straight down the wall."

Alicia led us to the hallway that ran across the back of the
entrance hall. It was really more of an open arcade, supported by a
row of cherry-wood archways. One side of the hall opened into a
kitchen with a large bay window, a row of throw pillows arranged
neatly on the window seat.

The other end of the hall terminated at three doors—left, right,
and center.

Alicia pointed to the left. "This one leads to the hallway we all
share, because it has the only staircase to the basement. The laundry
machines are down there. At one time, I thought that was the main
reason the rent was so cheap, because everybody has to go and do

their laundry in the basement." Alicia let out a little humorless laugh.

"That one leads to my bathroom," she continued. "My bedroom used to be the front parlor, I think, back when it was all one big house with one rich family. But now, this door..." She pointed to the one on our right. "That's where I think he really goes."

"His lair?" I asked.

"Yeah. That's a good word for it," Alicia said. She opened the door, revealing a flight of stairs that ran underneath the main staircase. It was blocked off by cardboard boxes about halfway down.

"Where do those stairs lead?" I asked.

"I guess they used to go to the basement, but they're sealed off now," Alicia said. "That's Mr. Gray's apartment down there. We just use this stairwell for a storage closet."

I peered down the dead-end basement steps, illuminating them with my flashlight. My Mel Meter found yet another spike of energy right at the doorway.

"When I saw him climbing down the wall, he left through here," Alicia continued. "First he looked at me, though. He froze, like a cockroach when you flick on the lights, like he didn't expect to see me. His head turned sideways at me, and his neck twisted in a way...a living person couldn't do that. He kind of stared at me with that blank shadow face. Then he scuttled away inside, even though the door was closed."

"He goes from closet to closet," I said.

"Another night, I woke up from a bad dream and went to the kitchen for some water. When I was coming back, I saw him right here, crawling toward *this* door again. Well, he jumped right off the wall, right at me...and right *through* me," Alicia said. "I felt so sick I thought I would die. I got dizzy and nauseated and almost fell over.

"He slipped right through that door and out of sight," she said. "It was a minute before I saw my dress was torn and bloody. They say piranhas can eat your fingers so surgically you won't even know they're missing until you see the blood. That's what this was like." Alicia lifted the front of her shirt, showing us three long, scabby scratch marks across her stomach. "I was bleeding all over and didn't even know it. I can't tell you how scared I was. I work the ER, I'm used to blood, but there was no reason for me to be cut up like that. It meant the ghost was real, not just in our heads.

"I looked in on the kids—good thing they were sleeping and didn't see me like that. I cleaned up, and I just sat out here on the couch, shaking, for the rest of the night. I was scared it would come back and hurt the kids. I was too scared to open the door and go after it, and what could I have done?" Tears glistened in her eyes and she wiped them away. "That's when I knew I had to do something. Bring in some experts. And now you're here. So can you get rid of it?"

"We usually can remove unwanted entities," I said. Stacey gave me a look, either hearing the tremble in my voice or noticing something about the expression on my face. My confidence was crumbling fast.

I kept to my usual script with Alicia, though, mainly because it was the best way to keep myself composed.

"We're going to need to study your situation a little more," I said. "Have you told us everything you've experienced?"

"That's all we've seen so far," she said.

"You mentioned a laundry room in the basement. Have you ever seen or heard anything strange down there?"

"I never liked the basement," she said. "Always feels like somebody's watching you. At first, I thought it was just because it's such a dim, ugly place. It's also right next to Mr. Gray's apartment, so maybe that had something to do with it—Mr. Gray could just walk through the door at any time. I always thought it was just my nerves or my imagination bothering me, but I never went down there during the day. And after this..." She gestured at her stomach. "I trust my instincts more. Could be something there. I'll show you."

Alicia unlocked the door across from the dead-end basement stairs. She led us into a short, paneled side hall. An ornate Victorian door, trimmed in panes of colored glass and surrounded by windows, looked out on the side portion of the wraparound porch. The hallway had three interior doors, including the one from Alicia's apartment and another directly across the hall, which led to another apartment, labeled with a big brass "B."

"Here it is." Alicia opened the third door, the one to the basement. Old wooden stairs led down into a dark, humid brick chamber with a row of three coin-operated washing machines facing three dryers. One dryer chugged and rattled, with an occasional hard thumping sound like there was a shoe inside. A couple of hanging fluorescent bars cast weak, sour light that left much of the room in shadow.

"It's cold," I said, feeling the cool air as I stood in the doorway.

Alicia nodded, keeping her distance from the door after opening it.

"That's weird for a laundry room," Stacey said.

I felt sick and afraid as I looked into the darkness of the basement. It wasn't just fear, it was dread, the deep certainty that something horrible was about to happen.

Something horrible already had, I supposed—the monster had returned.

I pointed my flashlight down the steps, but had no real desire to descend into the basement just yet. It might be down there...and it might remember me.

"Have you asked your landlord whether anyone else has had these experiences?" I asked. "Or if there's any dark history to the house?" Last time, Calvin and I had been unable to determine the identity of the ghost—if it had a human identity at all. It might have been what Calvin called a *demonic*, a theoretical intelligent spirit that had never been born into flesh.

"Oh, I called the property manager," Alicia said with a scowl. "I told him what was happening, and he implied it was all a mental-health issue on my end. Only he didn't say it that nice. He called me hysterical and reminded me illegal drugs aren't allowed in the building." She shook her head, a little snarl forming at the corner of her lips. "I'm trying to save up enough money to move, but there's not much to spare. The rent's cheap, but there's a big penalty for breaking the lease."

"What about your neighbors? Have they seen anything?" I asked.

"I don't know the Fieldings or Mr. Gray very much. We hardly talk," Alicia said. "I suppose we could ask Michael and Melissa." Alicia pointed up the staircase behind her.

"Do they have any kids?" I asked.

"I would hope not! They're brother and sister. Melissa is seventeen, and she watches my kids sometimes. We can see if Michael's home."

"That would be great," I said.

Alicia led the way up the dark hardwood stairs, the antique grain absorbing the light from the windows alongside them. We crossed a second-floor landing, where there was nothing but a single closed door. She told me it led to the Fieldings' apartment, and they probably left it locked all the time. It looked like the area around the door had been sealed off long after the house was built—the wall was blank and white instead of paneled with wood.

Two more flights brought us up to another small landing, where there was nothing but a single door. A brass letter "C" hung beside it.

Alicia knocked. After a minute, she knocked again, then shrugged.

"He's probably at work," Alicia said. "He's a firefighter and an EMT, works twelve-hour shifts at the station."

"A fireman and a medic?" Stacey's eyebrows raised. "Is he cute?"

"Stacey." I shook my head.

"Hey, just asking."

"Do you have any idea why they don't live with their parents?" I asked.

"The parents are gone," Alicia said. "Father ran off, mother passed away. Michael's taken care of Melissa since then."

"Aw, and he takes care of his little sister?" Stacey asked. "He sounds great."

"Stacey, aren't you dating Jacob?" I asked.

"One date. We haven't talked exclusivity..." She glanced at Alicia and blushed. "Uh, anyway..."

"He helps us out, fixing things around our apartment. Electricity, plumbing...thank goodness, because I can barely get the property manager to return my calls when something breaks."

"So he's good with his hands," Stacey said. "Wait, are you like, romantically involved with him, Alicia?"

Alicia shook her head. "Nice guy, just...not my type."

"Next time you see Michael and Melissa, can you ask them to speak with us?" I asked.

"I certainly will."

As we descended the stairs again, I was deep in thought, worried about how we would handle this case. It sounded like the same entity from the Wilson house had slipped over into this apartment building. It had bested us last time, so what could we do now?

I needed to talk it over with Calvin, urgently. And Stacey needed to be brought up to speed.

"Mrs. Rogers," I said when we reached the ground floor, "I think we might have some insight into what's happening here, but I want to do some research and get back with you. We also need to schedule an overnight observation." *Which will hopefully show that I'm wrong about all of this*, I thought. "We can do it as soon as it's convenient for you, but I recommend we get moving as soon as possible."

"I agree with that," Alicia said.

"We'll have to come in and set up cameras, microphones, and other gear around your apartment," I said.

"Do it as soon as you can," she said. "I'm about to lose my mind here."

"Anybody would feel that way after what you've been through," I told her. "We can start tonight."

Alicia agreed. She led us out to the front porch, and I walked to the corner and pointed to the boarded-up Wilson house. "Have you or your kids ever gone over to that house?"

"That scary old place? They better not have," Alicia asked. "Why? Is it haunted?"

"It has a history of being haunted," I said. "We've investigated it before."

"What happened?" Alicia asked.

"The entity vanished without a trace before I could trap it," I said.

"Wish this one would do the same," Alicia said. "It can start vanishing anytime it likes."

I gave her a laugh. "We'll be in touch a little later today."

Stacey and I left the porch and returned to the van, where I stopped and grabbed a crowbar out of the back, adding it to my toolbox. Then I continued on down the sidewalk.

"Um, where are you going?" Stacey asked. "Aren't we leaving?"

"We're walking to the next block. I want a closer look at the Wilson house."

"Not that creepy tall one with the boarded-up windows?" Stacey asked.

"Exactly that one."

"Ugh," Stacey said. "I'd better bring a flashlight."

Chapter Three

The next street had large antique homes as well, set back behind ornate but mildly aggressive fences that seemed to dare you to try and climb over their black iron teeth.

The boarded-up old Wilson house loomed over the neighborhood like a blind watchtower, much taller than it was wide. Its yard was a crazed jungle of weeds and wildflowers under the thick shade of the trees.

The air felt chillier as we approached it.

"What exactly happened here?" Stacey whispered.

"The Wilsons," I said. "They experienced what Alicia was just talking about. Monsters in the closet. A shadowy crawling thing that can take the shape of your fears."

"And you didn't catch the ghost."

"We couldn't *identify* the ghost, so it was hard to trap. And then..."

"Yes? Still listening over here."

"I'll have to let Calvin tell you about that part," I said. "But this ghost was very dangerous. Not just psychokinetic, but psychotropic. Able to induce hallucinations."

"Sounds fun," Stacey said, her tone sarcastic. She looked up at the tall, sealed-up house and let out a slow sigh. "What kind of hallucinations?"

"Whatever you're afraid of." I walked along the fence, then glanced around to see whether anyone was watching. Of course, anybody could have been peering at us through their windows, but the only person on the street was a mail lady in a white Jeep. I waited for her to continue on down the block, then I set my toolbox on the ground.

The fence was about four feet high, the gate padlocked. It wasn't impossible to climb over—just very, very tricky, with the iron spikes all along the top. I placed the toe of my boot on the middle rail.

"Uh, Ellie? It looks like you're about to climb over that sharp fence, there. Am I seeing that wrong?" Stacey asked.

"Give me a boost," I said. "I'll be less likely to impale myself that way."

Stacey helped me over the fence, then handed me my toolbox. I stood in high, tangled weeds.

"You can stay here and keep watch," I told her.

"For what? Old ladies walking Yorkies?" Stacey handed me her camera bag, then vaulted easily over the fence.

"Show-off," I said.

"I did gymnastics in high school." She shrugged, then looked up at the house. "Seems even colder on this side of the fence. Probably just the extra shade, right?"

"Probably." I brought out my Mel-Meter to check the temperature and any electromagnetic fields in the area. As I walked slowly toward the front stoop, stepping over thorny invasive plants and hidden stones on the ground, the meter ticked just a little.

"Are we finding anything?" Stacey looked over my shoulder.

"Just a milligau or so, but even that's unusual. Considering the house looks abandoned and locked up, I'm doubting there's any electricity flowing into it." I glanced up at the power lines, as if that would give me some clues. It didn't, of course.

I walked slowly around the perimeter of the old house, trying to see if the readings picked up.

"So, what happened? They just abandoned the house?" Stacey

asked.

I didn't really want to talk about it, but I had no choice. She had to know what we were up against.

"We couldn't get rid of the ghost," I said. "We couldn't trap it, and it started to get very good at hiding from me...Finally the family fired us since we couldn't help. It kept going after their kids, and I guess they couldn't sell the house. They just packed up and left town."

"That must have been a serious haunting," Stacey said. "This house looks expensive."

"Very serious," I agreed. We walked along the side of the house, then around to the back. My Mel-Meter continued flickering, indicating some kind of activity within.

"So tell me about the ghost—hey, are you doing what I think you're doing?"

I'd brought out my crowbar and placed the flat end against the plywood covering a small window at the back of the house.

"Yep," I said. I pointed the end against the edge of the wood and the brick frame of the window sill, and I slapped my hand against the curved end of the bar, hammering it into place.

"So we *are* breaking and entering?" she asked.

"I just want a quick look around."

After many difficult and sweaty minutes of work, during which Stacey kept glancing around with a worried look on her face waiting for somebody to bust us, the slab of wood pried away with a crack and tumbled into the weeds below the window.

"Little harder than I expected," I said, using my shirt to wipe sweat from my face.

Stacey peered inside the open window, up on her tiptoes for a better view.

"Whoa, somebody wrecked this place," she said.

I looked in alongside her, shining my flashlight into a bare, dusty room where the walls and ceiling had been ripped open.

"It looks like thieves stripped out wiring and pipes to sell for scrap," I said. "That can happen when houses stand abandoned like this. I guess they boarded up the windows a little too late."

"Yeah, those plywood sheets really provide a lot of security," Stacey said, looking at the sheet of wood I'd just pried loose.

"Why don't you gymnast-vault on in there and have a look around?" I asked.

"By myself?" Stacey blanched. "In an abandoned old house?"

"What, are you scared of ghosts?" I asked.

"It's just..." She shook her head. "I never told you about the first time I ran into a ghost."

"It wasn't a college project thing you were shooting at Colonial Park Cemetery?" I asked. That was how Stacey had introduced herself to us, with video footage of ghosts from around the city. She'd told us that she'd caught one on camera by accident, then started intentionally pursuing them. With a regular camera, you're lucky to get a flicker of a shadow, maybe an orb or two. The amount she'd collected, and her obsession with finding more, had impressed my boss, Calvin Eckhart, who'd been looking for someone to help me in the field.

"No..." Stacey shook her head. "That was when I started collecting ghost images. Something else happened back home, when I was a kid."

"Tell me while we look around." I boosted myself up onto the window sill, then into the dark old house. Stacey followed me inside. I hadn't had any intention of sending her in alone.

"Where I grew up, right outside Montgomery, there was an old mansion like this. Well, not quite like this, not as tall, but it was a sprawling old antebellum place. Some parts of the roof had caved in, and it was so old, I can't believe any of it was still standing." Stacey swept her light through the dark room. We continued on into a hallway, and I watched my Mel-Meter for any increase in the electromagnetism around us. "I guess it used to be a plantation house, but most of the land around it was strip malls and stuff...but if you went deep enough into the woods, you could find it standing there, overgrown with thorns and poison ivy. A lot like this place."

I opened a closet door, and my Mel-Meter ticked up to two milligaus. A strong residual or a weak active presence.

"I'm guessing you went inside?" I asked.

"Yeah." Stacey stepped over a broken heap that might have been a wooden chair at some point in its existence. "Right before Halloween, what a shock. My brother was going with a couple of his friends—Kevin was thirteen, and I was eleven. Our older brother, Patrick, was in high school and busy with his own friends.

Kevin didn't want me to come either, but I threatened to tell our parents where he was going if he didn't take me with him."

"Bratty little sister," I said.

"Exactly." Stacey said it with a weak half-smile. "So we broke in there that night—well, we didn't really have to break in, because the back door was missing. The place was all in ruins, all rotten inside. The floors creaked and groaned like it was fixing to collapse under our feet, and there were a couple of big holes where you could fall through into the foundation, or whatever was under the house. We didn't have great flashlights like this." She waved her heavy-duty tactical flashlight.

While Stacey talked, I continued checking the rooms of the old Wilson place, particularly the closets, where the EM activity was a little higher. I led her up the steep, winding stairs to the second floor. The place felt like some kind of network of caverns, completely lightless. The air had a stale, sour smell from being sealed inside so long.

I tried to suppress the memories that wanted to boil out at me at each turn—screaming children, the dark mass of the ghost crawling in its spidery fashion across the ceiling, and finally the blood. Blood everywhere.

"We heard something at the back of the house," Stacey said. "Like a scratching sound, over and over again. My brother insisted we go check on it. He said it was probably just a dog or some animal trapped inside the house...I was scared, but I was even more scared to be alone. So I went with them.

"It was creepy, because there were trees growing up through the house, and moss everywhere, like it was half-house, half-forest. The scratching got louder as we advanced, room by room, trying not to fall through the old floorboards.

"Kevin walked up to this old door near the back, and he and his friends dared each other to open it. Every time the scratch sounded, the door bumped a little. There was a latch holding it closed on our side, but it was really loose, a couple of the screws had come out of the wall. I had a bad feeling about it, but if he was right and it was some kind of trapped animal, I wanted him to let it go...so I didn't say anything. I should have."

"Did you open it?" I led Stacey up to the third floor. Three of the Wilson children's rooms had been up here—that meant three bedroom closets I had to check. I walked into the nearest bedroom, where a Cookie Monster poster still hung on one wall. The folding doors to the closet were closed. I set my toolbox down beside them.

"Not me, no way," Stacey said. "Holy cow, I was shaking so hard. My brother was the one who finally did it—lifted the latch, pulled the old door open. I'll never forget that awful rusty squawk from the hinges."

"What did he find?" I tensed and drew open one folding door, half-expecting my worst fears to jump out at me, maybe claw my face off, maybe kill me. Maybe leave me in a wheelchair for the rest of my life.

My heart was thumping as I jabbed the flashlight into the shallow rectangular space of the closet. It was full of cobwebs, and a few forgotten hangers dangled on the rack. More hangers lay on the floor, among abandoned stuffed animals, Barbie dolls, and a pair of very small pink Nikes.

The Mel-Meter ticked up briefly, then subsided.

"When my brother opened the door," Stacey said, "I thought something would jump out at us, the way it was scratching and clawing on the other side. But nothing did. The door opened, the scratching stopped, and we were looking into a small, dark room, with a little moonlight leaking in from a window.

"The smell hit us a couple seconds later—a gagging, dead-thing-full-of-maggots smell. We all kind of choked, but my brother pulled his shirt over his nose and stepped in there anyway. He was always the brave one, you know. Patrick, my oldest brother, was the popular one, and he stayed out of trouble. Kevin could create trouble out of any situation, even a church barbecue."

"What was inside the room?" I asked, while leading us into another dark bedroom. Crayon drawings adorned one wall, animals with big teeth and claws, nightmarish things drawn by a little boy. A small bed lay in one corner as if it had been shoved there haphazardly.

"A dead squirrel," Stacey said. "And that thing had been dead for days, its eyes and guts were all eaten out—"

"I get the idea."

"It was gross. But it definitely hadn't been scratching and pounding on any doors anytime that night. And there was nothing else in the room. We shined our flashlights all around—well, *they* did. I just stayed outside the door and watched.

"The scratching sounded again," Stacey said, and her voice was very low now. "From inside the wall."

I checked the closet, and again my meter flickered upward, almost two milligaus this time, though there was nothing visible inside. I knelt by the bed and eased up the edge of a blanket to shine my light into the darkness beneath it. Again, I tensed myself for an attack, but found only dust bunnies, and not particularly feral ones. My meter again ticked up a notch.

A banging sounded upstairs, startling me into scampering back from the bed. Stacey gasped, shining her light up at the moisture-damaged ceiling.

"What was that?" she whispered.

I opened my toolbox and brought out our goggles—thermal for me, night vision for Stacey. We strapped them onto our foreheads, ready to drop them over our eyes if we needed them. I cued up a Karamanov symphonic work, a little Eastern Orthodox gospel to blast at the ghost. The right music can be a powerful weapon against troublesome spirits, slamming them with enough emotional energy to jar them for a little while. Or send them running, if you're lucky.

The banging continued overhead.

I motioned for Stacey to follow me.

We ascended the steep, narrow stairs to the fourth floor, approaching the repeated banging above.

There were only two doors at the top. A weird light flickered below one of them, in time with the banging. The sound clearly came from that direction. I pointed at the door, and Stacey nodded.

I pushed it open. We walked into a room with exposed timber rafters and a slanted roof, which had been the bedroom of the oldest Wilson child.

A bit of light flashed at me, then vanished, and the banging sounded again. I turned my flashlight toward it.

The plywood panel covering one of the narrow, rectangular windows had come loose. A stiff wind was blowing in through the broken glass, whipping the panel so it banged against the window frame, letting in brief flashes of light from outside.

"It's the ghost of the haunted window," Stacey said, in such a dead-serious, solemn tone that I had to laugh.

"About as dangerous as your dead squirrel," I said. I inspected the fireplace with my flashlight and Mel-Meter. Again, it hovered between one and two milligaus.

"That wasn't the end of the story," Stacey said. "While the boys were poking around in there, something came out of the corner. I mean it didn't come from a window, and the only door was the one where I stood. One minute, there's nothing there at all. Then, all at once, a heavy black mass, like a dark cloud, fills that whole corner of the room.

"Kevin's two friends backed away. Kevin moved toward it, though, shining his little orange pumpkin flashlight, just a cheap thing from the Halloween section at the grocery store. And the darkness absorbed the light.

"She took shape from the black mist. A woman in a hoop skirt, a bridal veil. Her dress was transparent in the moonlight, so you could see the rotten skin and bones beneath. Her face was decayed, you know. But her eyes were pale blue, and they just about glowed. I can still see them." Stacey shivered.

I approached the closet door.

"You saw a full apparition," I said.

"More than full. Overflowing. She looked at my brother, standing right in front of her. Then she bared her teeth and lashed out at him. Her skeletal little hand was like a shriveled claw, and she left scratch marks across his cheek." Stacey demonstrated with her own fingers across her face. "It was ugly."

"What did you do?" I slid open the folding door to the closet. A dark, deep space with a low ceiling, more like a crawlspace than a closet, looked back at me, daring me to come play with the spiders and the restless dead.

"We all screamed and ran," Stacey said. "One of the floorboards broke beneath me, and I fell on my face. I used one of those trees to pull myself up, and I remember the trunk was soft and rotten, and I could feel insects crawling over my fingers, but I couldn't see them. I had no idea where my flashlight was by this point.

"So I got to my feet and ran back through the house, out the front door with the other boys. Kevin's friends jumped off the porch and started running for the woods.

"I yelled after them, asking where my brother was. One of them turned and pointed into the house. The other one didn't even look back.

"I screamed for them to come back, but they were gone, off into the woods. Leaving me there alone, with my brother somewhere inside the house. So I went to the front door and started screaming for Kevin. He didn't answer me.

"Finally, I just went back inside to look for him, even though I was scared to bits by this point. In one of the rooms, which had about four good-sized trees growing through it, most of the floor was missing. In the dark space below, I could see the pumpkin-orange glow of Kevin's flashlight pointed at the old rock foundation of the house. It was lying on top of all these broken floorboards. I mean, there was almost no floor left in that room, I couldn't have crossed through it if I'd tried.

"So I yelled his name, you know, 'Kevin! Kevin!' And I thought I heard him groan down there, but I wasn't sure. I couldn't see him at all, the way his flashlight was pointed.

"Then I felt the air get cold, like really, *really* cold. I felt her looking at me before I saw her. She stood on the other side of the open pit, staring at me."

"The rotten dead bride chick?" I asked.

"Yeah, the dead bride chick. And she spoke to me. It was just a whisper, but I could hear it clearly across the room. 'Don't cry for him,' she said. 'All men are devils under the skin.'"

"Early feminist thought of the antebellum South," I murmured.

"Well, she disappeared. Just whoosh, gone. And then chunks of the old ceiling started coming down on me, and the floor groaned under my feet, and it started to sink. She was trying to kill me with that old house.

"I shouted to my brother that I'd get help, but I didn't hear him say anything back. I got out of the house as fast as I could, but my ankle started burning. I guess I'd turned it when I'd fallen through the old board earlier, but I hadn't noticed yet. I noticed it then. It was all I could do to hobble to the front door while pieces of the ceiling and walls crumbled down on top of me.

"The front porch stairs were old and collapsed, so I had to sit down and slide off the porch. I moved as fast as I could, through the weeds and briars, sort of hop-dragging with my swelling ankle. I looked back, expecting to see the whole house shaking like an earthquake, but it was dead calm. A pale light glowed in one of the windows, like somebody was holding a dim candle. I think that was her, watching me.

"I made it into the woods and kept going. It was maybe a half mile to the nearest road, which normally wouldn't seem that far, but my ankle was screaming in pain with every step. I had to drag myself through those woods, using low branches to support me. I stumbled that way for a long time, and I kept looking back, sure the lady was going to pop out of the woods and kill me.

"Finally, I made it to a break in the woods, one of those strips they carve out for power lines, you know, with grass growing under it. I followed those out toward the highway. My ankle was killing me. I finally felt some relief when I saw that bright red light, and that big freckled girl smiling down at me...it was a Wendy's sign.

"I limped inside, all scratched up and dirty from the woods, and leaned against the wall so I didn't collapse to the floor. The manager called the police and my parents, and he gave me a free chocolate Frosty since I didn't have any money.

"It felt like forever waiting for my parents and the police. I wanted to go back into the woods with the cops, but they wouldn't let me. I couldn't actually walk. My dad went with them, my mom stayed with me. She basically set me in the car and yelled at me." Stacey sighed. "So why do you keep staring into the closets, Ellie? Is this thing really a closet monster?"

"We're looking for the boogeyman," I said.

"Okay, but seriously..."

"Seriously. *Babau* in Eastern Europe. *Busseman* if you want to get German about it. *Saalua* or *lulu* in the Middle East. *Dongola Miso* in parts of Africa. The monster that hides in dark places and comes out to torment children at night." I peered into the deep crawlspace-closet. Black widow spiders perched in there, watching me from their webs. Ugly little dark-shelled palmetto bugs scurried away from my light. "It's a species of specter known all over the world."

"Whoa," Stacey said. "And it knows what scares you?"

"It feeds directly on fear," I said. "Remember the Paulding case, with the poltergeist? Poltergeists feed on anger, particularly the frustrations of adolescents and children...probably because their emotions are more powerful and less controlled."

"Low-hanging fruit," Stacey said.

"There's more energy to take, and it's easier, compared to adults," I said. "The paranormal journals call these entities fearfeeders or fearmongers, I guess because *boogeyman* just doesn't sound sciencey enough. They feed on the emotional energy released by fear, so they've developed methods of causing people to feel as much fear as possible. Like I said, they focus on children because that's where the energy is, but that doesn't mean adults are immune. Not at all."

"Great. And things went wrong last time?"

"Very wrong. You never finished your story," I said. My Mel-Meter had given me readings similar to the other closets, so I closed the door and headed downstairs.

"Right," Stacey said. "Where was I?"

"At Wendy's, getting yelled at by your mom."

"Yeah, so my dad and the police went to find Kevin. I guess the cops knew right where to go. It probably wasn't the first time kids had decided to sneak into the haunted old mansion in the woods." She shook her head. "It turns out my brother had landed on some big nineteenth-century nails. His heart and lungs were punctured. He was probably dead before I even escaped the house."

"Oh, my God, I'm sorry," I said, touching her arm. I felt genuinely horrified. "You never told us about any of this."

"I don't like to talk about it." Stacey was looking away as we rounded a landing and continued down the steps.

"I understand."

"I did tell Calvin, though. I just asked him not to tell you."

"Why?" I looked back at her, but she wasn't meeting my eyes.

"I kind of felt like you didn't want me around." Her voice was so quiet I could barely hear it over our echoing footsteps. "I didn't feel comfortable with you knowing that about me."

I stopped and turned back to face her as we reached a lower landing.

"It wasn't about you," I said. "I didn't want...honestly, I didn't feel like I was ready to train anybody else. I'm still learning so much myself. And you've seen how dangerous this work can get. I didn't want to be responsible for somebody else's life. Or for their death. I'm really sorry to hear about your brother."

"It was a long time ago. It doesn't always feel that way, though."

"I know." I didn't need to tell Stacey about Anton Clay, the fiery ghost who'd burned my house down and killed my parents when I was fifteen. Both of us had lost family members to ghosts. "So you weren't just some aw-shucks kid who happened to catch a ghost on her video camera. You were searching for them, weren't you?"

"I've been searching for them since my brother died," Stacey said. "I used to sit alone in my room with a Ouija board. The whole occult thing. I hid it from my family, of course. It would have horrified their United Methodist sensibilities."

"How do they like you working here?"

"I haven't...totally told them what I do," Stacey said. "They think I'm a production assistant for a company that makes commercials and stuff."

"So you haven't told them at all."

"They'd think I was crazy. Or into Satan or something."

"That's what my Aunt Clarice thinks," I said. "She's the one who took care of me after my parents..."

"She thinks you're into Satan?"

"Probably." I snickered. "She thinks we're all crazy, selling pure craziness to people even crazier than ourselves."

"Sounds about right," Stacey said.

We climbed back out the window. After the relentless heavy darkness inside, the sunshine outside came as a blinding shock.

Chapter Four

I wanted to speak with Calvin about the new case right away, but we also needed to spend some time at the city archives for background research before it closed at five p.m.

Our first job was to sort through the property titles of the house and identify who had lived there and when, establish a complete history of ownership. This process was about as much fun as it sounds—lots of old file folders and faded type on yellowed paper.

"Done," Stacey sighed, when we'd traced the owners back to the house's construction in 1889. It had most recently been acquired by Keystone Properties, a company whose sign I'd seen on small apartment and office buildings around town.

"Now, all the neighboring houses," I said.

"You're kidding." She slumped back in her hard wooden chair.

"Now that we know the entity is mobile, we have to cast a wider net," I said. "The Wilson house wasn't built until 1925. There wasn't a house there before—the area where it stands was part of the garden belonging to the house next to it. That's why the house is so tall and narrow, because the lot is small. We investigated the older house next door last time, the one that used to own the property, but it didn't give us any good leads. Now we know to look all around, at houses on both streets."

"That'll take forever," Stacey said.

"Let's get digging," I said, approaching the row of file cabinets. A rotund, middle-aged archive clerk with a walrus mustache watched me from a desk.

"Don't re-file anything," he said, for the fifteenth time that afternoon. "We have a very specific system. Leave it all on the table when you're done."

"I will," I assured him, also for the fifteenth time.

He raised the *Better Homes and Gardens* magazine he was reading, but he kept his eyes on me, clearly suspicious that I would attempt to re-file something if he glanced away for a moment.

I returned to our table with another heap of folders. Stacey gave just the slightest pout at the sight of them.

"This is great," I said. "We'll have to find something, finally."

"Yeah, great," Stacey said, in a not-so-thrilled tone of voice. She didn't immediately leap to open the folders and start searching. "So, what about this alleged hot fireman guy?"

"What about him?" I sat across from her again and began reading through more exciting property-title records.

"When do we get to talk to him?"

"We need to get this done, Stacey. The archive's closing soon."

"I know that! I just meant, you know, he lives in the building, too, so he might have witnessed something. And his little sister or whatever might have seen the ghost."

"Right, witnesses. That's why you're so interested."

"I'm all business." She winked. "Still...hot fireman guy. Just think about it."

I slid her a stack of folders. "Just think about tracing the ownership of the old Greek Revival house on the corner."

She sighed and got to work.

The walrus-mustached clerk began clearing his throat about ten minutes before closing time, and he kept clearing it. We'd churned up a heap of stuff for him to re-file.

When I said it was time to go, Stacey jumped to her feet and all but flew to the door.

"Sorry about the mess," I said to the clerk as I walked past him, giving him an apologetic smile.

"You didn't re-file anything, did you?" he asked, looking suddenly alarmed.

"Not one piece of paper, I promise."

"We have a very specific system here."

"I understand."

He hefted to his feet as I left the room, and he hurried to close the door behind me.

We drove out of downtown, to the fairly scary-looking industrial district where our office is located. The largest area of the office is the workshop in back, where we park the van and store all our gear. I sat down with Calvin at the long worktable in at the center of the room while Stacey poked around in the refrigerator. Hunter, Calvin's bloodhound, nosed around her, clearly curious what she might do with the food.

"Who wants salad?" she asked, grabbing out lettuce and a tomato.

"I'm not hungry," I said. I'd been dreading telling Calvin about the new case.

"You look upset," Calvin said.

"I know you must have noticed the location of our new client," I said.

"I did."

"I think it's a fearfeeder," I said, and then I filled him in on the details.

"That sounds like our old friend the boogeyman," Calvin said, with a smile that didn't have the least bit of humor. "Maybe you should just advise the family to move. Leave this case alone."

"I can't do that," I said. "Neither would you, in my position."

"You can't place yourself into that kind of danger."

"Pickles, anyone?" Stacey asked. "I like bread and butter pickles on my salads, but other people seem to hate that..." She looked at the haggard expression on Calvin's face, then at whatever fear or anxiety was showing on mine. "What are we talking about? Why does everyone look like we all just got called for jury duty or something?"

"Did you tell her what happened during the Wilson case?" Calvin asked me.

"I thought I'd let you explain," I said.

"Are we sure nobody wants salad? I brought Bacon Bits." Stacey shrugged, then sat down with a bowl and started crunching. "So what's the mystery? Ellie told me you never caught the ghost last time."

"We nearly did," Calvin said. "We couldn't identify the ghost, and we couldn't lure him into a standard trap with just candles for bait. So we set up the bear cage in the attic area on the fourth floor."

"Bear cage?" Stacey raised her eyebrows.

"We mainly call it that because it's a bear to transport and set up," I told her. "We haven't used it since...well, it's been a long while." I walked to a storage closet, which I opened to reveal a roughly phone-booth-sized object draped in a tarp. It stood next to shelves crammed full of soldering irons and baskets of sharp hand tools and spools of wire.

"And it's big enough for a bear," Calvin added, watching us from the table. He was shuffling a deck of cards, something he did at times to keep his hands busy. Calvin loved the cards—he had a running poker game with a few old friends from the city police force. He'd worked with them as a homicide detective before retiring to hunt ghosts full-time.

"And even if it works, you *barely* survive." I gave him a smile. We were resurrecting an old inside joke from before Stacey's time, from the day we'd set up the trap after carrying it, piece by heavy piece, up the four stories of the house. We'd tried to use the word *bear* as many times as we could. "Anyway, we had to bear it all the way up to the attic. That's when I decided I preferred basement ghosts to attic ghosts."

"Let's see it," Stacey said, walking over to help me pull the tarp off the big trap. While the canvas thudded to the ground, her eyebrows rose. "Holy...you could fit a cow in there. Well, a small one."

The cage, mounted on a platform with lockable wheels, was indeed big enough for a small cow. It had leaded-glass panes on every side, done in a Victorian array of colors that made it resemble a set of church windows welded together into a cage. Either that or some crazed lighting fixture from the nineteen-seventies.

"There are two doors," I said, while I unlatched and opened

both of them. The narrow doors were on opposite sides of the colored-glass cage, so that you could run straight through it without slowing down—which was pretty much the whole idea. "It's for ghosts who won't respond to other kinds of traps, but who will chase and attack any nosy ghost removal specialists in the area. Ghosts who are only tempted by live bait."

"And we're the bait?" Stacey asked.

"We hate this trap," I said. "For obvious reasons. It's a bear to move and a bear to keep charged. But we eventually had to resort to it for the Wilson case."

"Did it work?" Stacey peered inside. Fine copper mesh lined every surface, fitting together and overlapping at the corners of the cage. When charged, the layer of mesh created an electromagnetic prison for ghosts.

I looked at Calvin.

"I was the bait," he said. "Still had my legs under me back then. Ellie had your job, Stacey—out in the van, monitoring the house. There was a lot of scattered activity in that place, aside from the fearfeeder."

"That's what we're calling the boogeyman, right?" Stacey asked. "You were boogeyman bait."

"Only I didn't boogie fast enough, it turned out," Calvin said. His face was perfectly stoic while he made the little joke, framed by his overgrown gray hair and granny glasses. "By this point, the family was out of there for the night, staying at a relative's place. I was alone in the house, and it was so active....the boogeyman brings his pack of stolen souls with him, you see. He's looking to add a new one, sooner or later. A child. But first he feeds on the living for as long as he can, until he picks which child he wants to take away with him. Then he's gone, dormant, like a bear that's filled its belly for the winter. That's how these fearfeeders usually operate."

"So the boogeyman was in this trap?" Stacey said, regarding it with new curiosity.

"By the time the entity finally came for me, I'd been alone in that dark house full of whispering, creaking, and knocking for several hours. I'd seen apparitions of dead children. I told Ellie everything was fine, but...I could feel that place eating into me." Calvin said. "I should have called it a night. I was too worn by the time it arrived. Worn down by fear."

Stacey had returned to her chair, leaning on the table and

listening to Calvin, her salad long forgotten.

"He pursued me—as he'd already done the night before, as I knew he would do—and I led him right into the trap. Ellie was watching on video and monitoring the trap's sensors. She had a remote control ready to slam both doors once the entity was inside, just as soon as I ran out the second door. That was the plan.

"He chased me into that trap. While I was inside, just before I made it to that second door, I turned and looked back." Calvin winced and shook his head. "Never look back, that's what they say. They're right. I just glanced over my shoulder—I was wearing night vision goggles—to see if he'd followed me. And that's when I saw him."

"What did he look like?" Stacey asked.

"He'd reached in and found something that scared me when I was younger, when I was in uniform," Calvin said. "Something that lurks in the mind of every cop on the beat, or every time you stop a motorist. It's the quick-draw devil, the one that gets the drop on you, the one that puts a bullet in you. That random, armed madman who pulls a gun instead of his driver's license. You never know who it's going to be. Odds are you'll never see him at all, but he could show up anytime. He could look like anybody at all.

"His clothes were nothing you'd notice, just the plainest street clothes, gray flannel, faded jeans. His face was about as vanilla-average as any you could cook up, except for two things—his black sunglasses, where I could see two images of myself looking back at me. They weren't exactly my reflection, though. They were my younger self, in my uniform days, looking scared as all get out, like I'd seen the devil himself rising up from the soil.

"The other thing was his smile. Sly. Knowing. Because he had the drop on me.

"I barely had time to notice his weapon—it was a fat, six-barreled pepperbox revolver, like something out of the back room of an antique store. He was already shooting at me, the barrels rotating and blasting hellfire.

"I felt those things tear through my chest and stomach, hot metal slugs that slowed and rolled as they passed through me. He fired all six shots and never missed one. I was on the floor of the cage, with my blood everywhere. There was no chance for Ellie to close the trap, because I couldn't move—my legs were useless already.

"The armed madman shriveled up and turned into the entity's real shape, the faceless black shadow. It crawled away across the ceiling, upside down, like a bug. Its movements are all jerky but almost too fast to see."

"It shot you?" Stacey was horrified. "Ghosts can shoot you?"

"The bullets were just an embodiment of *my* fear," Calvin said. "They didn't exist for long. Nobody ever found a single one of them, either in the room or inside me. Ectoplasm bullets...there when you need them, gone when you don't. The ghost was just punching holes in me with its psychokinetic energy. Got me right in the central nervous system."

"That's terrible!" Stacey said. "I'm so sorry."

"I'm used to it," Calvin said. "It's been about eighteen months now. Anyway, that eventually led to a job opening for you, so it all worked out." He forced a smile.

"And so he got away," Stacey said. "That's the one we're dealing with now? We'll get him for you, Calvin!"

"I appreciate your enthusiasm, but this is a tricky entity," Calvin said.

"I kept trying to capture it by myself," I told Stacey. "Calvin didn't want me to, but I spent the next week at that house. The family finally told me to give up, because they weren't coming back."

"That was the one good thing about what happened to me," Calvin said. "It convinced that family the house was too dangerous for their children to ever set foot in again. They escaped with all their children. Another family hadn't been so lucky." He shook his head. "I can't believe he got the drop on me."

"What happened to the other family?" Stacey asked.

"The McAllisters. They lived in that house in the early seventies. They had a child go missing, six-year-old girl. No evidence, no sign of a break-in, no leads. Most kidnappings are done by people who already know the kid—the perp's identity is something you figure out in the first thirty seconds. There was nobody like that in her life. The girl had screamed about demons in her closet to the point where her family brought her to a kid psychiatrist. Then, one night, they tuck their little girl into bed and she disappears before sunrise. Nobody ever saw that girl again."

"We aren't just looking for violent deaths this time," I told Stacey. "Now that we know it moves from house to house, we have to look for missing children connected to all the surrounding houses, going back as far in time as we can dig."

"So basically we're just going to live at the library every day until we solve the case," Stacey said. "We're still identifying the past owners of all the houses."

"Let me see what you have," Calvin said, glancing at our notes. "I'll start checking missing persons databases for all the families who've lived at those addresses, but that will only take us so far back in time. I can ask my friends at the department to look through older missing person files, but we'll need to give them much more specific details than what we have here."

"How can we find out about the older cases?" Stacey asked.

"Maybe call your boyfriend," I said, and she blushed a little. "We can have Jacob check the house, then walk around the block and see if he picks up on any missing kids over the centuries. He probably won't be able to give specific names and dates, but at least locations and eras. That could narrow it down."

"So we should bring him in soon?" Stacey asked. "I'll call him."

"As soon as possible," I said. "If he could come tomorrow night, that would be great."

"Why not tonight?" she asked. "I mean, if he's available."

"We have enough to do tonight, setting up the observation gear and trying to talk to Alicia's neighbors," I said. "If we wait and get a clearer picture of what's going on, we'll have a much better idea of how we want to use Jacob. Well, I guess we all know how *you* want to use him, Stacey, but—"

"Change of subject," Stacey said, blushing now. "Away from my love life. So how do we trap this guy, or this thing, when you haven't been able to do that before?"

"That's why we're looking into missing-child cases," I said. "The oldest cases might give us a clue about the origins of the fearfeeder."

"You mean the boogeyman? But we're not even sure if he's human, right?" Stacey asked.

"We'd better hope he is," Calvin said. "If it's a demonic, it could prove impossible to trap him."

"Well, yay," Stacey said. "Can't wait to get started."

Chapter Five

Evening was already coming on, darkening the street with shadows as Stacey and I returned to Alicia's house. We had to park halfway down the block, since only street parking was available.

"Can't wait to carry this junk all the way to the house," Stacey grumbled as we hopped out of the van. She pulled the strap of her camera bag over her shoulder. We'd be making a few trips to bring in all the cameras and tripods.

"What are you complaining about?" I asked. "I thought you liked going on long hikes with a heavy pack on your back."

"That's different," she said, while we walked toward the big Queen Anne house. "That's in the woods or the mountains."

"Then pretend you're in the mountains," I said. "Problem solved. Look, deer! And...monkeys!"

"There are no monkeys in the Appalachians," Stacey said.

"So it's an exciting adventure already." I led the way onto the porch and rang the bell.

Alicia smiled when she opened the door, though it looked like she was struggling to make the smile happen. The TV was blasting in the living room behind her, some singing-kids show that was probably on Sprout or the Disney Channel.

"Hi!" said a young girl by Alicia's side, who I recognized as Mia from her pictures.

"Mia, this is Miss Ellie and Miss Stacey," Alicia said.

"Nice to meet you, Mia!" Stacey gushed, while I nodded and waved.

"Are you the monster catchers?" Mia asked.

"That's us," I said, while Alicia ushered us inside.

"How do you catch them?" Mia asked.

"We have special traps," I told her.

A boy with thick glasses watched us from the couch. Math textbooks and worksheets cluttered the coffee table in front of him. Math camp, I remembered. I would've hated that as a kid.

"And this is Kalil," Alicia said.

Kalil stood up and offered his hand.

"Hello, it's nice to meet you," Kalil said, as professional as any business executive. Stacey and I shook his hand. "Please let me know if I can assist."

"You're the future astronomer, aren't you?" Stacey asked.

"Astrophysicist," he corrected. "I want to help search for Goldilocks planets."

"What are those?" Stacey asked.

"Like the Three Bears," he said. "Not too hot, not too cold...not too close or far from its star, but just right. A planet must have liquid water for life as we know it to emerge."

"That's interesting—" Stacey said.

"There could be as many as forty billion planets the right size and location for life," Kalil said. "That's just our galaxy alone."

"Amazing!" Stacey said, looking genuinely impressed. "Huh. That gives you a lot to think about."

"Want to see me do a cartwheel?" Mia asked Stacey, as if jealous of the moment of attention Kalil was getting. The girl didn't wait for an answer, but went right into three cartwheels that took her all the way across the living room.

"Very nice!" Stacey clapped.

"Okay, kids, they have work to do," Alicia said. She turned to me. "What's next?"

"We'll set up our observation gear to try to get a look at what's happening here," I said. "Cameras, most importantly. We need to place those in the paranormally active areas of the house."

"The hauntspots," Stacey said, making me cringe a little.

"He's in my closet," Mia said, looking very serious now. "Fleshface. You have to get him!"

"That's the plan," I told her. "Mrs. Rogers, we'd like to put gear into both kids' rooms for us to watch overnight, if that's all right with you."

"That's fine," she said. "Call me Alicia, though. I'm not that much older than you, am I?"

"No, ma'am," I said, and she rolled her eyes and laughed a little.

"I'm surely not *that* old, either," she said.

"What kind of equipment do you use?" Kalil asked.

"I can tell you all about that!" Stacey said. "Especially if you help me carry it in from the van."

"I want to help, too!" Mia said, stepping in front of her brother.

"Great," Stacey said. "Let's get moving."

Alicia followed us outside. With her help, and the kids carrying tripods, we brought in the gear in just a couple of trips.

I frowned at the purple sky above, while the last orange embers of the sun died away somewhere beyond the west end of the street. It was better to set up during daylight hours, so you don't have to go into the hauntspots after dark when the ghosts might be getting active.

Hauntspots. Stacey's word had crept into my thoughts like an unwelcome party guest.

"Let's start in my room," Kalil said, after we'd deposited our gear in a heap in the living room.

"No, my room!" Mia countered. "I have the worst ghost. You just have aliens."

Kalil cleared his throat. "Have you ever encountered extraterrestrials?" he asked me, dead serious.

"Not so far," I told him. We lugged gear up the stairs. "We think that what you're dealing with has the power to take the shape of whatever you fear. That's why you each see different things."

"Aliens could be real," he said. "The universe is probably

loaded with species more intelligent and capable than we are."

"I certainly hope so!" I replied, but he didn't seem to find it funny.

"If there aren't aliens, then what's in my closet?" he asked.

"It's a kind of electromagnetic entity imbued with consciousness," I said, thinking he'd dig the scientific terms.

"Huh?" Mia asked, pausing by the door to her room, holding a tripod in both arms.

"A ghost," Stacey said. "A ghost that can pretend to be other things."

"Oh," Mia said. "Like Fleshface."

"Exactly. It's not really Fleshface. Fleshface is just a made-up character from a movie," Stacey said.

"Maybe." Mia did not look convinced.

We set up thermal and night vision cameras in her room, pointed at her closet door, along with a high-powered microphone and EMF and motion detectors. We didn't want to miss anything in the kids' rooms.

Stacey explained to a very curious Kalil how ghosts draw energy from their environment, creating cold spots and shapes we can detect on thermal, and how we use EMF meters to check for unusual electromagnetic activities.

We moved on to Kalil's room.

"We'll watch your kids as closely as we can," I said to Alicia. "But the house is full of blind spots, and we won't be able to fully track the entity's movements unless we can get your neighbors to agree to cameras, too."

"I don't know," Alicia said. "I really don't know the Fieldings or Mr. Gray. What do we say? 'Hi, remember me from the mailbox and the laundry room? Can I set up cameras to check your apartment for ghosts?'"

"How about your neighbors on the third floor?"

"I told Michael and Melissa what we're doing," Alicia said. "They're expecting y'all to go up and ask some questions, but I don't know about cameras..."

"We'll make that one of the questions," I said. "Stacey, how much longer up here?"

"There's a lot to do," Stacey replied. "We need a few downstairs, too."

"We need to go up and speak to the third-floor neighbors."

A wicked smile broke across her face—Stacey thinking of the mysterious hot fireman, no doubt.

"Hey, I've got this covered," she said. "Especially with the kids helping me. Why don't you go on up?"

"Seriously?" That threw me off-balance for a second. I'd thought she wanted to meet Fireman Michael pretty badly, the way she kept bringing him up.

"Yeah, you can fill me in on the highlights later." Stacey winked.

My cheeks burned a little as I realized what she meant. She wasn't interested in the guy for herself, but for me. That made me feel embarrassed somehow.

"I'll take you up there," Alicia said. "Kids, put yourselves on Grade A behavior. I'll be right back."

Kalil mumbled something and nodded, not even looking up from the technical manual for Stacey's thermal camera, which he was studying as though he had to memorize it. Mia was showing off her somersaults to Stacey and didn't respond.

"Mia, what did I say?" Alicia snapped.

Mia rose up from a somersault, held out both arms, and sang out "Grade AAAAA!" dragging out the "A" sound as if it were the dramatic crescendo note of a musical.

"That's right," Alicia said.

Alicia led me back downstairs, into the short side hall that provided the apartments shared access to the basement. I opened the basement door and looked down into the flickering darkness below.

"We should really get a camera down there, too," I said.

"I'm not sure all the neighbors would agree," Alicia replied.

"Maybe I'll have Stacey hide one in a laundry basket or something." *But I'm not sending her down there alone*, I thought.

"I didn't want to say anything in front of the kids," I told Alicia, while we walked up the stairs. "But if this haunting is what I think it is, the entity is very dangerous. It may have taken a five-year-old girl who lived here a few decades ago. It...injured my boss, Calvin Eckhart. Paralyzed him."

"So my kids aren't safe here."

"Is there anywhere they could go?"

She sighed. "Not in town. I could have Mia stay at a friend's house for a night maybe. Kalil, he's a little more difficult. He doesn't have a lot of friends, and he'd rather stay home and read..."

"Have you considered moving out?"

"Naturally, but that's so expensive. I had to put down a deposit and a month's rent, and there's a big penalty if I break my lease, then I'll have to come up with a lot more money to move...and I didn't want to take the kids away from their school, but there's not much we can afford in this district. That's why I called you."

I nodded. "From what I've read about these entities, they feed on their hosts a long time before taking them, if they take them at all. Bonnie McAllister dealt with it for over a year before she vanished."

Alicia stopped a few steps down from the third-floor landing. She looked at me, studying me for a moment.

"Can you get rid of this or not?" she asked. "If my kids are in danger, we'll run, even if we end up homeless and living in the car."

"If we can't, you'll be the first to know," I said. "You should all be safe while we're here, because Stacey and I will watch the house at night until this is resolved. We haven't even verified that this is the same ghost from the other house...but it certainly sounds like it."

Alicia shook her head, not looking reassured at all. I couldn't blame her.

"What happened to your boss?" Alicia asked.

"He was attacked while trying to capture the entity. It was evasive—it hid from us for most of the investigation, and then it fought back viciously. At the moment, I'm worried it will remember me, and it just won't come out at all." *Or it will try to kill me*, I thought, but I didn't see any need to distress her further. She knew the situation was dangerous.

"It usually goes away just before I get there," she said. "One of the kids screams for me, I go up there...nothing. Except for the times I told you about."

"How often do they see it?"

"Couple of times a month."

I nodded. "It hasn't built to the truly dangerous point. It's still sniffing around. I spent some time studying these kinds of entities when we investigated the Wilson house—"

"How many kids has this one taken?"

"Just one that we know of, and that was forty years ago," I said.

"We're researching the history of both streets to see if there are any more cases, but that will take time."

"I want to get back to my kids." Alicia knocked on the door to the third-floor apartment. "Mind if I introduce you and run? Or do you need me?"

"I'll be fine, thank you."

The door opened, and warm air that smelled of tomatoes, spices, and toasting bread wafted out, reminding me that I'd skipped dinner, too worried to eat.

"Hey, Alicia." The teenage girl who opened the door smiled at her, then gave me more of a tentative look. She was tall, freckled, and gangly, dressed in glittering jeans and an absurd number of little bracelets.

"Melissa, this is the lady I was telling you about," Alicia said. "Her name's Ellie."

"Hey," Melissa said, smiling tentatively. "Y'all come on in."

"I have to run," Alicia said. "Before my kids drive the other ghost exterminator crazy. You're still watching them for me tomorrow afternoon, aren't you?"

"Of course." Melissa turned and stepped back into the apartment. The place had irregular ceilings, sloping low to the wall at some points. The floor was dark hardwood, like the stairs, with several colorful rugs scattered around. I saw a large saltwater tank, home to some exotic-looking fish. An old-fashioned cuckoo clock, shaped like an ornately carved little rustic cottage, hung on the wall.

I followed Melissa into a living room, where the TV was off but the stereo by the brick chimney—no fireplace, just a chimney from the lower floors—blasted some old blues. "Michael! The ghost hunter person is here!" she shouted, turning down the music.

She'd been yelling through a cutaway wall into a small kitchen, where her older brother stood at the stove, his back to us. The firm muscles of his back were fairly apparent through his thin white t-shirt.

He turned around and I got my first look at him: brown hair, a little shaggy, eyes bright green and intense. A playful, devilish look, especially around the lips. He was taller than me by a head, and I'm not short.

Hot firefighter guy.

Let's try not to call him that to his face.

"Hi," I said, while he stepped around to greet me. Clingy white t-shirt, old jeans. "I'm Ellie Jordan, lead investigator with Eckhart Investigations. I'm not sure what Alicia told you—"

"You're here to look for ghosts," he said, and there was that hint-of-devil smile again. I wondered if he were secretly laughing at me. If so, at least he had the decency to keep it secret.

He held out his hand, and I took it. Warm, strong, rough around the edges.

"Michael Holly," he said. His eyes glanced over my face, taking me in with quick little flashes. "Good to meet you."

I could say that I wasn't suddenly looking forward to the interview ahead, but I'd be lying.

Chapter Six

"Do you catch a lot of these ghosts?" Michael asked, leading me back to the kitchen, the source of the tasty aromas that had greeted me at the door. His sister Melissa was still in the living room, in body but not in spirit—her eyes were glued to her phone, and her purple thumbnails clacked the screen as she hammered out a message to somebody.

"I do my best. Have you ever seen anything unusual in this house?"

"One second." He picked up a wooden spoon and stirred a pan of spaghetti sauce with four large meatballs in the center, then sprinkled in a pinch of freshly-pressed garlic. *He cooks, too,* I heard Stacey whisper in my head, and I wanted to scowl at her for putting me in this state of mind. I was here to work, not make an idiot of myself trying to flirt with a guy who was probably a couple degrees too hot for me, anyway. That kind of thing was well outside my comfort zone.

He tasted his concoction, then nodded. "Do you like

spaghetti?"

"Sure...I'll only take a minute of your time."

"Have a seat, I'll bring you some." He gestured toward a rough-plank table just beyond the kitchen area, positioned in a corner with tall but shallow bay windows on each side. These looked out onto ancient trees, the twisting oak limbs lit by the streetlamps below.

"Bring me some? Oh, no, you don't have to do that," I said.

"Suit yourself, but it's going to get awkward with the two of us shoveling spaghetti in our faces while you watch. Plus, there's garlic bread." He pointed to a small bread basket, where slices of toasted, buttered French bread were nestled in the white cloth. The meal was Carb City—how could he eat like this and still look good in a t-shirt?

He transferred the spaghetti into a large serving bowl, then carried that and a big salad out to the kitchen table. I found myself carrying the bread to the table for him. It was all weirdly domestic.

"Here you go." He pulled out a chair for me, facing one of the big windows, the one that looked out over the sidewalk and street. "Melissa! Come set the table. Melissa!"

Melissa looked up, jarred back into our own dimension by his voice. "What?"

"The table," he said again.

"Is she having dinner with us?" Melissa squinted at me.

"You don't have to—" I began.

"She's just going to watch us eat, but give her a plate and fork in case she changes her mind," Michael said as he returned to the kitchen.

"Oh...kay." Melissa gave him a you're-a-freak-look, one eyebrow raised, and began setting the table. "You have to excuse my brother. It's the firefighter thing. I think all the smoke goes right to his brain."

I smiled at her while she sat down.

"So, have you ever—" I began, ready to start talking ghosts. Anything to keep me from watching Michael's shoulders move inside his shirt.

"Beer? Or wine?" Michael offered. He opened a cabinet and looked inside. "I mean, uh...beer?"

"Just water, thanks," I said. "I'm technically at work right now."

"That's right. On duty." He pressed a glass against the filtered-water dispenser in his refrigerator, then set it in front of me, alongside the empty dish and silverware Melissa had put out for me. Now it would be weird if I *didn't* eat. It was like I'd been sucked into a Venus flytrap of Southern hospitality.

As Michael sat across from me, holding a bottle of a local microbrew called Southbound, I considered that maybe I wouldn't mind being trapped here. For a little while.

We served ourselves family-style, using tongs for the salad and a giant spoon for the spaghetti. I assumed they weren't crazed psychopaths who invited people into their homes for poisoned garlic bread.

"You should grab one of those meatballs," Michael advised me, pointing to them as if I couldn't see where they were. "I learned that recipe from my friend Serge at the firehouse."

"Oh. Is he Italian?"

"Russian, I think. But he makes great Italian meatballs."

"I'm not really that hungry—" But I *was*, that was the problem. The food smelled amazing, and I didn't want to go into pig-mode just now.

"Try it." He served one big meatball and a nest of saucy noodles onto my plate. Now I *really* had to eat it.

I did, and it was good. Spicy, right up on the edge of too spicy but without going over. My stomach growled.

"What did I tell you?" he asked.

I nodded, because I wasn't about to open my noodle-and-sauce-filled mouth. I took a sip of water before answering.

"It's good. Do you learn all your recipes from the fire department?" I asked.

"Most of them. We spend all night waiting for calls. Occasionally we have to go put out a burning building or respond to a car crash, or a heart attack...the rest of the time, we're cooking and eating."

"Which could only lead to more heart attacks," I said.

"Exactly." He smiled. "So how exactly do you do it?" he asked.

"Do what?"

"The ghost thing. Same kind of work? Hang around waiting for supernatural emergencies?"

"It's a lot of watching and listening," I said. "I guess there's a good amount of waiting. That's what we'll be doing tonight in Alicia's apartment."

"Have you seen anything there yet?" Melissa asked, looking up from her phone at last.

"We've only just started. What about you?" I looked from her to Michael. "Have either of you seen anything strange in this house?"

"I saw my brother in a Speedo once," Melissa said.

"Not true," Michael countered. "I only wear trunks."

"Anything scarier than that?" I asked.

"Scarier than Speedos?" he asked.

"He used to wear Crocs," Melissa said.

"I thought we weren't going to bring that up again," Michael replied, looking solemn.

I smiled, keeping my mouth firmly closed. Spaghetti is a poor choice for a date meal—you've got noodles and sauce constantly on the brink of spilling everywhere. Not that I was on a date. It almost felt like that, though, some sort of nineteenth-century Victorian date where we had to be chaperoned by his sister because unmarried men and women couldn't be trusted alone.

I shoved that sort of thinking out of the way as best I could.

"How long have you lived here?" I asked them, attempting to steer the conversation back on course.

"Two years?" Michael glanced at his sister. "Two and a half?"

Melissa shrugged and looked down at her food.

In that silence, I could feel something heavy hanging in the air between them, like a dark cloud over the dinner table. It probably related to how they'd ended up living here in the first place, brother and sister with no parents. I decided to back away slowly from that topic—they'd only just met me, and I had no right to ask about their personal tragedies.

"Have you seen anything unusual in that time?" I asked. "Other than questionable swimwear?"

Michael looked at me for a long moment, his lips parted, forkful of spaghetti forgotten halfway from his plate. He was studying me again with those intense eyes, but I had no idea what he was thinking.

Then he turned to look at Melissa, as if expecting her to speak.

"Go on, Mel," he finally said. "You want to tell her?"

Melissa sighed and poked at her spaghetti for a bit before

looking up at me.

"It's kind of...embarrassing," Melissa said. "I'm not even sure it was a ghost. More like a nightmare I kept having."

"Now it's just a nightmare." Michael shook his head. "That's not what you used to say."

"Well, it's been a while..."

"Can you tell me what happened? From the beginning?" I asked her.

"Okay." She took a breath. "Okay. So, I was like fifteen, and I was at my friend Callie's house. She was from my dance group. I do modern dance and ballet. Anyway, a bunch of us slept over there, and when it was really late, somehow we decided to play Bloody Mary. You know that game? You stand in front of a mirror and say 'Bloody Mary' three times, and this crazy ghost lady is supposed to appear."

"Sure," I said.

"So we crowded into her basement bathroom—that's where we were hanging out, you know, down in the basement, there's some old couches and a TV and stuff. We turned out the lights and lit a candle, this pink thing that smelled like cotton candy.

"We're all kind of spooked already, and we started daring each other to say it, because nobody wanted to start. Finally we decided to all say it at the same time. We were kind of whispering it, and it was creepy, like six girls going..." Her voice dropped into the softest possible whisper. "'Bloody Mary, Bloody Mary...' We whispered that three times." Melissa threw a worried look at each of the big bay windows that flanked her, turned into partial mirrors by the dark night outside. I realized she'd been afraid to say the name a third time, even now as she recounted the story.

I found myself leaning forward, waiting to hear what happened next, my delicious spaghetti totally forgotten.

"Then we waited," Melissa said. "Angie—that's this other girl—started making little 'woo-ooh' ghost noises and we told her to hush. Then we whispered about it and finally decided to do it again, but we had to say it louder this time. Simona was already freaking out and wanted to leave, but we wouldn't let her.

"Anyway, we did it again. We said the name three times, but

louder, like a normal talking voice," Melissa said. "Then we got braver and did it *again*, and again, and by then we're all like trying to be louder than each other and just yelling it at the top of our lungs. Like we totally forgot her parents were asleep upstairs.

"I really don't know how many times we said it, but then there was this thump outside the door. She had a dog, so maybe it was the dog trying to get in, or maybe not...But nobody was thinking about the dog, you know? Not right then.

"So we all got quiet, totally frozen, and I was watching the door in the mirror So I could see all of us there in the mirror, but the girls at the back were just dark shapes because the candle was burning down.

"I'm looking and looking at the door in the mirror. That's when I saw her." Melissa chewed her lower lip, falling silent.

"What did you see?" I asked, as gently as I could.

"The face. *Her* face. Like a young woman—I mean, older than I was, like in her twenties, and she was really pretty, or you know, she used to be. There was blood." Melissa traced her fingertips from her eyes down across her cheeks. "Her eyes were full of red, and she was crying blood. Her lips were bloody, too. She was dead, like someone had stabbed her to death through the eyes. And she was just standing there, facing me in the mirror.

"Then she turned her head a little bit, like she was trying to see everyone in the room—which is weird, because she didn't have any eyeballs, just bloody holes—and that's when I screamed. And everybody else screamed, and we all ran out of there."

Melissa had long since abandoned her dinner fork. She repeatedly twisted and crunched a paper napkin in her hands, looking stressed.

"That sounds pretty scary," I said.

"Totally." Melissa nodded. "Hey, you're a ghost expert. Do you know anything about Bloody Mary? Like who she *really* is?"

"My first response would be that most cases are probably a combination of self-hypnosis and the Caputo effect," I said.

"The what thing now?" Michael asked.

"A psychologist in Italy had test subjects look at a mirror in a dim room for ten minutes each," I said. "They saw their faces change—sometimes into other people, sometimes into monsters. It's some kind of hyperactive processing in the brain's facial-recognition software, as far as anyone can guess."

"And that scientist grew up to be a guy named Caputo," Michael said.

"Sure...on top of that, you all expected to see something scary," I said. "You'd psyched each other up for it. So, combine those two effects. What did the other girls see?"

"A scary woman's face," Melissa said.

"Just like yours?"

"Um..." Melissa sat back in her chair. "Simona said it was like a shriveled old woman with black eyes. Callie said it was more like a skull with red hair."

"So you all saw something different?"

"I guess. You think we just made it all up?"

"That's the most likely possibility," I said. "But there are a couple of others..."

They both looked at me, waiting. Matching pairs of vibrant green eyes.

"Your ritual activities could have attracted any loose spirits in the area," I said. "Your state of mind could have made you more sensitive to seeing them. And there are a few ghosts who use mirrors as a kind of doorway. The symbolism of a mirror attracts them. It can be difficult to explain."

"Doorways to where?" Melissa asked, her voice a whisper.

"Wherever they go when they're not here," I said. "Sometimes they're here, sometimes...*there*. The other side."

"What's on the other side?" Melissa asked, and Michael leaned in a little, like he wanted to hear.

"I don't know," I said. "Who does?"

The room was quiet for a minute after that, everybody poking at their food but not eating very much. I was a real downer, I guess.

"So," I said, clearing my throat. "Is that the whole story, Melissa?"

"I wish!" Melissa said, perking up again. She hopped to her feet. "Come on, I'll show you."

I glanced at Michael, who shrugged, gesturing for me to follow her.

Melissa led me to a low half-wall under a slanted roof. She knelt by a kind of hobbit door, much lower and wider than a normal door. It sort of reminded me of a barn gate, actually.

She pulled the knob at one end, swinging it open. I expected to see a crawlspace beyond, or maybe a storage closet with an inconveniently low ceiling.

Instead, it opened onto another room, with a single bed and wooden dresser with a large mirror framed by ornate little shelves and columns. Dance trophies adorned the shelves, tall plastic figurines colored to look like gold, on plastic pedestals colored to look like wood.

Melissa hopped down into the room—the floor was a few feet lower on the other side of the door.

"Watch that first step," she said.

"Interesting doorway," I said, squatting down and swinging my legs through.

"I think the house originally had multiple attics or something," Michael said. His voice startled me because it was so close—I hadn't realized he'd left the table, but now he stood over me, watching me with a little lopsided devil-grin. "Things didn't line up when they fused all the third-floor portions together."

"It's pretty neat," I said. Melissa's room was small and rectangular, with a pair of windows in one of the long sides of the room. Her single bed lay under one window, but the other window was mostly blocked by the big dresser and its mirror, which were jammed against the foot of her bed. It didn't seem like the most logical use of the space.

"My dresser used to be over there," she said, pointing to one of the short ends of the rectangular room. Then she pointed to her bed. Her headboard was against the other end of the rectangular room, next to her closet. "When I was in bed, I could see the mirror. It reflected my bed and my closet. So at night, if I woke up, I'd see myself and the closet beside me, too."

"Okay," I said, nodding for her to continue.

"About a month after that party, I woke up one night, and my room was really, really cold," she said. "It was August, so it was still hot outside, but I was freezing. My teeth were actually chattering together. I didn't even know that was a real thing until then. And it wasn't just the cold—I felt like something was watching me, or like somebody was in the room with me.

"I saw her in the mirror. The doors of my closet were like half open..." Melissa demonstrated, positioning the two doors. "So I couldn't see right into my closet, I could only see the inside of it in the mirror. It was Bloody Mary again, like she'd followed me home or something. Standing in my closet. Watching me from the mirror with her bloody eyes.

"I couldn't move. I was seriously frozen, not just from the cold. It felt like all the strength was draining out of me while I just lay there, looking at her in the mirror. I was too afraid to even close my eyes."

"What did she do?" I asked.

"She stood there for a minute, watching me. It seemed like it lasted hours, but it couldn't have been that long. Then she was gone, just like that. The room slowly got warmer, but I could still barely move at first. My muscles were like jelly. I was so tired, but I was still more scared than tired, so I turned on the lamp. I stared into my closet, but there was nothing there. I left the light on and somehow fell asleep later, after telling myself it was just a bad dream. The next day I saw a dress hanging in my closet, right about where Bloody Mary had been, and I told myself, yeah, I just was half-asleep and got confused.

"But it happened again a couple weeks later, and then again. Freezing cold. Bloody Mary watching me from the closet. I started sleeping in the living room. Finally Michael turned my dresser so I couldn't see the mirror at night, even though he had to jam it in between the wall and the foot of my bed."

"Did that take care of it?" I asked.

"Sort of," she said. "A couple of times I thought I heard a footstep in my closet. One time I heard some of the hangars kind of rattle together in the middle of the night. Why would they do that? I didn't open my closet to look. But it started happening less and less. It's been a year or something now since the last time. I haven't thought about it in a while. I guess I blocked it out. Everybody thinks you're crazy if you talk about seeing ghosts." She shrugged.

"Believe me, I know exactly what you mean," I said.

"Do a lot of people think you're crazy?" Michael asked.

"More than I'm comfortable with." *Do you think I am?* I wanted to ask, but didn't. "It comes with the work." I looked at Melissa again. "Is that it?"

"Is that not enough?" She frowned.

"Do you have any idea why it might have gone away? Did anything change in your life around then?" I drew my Mel-Meter and leaned into the closet, but I didn't find any unusual readings, not even a ghost of a ghost.

"I don't even know why it was here," Melissa said. "I figured she followed me home from Callie's party or something, then haunted me for a while until she got called away."

"Called away?"

"Sure. Think of how many kids are out there doing 'Bloody Mary.' It must be, like, thousands every day. Every weekend, at least. I guessed she finally got distracted. I didn't really think about it, I was just glad she was gone. But no, I don't think anything special happened in my life to end it." Melissa seemed to be concentrating very hard.

"Did anything change around the house?" I asked. "Somebody move in or out?"

"The Fieldings moved in last summer," Michael said.

"Do they have kids?" I asked.

"They have a boy. He's like nine or ten," Melissa said. "I tried to get some babysitting work from them, but they didn't hire me. They're not very nice. They think they're better than everyone else in the house, I guess because they have the biggest apartment."

I nodded. I wanted to speak to them now, especially the boy, but that sounded difficult to arrange.

"So what do you think? Was I haunted by the ghost of Bloody..." Melissa glanced at the dark, reflective window again. "Of her?"

"I don't think that's exactly it," I said. I looked to Michael. "What about you? Ever experience anything strange or unexplained in this house?"

Michael shrugged. "Just a creaky old house being old and creaky."

"That's not true!" Melissa said. "What about that one time in your room?"

"I told you that was nothing," Michael said.

"That's not what you said when you told Angelique about it." Melissa looked at me. "He won't admit it, but he saw something. I heard him tell his girlfriend."

"It was *not* a big deal," Michael said.

"I'd like to hear it anyway," I said. *Girlfriend?* Of course he had one.

"Come on." Melissa heaved herself up through the low half-door, back into the living room. I followed, feeling a little silly as I crawled on my hands and knees a few paces until I could stand without banging my head on the steeply sloped ceiling.

"Where are you taking her?" Michael asked, hurrying to cut off his sister.

"Your room." Melissa pointed to a door tucked on the far side of the brick chimney, almost out of sight.

"There's no reason to do that," he said.

"I just want to show her the closet—" Melissa tried to dodge around him, and he stepped sideways to block her. There was some wrestling as she tried to push past him, grinning the whole time like she was playing the world's greatest prank.

"You really don't have to show me," I said.

"See?" Michael said, relaxing a little. "She doesn't even want to see my room."

Melissa took advantage of the moment to dodge under his arm and open his door.

"Wait!" Michael said, hurrying after her.

"Wow, your room's a wreck," Melissa said, snickering.

"Just let me...can you wait here a second?" he asked me, looking flustered. He'd been laid-back and calm so far, but his little sister apparently knew how to annoy him. Not surprising. I was an only kid, so I didn't have the pleasure of a sibling making my life more difficult.

"What are you hiding in your room?" I asked. "A gorilla?" I don't know why I said *gorilla*. Guess I thought it would be funny.

"I'll be right back." Michael stepped into his room, and I heard him rummaging around in there. Melissa stood outside the door, giving me a smile.

"He's just hiding his My Little Ponies," Melissa said.

"I am not!" he shouted from behind his mostly-closed door, and Melissa cackled.

"Just leave the My Little Ponies out where I can see them," I said. "They're not that scary."

Michael opened his door. "Okay. Come on."

I stepped into his room. It was a very artist-in-a-garret situation, cramped under a sloping roof, except that it flared out at one corner. Two steps led up into the corner, but most of the area at the top of the steps was hidden behind a heavy blue drapery, like an old-timey bed curtain.

A breeze shifted that curtain, giving me a glimpse of the foot of his bed, which apparently sat on a small raised platform surrounded by arched windows in one of the house's turrets. The windows were open to let in the cool evening breeze.

I quickly turned my attention away from this odd-but-fascinating sleeping arrangement and looked at the narrow workbench set up on one side of the room, where Michael was standing. Tiny gears, cylinders, and disks were spread across the table, along with some odd little hand tools and spools of wire.

At one end of the table stood something that looked like a fanciful Bavarian dollhouse, with colorful wooden flowers trimming the bottom edge. A second-floor balcony with large doors sat under a clock face with Roman numerals.

"What's that?" I walked around and saw the exposed back, full of intricate little mechanisms.

"It's just an old automaton clock," he said. "I kind of...fix them up. It's extra money," he added almost apologetically, as if embarrassed.

"Automaton?" I asked. "Like a cuckoo clock?"

"Exactly. But this one's a gnome clock." He lifted up a wooden disk with four little gnome figures mounted around the edges. "Every hour, the balcony doors open, and one of these four guys pops out, depending on the time of day." One gnome leaned on a shovel, as if hard at work. Another snoozed on a mushroom bed, his hat low over his eyes.

"You made this?" I asked, and he laughed.

"No, I just find old ones and fix them," he said. "Some of them are in really bad shape. I like restoring these old things, bringing them back to life..."

"He's a freak," Melissa said, watching us from the door. "Just tell her about the ghost, Mikey."

"I don't know if it was a ghost." Michael sat down behind the bench and toyed with a weird little tool, like miniature pitchfork with the outer tines bowed out into a "C" shape.

"What did you see?" I asked.

"I was up here working one night, on this owl clock I'd found at an estate sale. Its eyes and wings moved when it hooted the hour. That's what it was supposed to do, anyway, but this thing was missing half its parts. I had to replace the weights, the pendulum rods, the winding chains, the eyeball mechanism. It was a great piece, though, made by Shaefer Brothers of Philadelphia in 1887—"

"Nobody *cares*, Michael," Melissa interrupted.

"I thought it was pretty interesting," I said.

"Oh-kay..." Melissa shook her head and gave me a perplexed look, as if I'd spoken an alien language.

"Anyway," Michael said, "I was sitting here working on that Shaefer owl clock one night. It was around one in the morning, and I had all these problems with the owl wing I was trying to fix. I was totally focused on this, but then out of the corner of my eye..." He pointed over to his arch-shaped closet door. "I saw the door open. And I was pretty sure a shadowy head leaned out and looked at me.

"I turned, and it dodged back into the closet." Michael dashed across the room, reenacting for my benefit. "I ran after it, but when I looked in the closet, nothing." He started for the door. "And that's it. That's all I saw."

"How long ago was this?" I asked.

"Two years, at least. Pretty soon after we moved in." He stood near his bedroom door, waiting for me.

"It was inside this closet?" I reached for the handle and pulled it open.

"Hey, don't—" he said, and then a couple weeks' worth of dirty laundry spilled out onto my feet. Jeans, socks, t-shirts, boxer shorts. There was a reassuring lack of Speedos. He'd probably jammed it all in there at the last minute.

Melissa cracked up.

"Oops," I said, then I drew my Mel Meter again and checked the closet, holding it over the dirty laundry. "I'm not picking up any sign of a ghost in here."

"Mike's socks probably ran it off," Melissa said.

"Can we go back to that part where we were out in the kitchen having a good time?" Michael asked.

"I probably need to get back downstairs, anyway," I said. "I guess we're done checking out your, uh...stuff." I backed up, shaking his underwear off the toe of my boot, feeling more than a little embarrassed. For both of us, really.

"We're setting up cameras and microphones all over Alicia's apartment tonight," I said, while making my way out of his room. Michael closed the door behind him, and I caught him giving his sister a quick scowl. "It's a long shot, but if we have any extra cameras, could we set up one at each of your closets?"

"A camera in my room?" Melissa frowned. "Who's going to be watching it?"

"Mostly my tech manager, Stacey," I said. "She'll be watching the whole house."

"Okay, a girl," Melissa said, relaxing a bit.

"We won't be looking at you," I told her. "We can position it right at the closet door."

Melissa shrugged and looked at her brother.

"Just the closet?" Michael asked. "I don't want anybody stealing my secret gnome-clock repair techniques."

"You're such a dork," Melissa whispered.

"So that's a yes from both of you, right?" I doubted we'd see much activity in their apartment, but I wanted to cover as much of the house as we could. Apartments B and D, the Fielding family and Mr. Gray, weren't available to us, so I wanted to get a foothold in Michael and Melissa's apartment. It wasn't just an excuse to come back and see Michael again. Though I couldn't say I minded that aspect of it at all.

"I suppose you can check our place for ghosts if you want," Michael said. He gave me a crooked smile, and the cuckoo clock on the wall sprang to life. Its little door opened and the wooden bird popped out and made its "cuckoo, cuckoo" sound several times, as if to say the idea of looking for ghosts was a bit insane.

I smiled, feeling pretty awkward, and returned downstairs.

Chapter Seven

"Check this out," Stacey said. I'd found her, along with Alicia and her kids, in Kalil's room. She was rigging up a small spotlight that plugged into the wall, and she'd aimed it directly at the closed door of Kalil's closet. "If anything comes out to bother Kalil, he can switch this on from a control by his bed. I rigged one up in Mia's room, too."

She flipped on the spotlight, soaking the closet door in its scorching white glare.

"Looks good," I said. "But we could have just loaned them a couple of tactical flashlights."

"True, but then I couldn't do this." Stacey tapped her digital tablet. The spotlight turned off, then back on again. "Remote control. Even if they're asleep when the fearfeeder comes out, I can torch it from the van."

"Nice." I nodded.

Kalil sat on the edge of the bed and pressed a button on his end table, wired to the spotlight, clicking it off and on.

"I have one, too!" Mia reminded me, beaming.

"So...how did it go?" Stacey asked with a sneaky grin. She stood and led me out of the room, while the kids stayed behind, taking turns clicking the spotlight. They seemed overjoyed about it, as if we'd given them a powerful weapon.

Ghosts hate bright lights, especially the sun. That's why Stacey and I carry high-powered SWAT-style tactical flashlights on our all jobs.

Unfortunately, no amount of light will really harm the dangerous ghosts or make them go away permanently—light is just a defense, and it doesn't always work if the ghost is determined to harm you. It still beats politely asking the monster to go away.

"Come on, I'll show you what I rigged downstairs." Stacey led me down the steps, then asked in a lower voice, "So?"

"They said we could put a couple cameras up there tonight. Do we have anything to spare? It's not that critical. They haven't had a lot of activity recently—none in the past year, but they have seen things in their closets in the past."

"What else?" Stacey asked, looking very amused with herself.

"The girl was haunted by Bloody Mary for a while after summoning her at a slumber party," I said, while Stacey led me toward a night vision camera pointed at the door to the old, sealed-off basement stairway under the grand front stairs. "You know, you look in the mirror and say her name three times..."

"I know," Stacey said. She stood by the camera, arms crossed, looking impatient.

"It's consistent with a fearfeeder," I said. "Taking the shape of something that scared her."

"That's all very interesting and great. Now tell me about the fireman. Is he hot?" She snickered. "Hot fireman. That's pretty funny—"

"Stacey, come on." I glanced upstairs to see if our clients had come out of the boy's room.

"Come on, what? Is he datable or not?"

"I guess." I double-checked the little display monitor on the closet camera to make sure the shot was lined up. I zoomed it out a little. "We want to get the area above the door. It likes to crawl on the ceiling."

"Your pretend lack of interest is totally not convincing," Stacey said.

"He has a girlfriend," I said. "*Angelique*."

Stacey snickered. "Is she French or what? An art student, maybe?"

"I have no details."

"Want me to ask him for some?"

"I do not." I checked the camera pointed at the dead-end basement stairs under the main staircase, and I made sure the door leading to them was closed tight.

"Milk the sister for information," Stacey suggested.

"I don't feel like milking anyone today, thanks." I heard footsteps on the stairs above us. "This camera looks good. Let's go set up in Michael's place. I want a hidden camera down in the laundry room, too."

"Why hidden?"

"So the neighbors don't complain. The Fieldings apparently aren't very friendly."

"No, they're not." Alicia came around to join us. "They only speak to me to complain. Kalil left his bike in the yard, or somebody played their music too loud, or Mia and her friends were practicing their dances on the front porch and the Fieldings had to walk *all the way* around them to open their door..." She shook her head.

"I have to wonder if their kid's seeing anything," I said.

"Good luck talking to them."

"We were about to head down to the basement. Do you happen to have a laundry basket we can borrow? Maybe a few towels to hide the camera?" I asked her.

"Sure. How was your talk with Michael and Melissa?"

"They've seen things," I said. "We're going to watch their closets, too, just in case. I'd like to get cameras all over the house. What about Mr. Gray? What's he like?"

"Quiet as a mouse," Alicia said. "You just see him coming and going. He's an older man who lives alone. That's all I know."

"Maybe I'll pay him a visit tomorrow," I said.

We grabbed our last cameras while Alicia brought us a laundry basket stocked with towels and a couple of blankets. Then Stacey and I headed out into the short side hall that connected three apartments with the porch and the basement.

I opened the basement door, and we looked down the wooden steps into the dim room below. One dryer was thudding along, rocking a little on the concrete floor. The hanging fluorescent bars swayed, casting shifting shadows that faded to complete darkness around the corners and edges of the room. The air was unseasonably cool.

Neither of us was in a hurry to start down the stairs. The air had an unpleasantly familiar heaviness, a cold thickness I'd learned to associate with strong, active ghosts. Goose bumps crawled up along my spine.

"Hey," Stacey said, "Let's go do the third-floor apartment first. Good idea, am I right?"

"The basement's not going to be less creepy if we come back later," I said.

"But we'll have less gear to juggle, in case we need to run out of the basement in a hurry."

She had a point there. We'd had some bad experiences in basements in the past. Ghosts are drawn to the dark underground areas of a house like bats to a cave. Maybe it reminds them of the graves where they belong. If we were going down there, I preferred to travel light.

So we went upstairs instead.

In the apartment, Stacey managed to distract Melissa by enthusiastically asking about the clownfish and anemones in the aquarium. Maybe it wasn't even an intentional ploy—Stacey does wildlife photography as a hobby. It fits right into her deplorable camping-and-hiking lifestyle.

She went to set up a tripod in Melissa's room, leaving me to handle Michael's room by myself. As he led me in, I noticed he'd crammed his dirty clothes into a laundry basket in the corner.

"So you're going to watch me sleep?" he asked while I set up.

"Just the closet," I said. "You won't even be in range." I glanced at his bed curtain, still swaying in the night air. "I can tell you're really into privacy by how you sleep surrounded by windows."

"I *close* the windows," he said. "If it's cold. Or...whatever."

"Uh-uh." I looked at the digital display screen. "Okay, if Closet Man pokes his head out, we'll see it."

"You're probably wasting your time up here," he said. "I only saw it once."

"Do you know any of the other neighbors very well? Besides

Alicia and her kids?"

"Not really. I met Hoss Fielding when he moved in—"

"Hoss?"

"Henry, but he prefers to be called 'Hoss.'"

"I find that hard to believe," I said.

"Me, too. He's a tall guy, seems like a car salesman or something. His wife is always scowling when I see her. Sometimes we hear them yelling at their kid."

"What about Mr. Gray?"

"I barely know that guy. Good neighbor. I'm surprised he puts up with the rest of us."

I sighed—I'd hoped he could help me talk to somebody who lived in one of the other apartments, but apparently the Fieldings were no more friendly to him than to Alicia. I would have to approach them cold, with a simple "Hi, I'm looking for ghosts in your building, can we spy on your apartment?" I couldn't see that going very well.

Then I glanced at his overstuffed laundry basket.

"Were you planning to wash those tonight, by any chance?" I asked.

"Uh...not really. I don't like to go down to the laundry room."

"I can see that."

"It's not that I'm lazy. The basement is just..." He shrugged.

"Scary? Spooky? Creepy?" I suggested.

"Right. It's like someone's watching you down there."

"That's just what Alicia told me," I said. "We have to go set up a camera in that room. I was thinking it would be convenient if you happened to be on your way down there."

"You're scared of the basement, too." He gave me his little devilish grin.

"I've had bad experiences with haunted basements. But if you're too busy, that's okay. I was just checking." I moved toward his door.

"Hold on. I didn't say I wouldn't go." He grabbed his laundry basket and followed me out.

Melissa and Stacey were back in the living room.

"What's up?" Melissa asked her brother. "Doing some night

laundry?"

"Just keeping the ghost hunters safe," Michael said, glancing at Stacey, who grinned.

"Sure." Melissa looked me over. "You've got my brother washing his clothes. That's amazing."

"Don't act like I never do it." Michael stepped out the front door of his apartment.

"He *never* does it," Melissa whispered to me. "Not until his socks are walking around on their own."

"Thanks for all your help," I said, giving her a smile.

"I know about the stuff Kalil and Mia are seeing in their rooms," Melissa said, suddenly looking serious. "They've told me about it. I hope you can take care of it."

"I hope so, too."

Stacey and I followed Michael downstairs. He was waiting by the open door to the basement.

"Ready?" he asked, already turning to start down the steps. I followed, noticing that this was my least favorite sort of staircase, wooden steps with no vertical risers, just dark gaps between the stairs where someone could reach up and grab your ankle.

The room was bigger than it had looked from the doorway. I clicked on my flashlight and swept it around the dark, dusty corners, finding lots of spiderwebs. Three of the walls were old brick, while one looked like stones crudely cemented together. Two basement-level doors led out of the laundry room, and I asked Michael about them while he dumped his laundry into a washing machine.

"That one connects to Mr. Gray's apartment," he said, pointing to the door set into a brick wall. He turned to the other door, in the rock wall. "That's just the furnace, I think."

"Mind if I look?" I approached the door and found it coated in dust and spiderwebs. It didn't appear to get much use.

"It's probably locked," he said.

I tried the cold, grimy handle, but it wouldn't turn. I wiped my hand on my jeans.

"Who would have the key?" I asked.

"You'd have to call the property manager," he said.

"Hey, what do you think about right here?" Stacey asked me. She was positioning Alicia's laundry basket on a counter that ran along one wall. "I can get...most of the room from here."

"Try to include this door," I said. "And as much of the ceiling as you can."

"Okay, but these aren't exactly ideal conditions." Stacey propped the camera on a rolled towel to tilt it upward, then packed in the other towels and blankets around it. She stepped back to look at her work. "That's probably the best I can do."

"You know, you've kind of trapped me here," Michael said.

"What do you mean?" I asked him.

"Now I have to come back in half an hour to move my clothes to the dryer," he said. "Or I'll get sour laundry issues. What if the ghost gets me?"

"I can come back with you if you want," I said. I thought he was kidding, but I wasn't totally sure. "And Stacey will be watching on the camera, too."

"I'd better give you my phone number so you can tell me if you see any ghosts down here." He was grinning—I still couldn't tell if he was kidding.

"Good idea." He told me his number and I saved it in my phone. Then I fished a business card out of my pocket and handed it over. "The second one's my cell number. If *you* see any ghosts anywhere in the house, call me."

"And you'll come bust the ghost?" he asked.

"Maybe." I took a last look around the cold, gloomy basement with my flashlight, then I headed upstairs.

Chapter Eight

"So, you gave him your number," Stacey said. She sat in the back of the van while the monitors came to life one by one, showing the feeds from the cameras we'd set up all over the house. The kids' room showed up in both thermal and night vision.

"I gave him my work number." I stood on the driveway, talking to her through an open door at the back of the van.

"Do you *have* another number?"

"It's just in case we see ghosts," I told her. "We condemned him to return to the laundry room, remember? And he'll let me know if *he* sees anything tonight."

"Then let's hope he sees a ghost," Stacey said. She smiled, straightening up on the narrow cot where she sat. "Hey, we could Scooby-Doo up a fake haunting so he'll have to call you!"

"We're not Scooby-Dooing anything."

"You sure? It would be a fun harebrained scheme. We make a sheet ghost and hang it on a clothesline, see, and run *that* past his bedroom window—"

"How are your monitors looking?" I asked. "Any adjustments needed? Any malfunctions?"

"Fine, go all Sally Serious on me." Stacey turned to the bank of little monitors built at the front of the cargo area, then checked her laptop and nodded. "All systems nominal, Captain. The *Enterprise* awaits your orders."

"Are your signals strong?"

"You know who *I* think was giving off some strong signals tonight—" Stacey began, and she looked like she was about to laugh.

"I'll mark that as a yes." I switched on my headset and walked away toward the big wraparound porch. "Testing, testing..."

"You could at least close the door behind you," Stacey said over my headset, while slamming the van door where I'd been standing.

"I thought you might enjoy the fresh night air." I glanced up, but I couldn't see any stars because of the row of wrought-iron streetlamps along the sidewalk. The old house towered above me, its small turrets, protruding windows, gingerbread trim, and recessed porches creating a labyrinth of shadows across its facade. Even at a casual glance, this place looked like a haunted house.

I returned through the front door. Alicia was in the living room, waiting for me.

"The kids are in bed," she told me. "I made you some coffee in the kitchen. Just help yourself."

"Thank you," I said.

"I'll probably go to my room, too. With you and your friend here, I might actually be able to sleep tonight. Wake me if anything happens."

"I will. Good night, Alicia."

She yawned as she walked into the first-floor bedroom and closed the door. I heard the sound of running water as I climbed the big entrance-hall staircase, like she was having a bath.

The doors to the kids' rooms were closed, and the upstairs was silent. I was camping out on my air mattress in the hallway to stay close to them, and I'd already placed my toolbox of gear and my digital tablet beside it.

I picked up the tablet and flipped through the various camera feeds. I couldn't see the kids, but I could see their closet doors were closed tight.

There was one camera in the hall, a thermal pointed at the door to nowhere with the decorative archway. Alicia had seen the entity leave through it. I glanced from the thermal image to the door itself. Nothing happening so far.

With a smile, I checked on Michael's closet door. Then I looked at his sister's door, then the laundry room, and the door to the dead-end basement stairs. Everything was coming in fine. Calm and quiet.

One end of the hallway terminated in a pair of narrow glass doors that led out onto a sunken porch. I stepped through them. Outside, I found myself in a small outdoor area, paved with brick and surrounded by solid walls on three sides, with an iron balustrade overlooking the garden below.

I had a clear view of the old Wilson house towering on its small lot, the moonlight painting the peeling exterior the color of washed-out bones.

I shivered at the sight of it. If this really was the same entity, I wondered how it had changed in the past couple of years. Was it weaker or stronger? Would it remember me?

"We're going to stop you this time," I whispered. "We're going to catch you."

The house stared blankly back at me, its windows and doors plugged with plywood.

Michael returned to the laundry room a while later, and Stacey made sure to alert me of the fact. I selected the night vision camera in the basement and watched him on my tablet. If anything supernatural jumped out of the shadows to grab him, I'd want to know about it.

He smiled and waved at the camera when he arrived, but glanced nervously over his shoulder a couple of times while he changed over his laundry. He gave another wave when he left, and said something, but we didn't have a microphone down there to hear.

"Did you catch that?" Stacey whispered over my headset.

"I think he said 'no ghosts.' Or maybe 'yo-yo.'"

"Yeah, probably 'yo-yo.' Because that makes sense."

Michael turned off the light as he reached the top of the basement stairs, and the camera adjusted, showing me the basement in shades of green, penetrating the shadows so I could watch the two closed doors.

"So, what did his room look like?" Stacey asked.

"Messy," I replied. "He sleeps in the turret."

"That's romantic."

"You're hilarious, Stacey. Can you keep your mind off my love life for a few minutes? Or years, maybe?"

"You have a love life?" Stacey feigned a surprised gasp. "Tell me all about it."

"Sorry, I didn't hear that," I said. "My headset must be going bad. We'd better stay quiet unless we see some otherworldly activity."

"Now you're being hilarious," Stacey grumbled.

It was a quiet night, for a while. We logged the first activity at two thirty-seven in the morning.

"Ellie," Stacey whispered. "The basement."

I checked my tablet. The camera's viewpoint was cut into two stripes by the laundry basket's plastic-weave design. I could see washing machines and the staircase on one side, a couple of dryers and the two basement doors on the other.

"Where?" I whispered.

"Watch by the last dryer. Maybe it'll come back."

After a moment, something flickered, but not where she'd directed me. It was farther back, by the door to the furnace. It was just a rippling curve that appeared briefly in the air, then it was gone.

"What was that?" Stacey whispered, in her best girl-about-to-be-slaughtered-in-a-horror-movie voice.

A suggestion of a shape appeared near the stairs, maybe the dim outline of a small person, but it faded just as quickly.

"I wish we had thermal down there," I said. I eyeballed the thermal down the hall from me, the one pointed at the door to nothing, and weighed the idea of carrying it down into the basement right away.

"We'll know for tomorrow," Stacey said. "Look, there's a..."

I saw it, and it faded before Stacey could even get the word out. A tiny, circular orb had winked across the room, near the ceiling.

"It's getting active down there," Stacey whispered.

We watched for the next half an hour as occasional forms and partial apparitions faded in and out, never very clear or lasting very long, making me think of a weak radio with poor reception, just the occasional hint of a voice or drop of music leaking through the static.

"Are you seeing anything up in the house?" I asked.

"Nothing."

The strange shapes continued to appear, increasing in frequency for several minutes. Then they stopped cold.

"Is that it?" Stacey asked after a few minutes of inactivity.

The laundry room lay quiet for a bit longer—then something emerged from the door in the rock wall. A dark shape rose from the top of the door, like a two-dimensional cutout made of black cardboard.

"The door," I whispered.

The dark shape slithered up along the wall, a roughly human-shaped shadow against the many shades of night-vision green. Its arms bent the wrong way at the elbow as it planted its hands on the ceiling.

Then the dark shape skittered across the ceiling, arms and legs bending at sharp angles that reminded me of a running spider.

"Holy cow," Stacey whispered.

The shape flickered toward the stairs, then it was gone.

"Where is it?" I asked. I was on my feet, ready to move, but I had no idea where to go.

"Not in front of any other cameras," Stacey said. "We need better coverage of this house. We focused too much on the closets."

I flipped through the various viewpoints in Alicia's apartment —the door that led beneath the stairs, the closets in the kids' rooms —watching for the thing to emerge.

"Ellie," Stacey whispered. "I think it's in the hallway with you. It's walking toward you."

I checked the feed from the thermal camera pointed at the door to nowhere. There it was. A faint pale blue shape moved in front of the archway, like the shadow of a man taking a walk.

It was moving toward me, toward the kids' rooms.

Then it stepped out of the camera's range, still heading in my direction.

I grabbed the thermal goggles from my toolbox and strapped them on as quickly as I could, never turning my back on the invisible figure. I could feel a growing chill in the air.

With the heavy goggles in place, I could see it again—a tall, broad-shouldered male shape, thin and blue. Walking, almost strolling, like it had all the time in the world.

I drew the powerful, three-thousand-lumen tactical flashlight from its holster on my belt, but I didn't click it on. The light might have chased the thing away, but the entity wasn't threatening anyone yet, and I was here to observe and learn.

My heartbeat kicked up as the pale figure passed close by me, my fingers trembling with a sudden blast of fight-or-flight adrenaline. The air grew even colder, and it seemed to seep into me, filling me with icy dread. I was definitely looking at something unnatural. If it hadn't been for my thermal goggles, though, I would have seen nothing, experienced nothing more than a cold draft drifting down the hall.

It stopped outside Kalil's room.

I tightened my grip on my flashlight, and also found the little iPod mounted on my belt, next to a small portable speaker. I was ready to hit the ghost with both barrels.

The ghost remained where it was, its faint blue shape fading in and out of sight, as if it were breathing in and using up sips of ambient heat in the room. I couldn't tell if it was preparing to manifest as an apparition or disappear entirely.

"Ellie, are you okay?" Stacey whispered. "I can't see what's happening."

"Mm-hmm," I hummed back, as low as I could, to avoid drawing the entity's attention.

After a long moment, it walked on down the hall, then stopped in front of Mia's room. The light blue blob of its head moved to one side, as though listening to something.

It froze there for several seconds, then vanished.

"I think it went into Mia's room," I said. "I'm pursuing."

"Let me know if it gets dangerous," Stacey replied.

I opened the door and pointed my unlit flashlight into the room, ready to blast the ghost and hopefully distract it from menacing the girl.

My thermal goggles revealed Mia's glowing red form in the bed, but no pale blue shape anywhere.

I tiptoed past the sleeping girl and approached her closet. As I reached for the knob on one of the closed sliding doors, I whispered for Stacey to stand by for activating her remote-controlled spotlight, in case I needed an extra-big flood of photons.

I couldn't help but tremble as I eased the door open. The entity that had haunted the Wilson house and crippled Calvin had the power to dig inside your mind. Not my favorite kind of ghost, not at all.

Nothing immediately jumped out at me, no movie monster wielding a chainsaw, no gray aliens wielding who-knows-what. No Bloody Mary emerging from the shadows like a reflection in a dark mirror.

The girl's clothes hung on the closet rod, neatly sorted by type and color, her shoes perfectly aligned on the rack below in her mother's typical obsessive-compulsive way. Tennis shoes, ballet slippers, black formal shoes with little white bows. No ghosts, as far as my thermals could see.

I raised the goggles off my eyes and clicked on my flashlight. I stepped down into the closet, blasting bright white into the dark corners. Nothing seemed amiss, and I didn't sense any kind of presence in the room. The Mel Meter found no change from the readings I'd taken earlier in the day.

Then I heard something: voices. One sounded like a child, frightened and whispering rapidly. An older male voice cut it off, angry and shouting.

I followed the voices to a wall and pressed my ear against it. It sounded like they were in the next room, but that was in the Fieldings' apartment, so I had no way to check whether these were auditory apparitions or regular living people. Most likely the latter, though.

I couldn't make out many words, and the conversation soon ended. I wondered if the Fielding kid had seen something. I needed to reach out and speak with that family as soon as possible, but the things I'd heard from Alicia and Michael didn't exactly make me look forward to it.

When their voices fell quiet, I left the closet, clicking off my light and closing the door firmly behind me. I slipped out of Mia's room and checked in with Stacey while scanning the hall with my thermals.

"All clear up here," I said.

"I've got a few hints of movement in the basement," Stacey told me. "Nothing anywhere else. Where did it go?"

"Maybe into the Fieldings' side of the house," I said. "I don't think that was our boogeyman, though. It didn't move the same way. And it seemed too weak."

"Another ghost?"

"Nothing attracts ghosts like a haunted house."

"The laundry room is a crowded ghost disco by night," Stacey said. "Why would all those spirits be crammed into the same place when they have this huge house?"

"We need to make a broader survey of the house." I turned the thermal camera in front of the arched doorway so it captured more of the hall beyond. "And monitor the basement in every way we can."

I watched the strange movements and shapes in the basement on my tablet, occasionally switching to the other viewpoints around the house. I didn't catch another glimpse of the dark, spidery shadow or the tall pale figure for the rest of the night.

Chapter Nine

Alicia awoke long before her children. It was still dark outside, but the sky was turning purple as we sat down at her kitchen table to give her a quick summary of what we'd found.

"The basement seems to be the most active area," I said. "We'll need time to analyze all the information we gathered, but Stacey clipped out some video footage for you."

Stacey nodded. She turned her laptop to show Alicia some night vision video of the basement in fast forward, with weird half-formed shapes blinking in and out of sight like bizarre creatures in a dark green aquarium. When the clip ended, she backed it up and played the last part in slow motion.

The spiky, spidery black entity crawled up through the door and across the ceiling. Stacey paused it while the entity was still visible.

"That's it," Alicia said. "That's what I saw in the living room. That's what got me." She touched her stomach where she'd been scratched. "Oh, it makes me sick just to see it."

"That was the last we saw of it," I said. "We think it went into the Fieldings' apartment over there, if it went anywhere at all."

"So it didn't go near my kids last night."

"No...but there was something else." I nodded at Stacey, and she pulled up the other clip she'd prepared, the glimpse of the pale blue figure in front of the dead-end door upstairs.

"What is that?" Alicia whispered.

"I'm not sure," I said. "I don't think it's the fearfeeder. An old house like this can have a number of ghosts." I gave her the quick summary of what the entity had done, how it had seemed to stop and listen at her kids' doors before vanishing. "It could be someone who lived here long ago. Anyway, it didn't seem very strong, based on the temperature reading. It might be a residual haunting, something that just repeats the same actions again and again. We'll gather more information as we go."

"And what about all those things in the basement?" Alicia asked.

"That seems to be the center of activity in the house," I said. "We'll monitor it much more heavily tonight."

"It could be hard to hide that much gear from the neighbors," Stacey said.

"I'll try to speak to your other neighbors later today," I said. "If they don't cooperate, we can probably still set everything up in the laundry room tonight. It seems like nobody in this house likes to go down there at night, so maybe there won't be anyone to notice the cameras and motion detectors."

"That's true," Stacey said. "Only Michael went down there last night...and only because you asked him."

"Good luck talking to Lulinda Fielding." Alicia shook her head. "I'd volunteer to introduce you, but she'd probably be *less* likely to speak to you then. That woman's a beast."

"I can't wait," I said. "In the meantime, we're going to dig deeper into the history of the neighborhood and see what we come up with. It's important to try and find some physical item that can be used to lure the ghost, something that had emotional significance in his life."

"I hope you can find a way to solve this mess," Alicia said. "My kids need to be safe in their home."

"I couldn't agree more," I said. "We'll get to work."

As the sun rose, we shut down our gear, retrieved the laundry basket with the hidden camera from the basement, and headed out to the van.

I dropped Stacey at her apartment and forced myself to attend an early-morning kickboxing class. Once I was there and felt the stress burning out of my tense muscles, I was glad I did it.

Then it was home, feed the cat, sleep for a few hours so I could get back to work with fresh energy.

By noon, I was back at the office. Stacey was already there, the little go-getter, reviewing footage with Calvin.

"Interesting," he said as I pulled an extra chair up to the video editing station, where three large monitors faced Stacey like a three-sided mirror in a department store. "I wonder who our mystery guest was."

"I heard something in the next apartment—" I began.

"Stacey told me. You need to get access to that apartment right away."

"Apparently the residents aren't the sweetest people in the world," I said. "Have you found anything?"

"A missing person file from 1994," he said, grabbing a stack of printouts from the long work table nearby. He rolled over to me and tossed them in my lap. The top page had a black and white image of a smiling boy with chunky braces, wearing a school-picture-day Izod shirt. "Kris Larsen, eight years old. Vanished one Friday night in September, never seen again. His family lived in the house that backs up to our client's. They first thought he'd slipped out and gone to a friend's house, but nobody saw him or heard from him that night."

"Was there any mention of closet monsters?" I asked, skimming over the brief summary from the missing-person database.

"Not in the police report, but that's not an area that your typical cop is going to explore," Calvin said. "We aren't exactly trained to consider supernatural perps."

"Maybe you should be, in this city. Does his family still live there?" I thumbed through more pages.

"Moved in 2001," he said. "The parents now live in Texas. Fourth page."

I flipped through papers and nodded. Too bad they were so far away. I would still try to contact them, but people have a funny way of not wanting to talk about sensitive and highly personal subjects with strangers who call them on the phone. They're even less responsive to emails than phone calls. Face to face is always much more effective, but we didn't have the time or budget for a plane trip halfway across the country.

"What else?" I asked.

"There's another one from 1985," Calvin said. "Bradley Carson, age twelve. It's hard to say whether this was related. The kid disappeared for several days but was found again. I tried to track him down, found out he spent some time in a state psychiatric hospital after that. That's all we know about him so far. I have a friend searching for that old case file."

"Which house?" I asked.

"Next door to the client's. Now, we already know about Bonnie McAllister, six years old, missing in 1973," Calvin said. "I gave Stacey a copy of the file to study."

I nodded. I'd just about memorized that file during our previous, ill-fated investigation. The little girl Bonnie had seen an old-fashioned devil in her closet, horns and hooves and red scales, the whole package. Her parents had responded with therapy and, ultimately, psychiatric meds. After fourteen months of the occurrences growing from once or twice a month to every single night, the girl had finally vanished and was never seen again. The case was still open.

"The databases we can access get spotty a few years before that," Calvin said. "You'll want to contact Grant to see what he can dig up at the Historical Association archives, but this is too wide a net to hand him. A dozen addresses over two centuries."

"Jacob said he can come tonight," Stacey said, grinning like a schoolkid hopped up on Pixy Stix. "I can walk around the block with him and see what he picks up."

"I'm sure you won't mind," I said. "Try not to distract him along the way."

"I won't!" Stacey gave me a sly smile and looked at Calvin. "*Ellie* met an interesting guy. He lives in the building we're investigating."

"That's a fascinating turn in the case," Calvin said. "Let's hear more."

"There's nothing to hear," I interrupted. "Stacey's been pushing me at this firefighter guy since she first heard of him."

"And she likes him," Stacey added, not helping things at all. I felt more embarrassed than annoyed, so maybe I *did* kind of like him.

"Sounds promising, Ellie," Calvin said.

"When did everyone become obsessed with my private life?" I asked. "Don't we have a dangerous ghost to catch here? Let's go call on our next witness."

I grabbed the piece of paper with the Larsen family's phone number on it and walked over to my desk, where I could sink beneath the walls and out of sight for a minute. Nobody answered my call.

"Let's load up, Stace," I said when I stepped out. "We need a full array for the basement, but I don't want to lose any of the camera positions we've already established."

"Look, she's all business now," Stacey said, and Calvin actually chuckled.

"Stacey, just assemble the gear," I told her.

"Yes, sir, captain, sir." Stacey grabbed a thermal and a pair of motion detectors. "Hey, should we go full-on laser grid? Really watch every square centimeter of that basement?"

"That's not a bad idea," I said. "Just remember we have to break down everything before sunrise, if the neighbors aren't cooperative when we visit."

"One multisided grid projector, coming up." Stacey walked to a storage closet.

"I feel like I should come with you," Calvin said to me.

"Come if you want," I said, "But we're still just observing. I'll let you know when we're ready to move on to trapping."

He nodded. "Any new ideas about how to trap this one?"

That was unnerving—my boss and mentor looking to me to figure this out. The responsibility felt a little too heavy.

"Maybe we'll turn up a human identity for the boogeyman," I said.

"If there *is* anything human under there," Calvin said.

"And if he's a pure demonic? Do we call the priest?" I asked.

"He's not a priest anymore," Calvin said. "Just a demonologist. I should give him a ring to make sure he's available." Calvin paused, reflecting. "And at least half-sober."

"We're all geared up for our mission, sir," Stacey said when she returned, giving me one of her mock salutes.

"Stop calling me 'sir.' You sound like Marcy from *Peanuts*," I said.

"Maybe I was talking to Calvin," Stacey said.

"Let's get to work," I said. "I want to squeeze in some serious library time this afternoon, too."

"Oh, please, let's." Stacey shook her head as we approached the van.

"Watch out for ghosts," Calvin said. I glanced back, giving him a grin, but he wasn't actually smiling. His look was dead serious. "Call me if you need anything."

I nodded. It wasn't like him to act so worried, but this was an unusually dangerous case. I was determined to make things right, to finally capture the ghost that had put Calvin in that wheelchair.

Chapter Ten

We spent another fantastic afternoon digging through old title deeds, property records, and faded photographs, still establishing a chain of ownership for all the houses around Alicia's home. There was much sighing and eye-rubbing on Stacey's part.

In the evening, we returned to Alicia's place, ready to set up more gear in the basement.

"Hi," Melissa said, answering the front door. In the big entrance hall-turned-living-room behind her, Mia was practicing handstands while watching cartoons, while Kalil sat on the couch reading a book called *Guns, Germs, and Steel*. "Alicia won't be home until after nine. Come on in. Need any help?" Melissa eyeballed the gear in our arms.

"We're good," I said, stepping inside and setting down a couple of tripods. "We just need to refresh the battery packs on the cameras."

"Did you see Fleshface?" Mia asked, swaying as she walked toward us on her hands.

"Or the aliens?" Kalil asked, pushing his glasses up on his nose as he looked up at me.

"We picked up some good evidence," I said. "We're definitely

on the trail of the one that's been bugging you. It's not really
Fleshface or aliens, did I explain that? It's a thing that can pretend to
be whatever you fear."

"But what is it really?" Kalil asked.

"It's a thing made of energy," I said. "It feeds itself by drawing
out the fear in people. The best way to weaken it is to recognize that
it's tricking you and resist the urge to be afraid."

"What's the *second* best way to make it weak?" Mia asked.

"Showing it courage," I said. "Even if you really feel afraid on
the inside...*act* like you're not afraid. That's what courage really is,
anyway. Shine a light on it. Throw a pillow at it. Shout at it to go
away."

"But what if that just makes it mad?" Kalil asked.

"At first, it might try to get even scarier," I said. "But if you
keep standing up to it, it will go away and sulk, or try to find
someone else to feed on. Because when you show it courage, you're
refusing to feed it. If it does try to make itself bigger and scarier,
that means you're winning, because you're making it use up more of
its energy."

"But what if you can't help being scared?" Mia said.

"I've faced a lot of ghosts," I said. "I still get scared. Your
natural reaction is to go very still, to make no movements or sound
and hope it goes away. With this type, that's *exactly* what they want
you to do. Take some action. Scream for your mom or your brother,
scream for Melissa or me or Stacey if we're here. And hit it with a
big blast of that spotlight Stacey set up for you. Ghosts hate light."

Kalil nodded and jotted notes on a pad on the table.

"All done down here," Stacey said. She'd been working on the
camera that pointed at the door to the dead-end stairs. "I moved it
for a broader view of the living room. Zoomed out as much as I
could."

"Did you get the—"

"It was hard to get the ceiling because it's so high," she said. "I
did get the stair railing, since Alicia saw it climbing there. Kind of a
steep angle, but it's something." She shrugged.

"Looks good," I said, after checking the display screen. "We'd
better get moving. Melissa, we need to change the batteries in your

apartment, too..."

"Go on up. My brother's home."

"Things sure would go faster if you took care of the third-floor cameras, Ellie," Stacey said.

"I'll tell him you're coming." Melissa was suddenly texting on her phone, her purple thumbnails flashing and tapping.

"Wait—" I began.

"Hey, Ellie, think fast!" Stacey said. I turned to see her tossing a camera battery right at me, and I barely had time to snatch it out of the air before it could wham into my ribs.

"Thanks a lot," I told her. "I said *wait*. I should go try to talk to the other neighbors first, before it gets too late to knock on their doors. Stacey, you take care of all the gear."

"Except the third floor, right?" Stacey winked.

"Hey, what was that?" Melissa looked between us, then focused on me. "Are you into my brother or something?" She had a weird little smile, like she was trying to decide whether to laugh.

"No." I felt my cheeks flush. "I mean, I've just met him."

"You're not into him?" Stacey asked.

"I'm into *working*. Which is what you should be doing, Stacey. The sun's almost down, and I don't want to be setting up in the basement at midnight." I walked to the front door, trying not to look like I was in a big hurry to leave.

I paused outside on the porch to take a deep breath of warm evening air. The sky was dark purple above us. I hated the idea of waiting until long after sunset to set up our gear in the clearly haunted basement, but we didn't have much choice if the neighbors didn't give permission.

I circled the house, past a fence thick with honeysuckle vines that blocked the view from the neighbor's yard.

Behind the house lay a small garden enclosed with high brick walls, a pleasant area edged with blooming pink roses. A bench and a covered wooden-bench swing faced a stone birdbath at the center. A pair of hummingbirds floated in the air near a sugar-water feeder on an old oak tree.

Narrow rectangular windows were set just above the ground, in the stone foundation of the house. They were dusty and dark, totally failing to provide any preview of the basement apartment or of Mr. Gray himself.

A pair of slanted doors were built into the back of the house, leading into the cellar, marked with a brass letter "D." Mr. Gray's apartment. From what I'd heard, it would be easier to talk to him than the Fielding family, so I figured I would start with the easy stuff and then let my evening go downhill from there.

I knocked on one of the slanted doors, feeling weirdly like I was visiting the home of some troll who lived underground.

No response came. I glanced at the little windows along the ground, but no light turned on, and there was no sign of activity.

I knocked again. "Mr. Gray?" I called. "Mr. Gray, are you home?"

Nothing. The evening gloom grew darker around me. The hummingbirds were gone, and three bats circled above in the rising moonlight, slurping their way through a cloud of mosquitoes.

I gave it a third knock, but the third time was not the charm. Mr. Gray didn't seem to be home, and if he was, he clearly wasn't planning to answer the door anytime soon.

I took a business card from my purse, circled my cell number, and wrote PLEASE CALL on the back, in the most girly handwriting, and drew a little smiley face. I thought it might reassure him that I wasn't there to harass him or anything negative. Then I stuck it into the crack between the cellar doors and walked away.

It was time for another deep breath as I ascended the porch steps, walked through the side door into the shared hallway, and knocked on the door to the Fieldings' apartment, which had a brass letter B mounted beside it.

The door creaked open. A woman stood there, wearing an inch or so of makeup, her hair an unnatural shade of yellow, her lips a garish shade of red. She was the type who was pushing forty but dressed like a teenage girl in desperate need of attention—high heels, low-slung shredded jeans, skimpy bra top to show off her tanned abs and the cobra tattoo crawling up her left hip. She was chewing gum as she looked me over, and her lips showed some distaste. I could hear a baby crying in the background, and *American Idol* blaring from a television.

"Who are you?" she snapped, by way of a greeting.

I told her my name and occupation, handing her a business card.

"Is this about the lawsuit?" she asked.

"What lawsuit?"

"The class-action against them birth-control bastards." She shook her head. "What do you want?"

"I'm investigating several houses in this neighborhood," I said. "I've been hired by some of your neighbors to look into possible disturbances. Are you Lulinda Fielding?"

"Who's there? Is it Joey?" A chunky kid emerged into the small foyer where she stood. He was pale and out of breath, draped in a Transformers shirt, his girth a weird contrast to his hardbody mother.

"It ain't Joey! Get out of here!" she shouted at him. She turned back to me, but the boy lingered behind her, slowly munching down a bag of Skittles while he stared at me like I was a vaguely interesting cartoon. "I have a lot going on. Would you hurry up?" Lulinda said to me.

"Sorry, ma'am," I said. "Some people in the neighborhood have complained of strange things happening in their homes, particularly at night. They see moving shapes, or things that appear to inhabit their closets—"

"What, like possums?" Lulinda asked.

"Nothing so easy to explain," I said. "We're talking about activity that seems...unnatural. Paranormal, even."

She stopped chewing her gum. "You mean ghosts?"

"Essentially. Though they may not actually be ghosts," I said. "These kinds of experiences can result from a number of explainable sources. Power lines, for example, can interfere with the brain, making it see things that appear to be—"

"Does that mean we can sue the power company?" she asked.

"Well, that's just an example," I said. "What we'd like to do is investigate your home for any possible supernatural activity."

"Uh-huh." She straightened up, stiffening her back and looking down her nose at me. "And how much does *that* cost?"

"I'm not trying to sell you anything—"

"Oh, yeah. Don't try to hornswaggle a hornswaggler. We are not buying anything from you." She began to close the door.

"Please, ma'am." I placed my hand lightly on the door, slowing it but not stopping it entirely—that would be a touch too aggressive. I felt like an old-timey door-to-door salesman, trying to hawk vacuum cleaners to housewives. "Haven't you or anyone else in your home seen scary or unsettling things at night?" I glanced from her to the kid who stood several feet behind her, slowly crunching his Skittles.

"Falcon, how many times have I told you not to eat outside the kitchen!" she snapped. "And chew with your mouth closed."

The huge kid, tragically named Falcon Fielding, frowned at his mom. "But—"

"Quiet!" Lulinda snapped. She turned back to me. "Why are you still there?"

"Would you mind if we just set up some of our gear in other areas of the house?" I asked. "We already have permission from the other tenants in this house. Just common areas like the back garden, or maybe—"

"I told you, we are not buying a thing. Good night!" Lulinda slammed the door in my face.

At least she hadn't thought to say *no.*

I walked around to the front door and let myself back into Alicia's apartment. Stacey was upstairs, reloading and double-checking the gear in the kids' rooms. I heard Kalil and Mia peppering her with questions.

"How did it go?" Melissa asked. She sat up on the couch and paused the TV.

"I met Lulinda Fielding," I said, and she cracked up. "She didn't exactly refuse to let us set up a ton of electronic monitoring equipment down in the basement, but I'm not sure she understood the question."

"Ugh, I hate the basement," Melissa said. "Are there ghosts down there?"

"Yes. That's where they all are, I think."

"I knew it! I totally knew it. You can ask Michael, I told him that yesterday."

"Any luck?" Stacey called down from one of the row of archways that looked out from the second-floor hall.

"They didn't say no," I said. "Nobody told me much beyond that."

"Jacob's going to be here any minute," Stacey said. "And you forgot to run the battery upstairs."

"Okay." I grabbed up the replacement battery from our little pile of basement-bound gear. Melissa narrowed her eyes just a little at me—I couldn't tell if she meant it playfully or not. Then she waved as if dismissing me and started her movie again.

"See you real soon," she said as I left. I don't know why that made me uneasy.

I carried the battery up the four flights to Michael and Melissa's apartment, slowly coming to understand how they could wolf down spaghetti and garlic bread dinners without gaining much weight. Their apartment was neat, and in a decent location near a big park, but I would hate to carry a couch up those stairs.

Michael answered the door. More of that blues music played from the stereo. He wore some ratty, worn-out khakis and a black t-shirt, but also a little pair of half-glasses that looked totally wrong on his face.

"Uh, hi," I said. "Ghost exterminator."

"Come in." He grinned as he closed the door behind me. "How's it going? Caught any yet?"

"No, but we're getting some bites. I just have to change out the battery in Melissa's room, then take the camera out of yours."

"Why's that?" His smile faltered a little, as if he were almost disappointed.

"We need a night vision for the basement. Your bedroom is the least active place in the house, so I'll grab it from there."

"You're saying there's not enough activity in my bedroom?"

"Right, there's—" I paused and blushed at the idea that he might be making a joke. "Not."

"I mean, you only monitored for one night. A *Monday* night."

"Are weekends more exciting?"

"Always. That's when I do most of my clock work."

He followed me to his sister's room and watched through her hobbit door as I switched out the camera batteries. "So...does this stuff really work?"

"This camera? Only if the battery's full."

"No, I mean..." He hesitated, looking at me with a little grin playing around the corners of his mouth. "You know. All of it. The ghost-hunter stuff."

"Are you asking if I'm a scam artist?" I crawled back up through the door. He offered me his hand to help me up, and I accepted. Why not? "Is that what you're getting at?"

"I guess. Not exactly. Yes." He smiled, as if expecting to remove any offense just by being kind of handsome. It helped. A little.

"If I were conning people, why would I admit it?" I asked.

"Maybe you'd have a moment of brutal honesty. A crisis of conscience. That kind of thing," he said.

"Nope." I ducked into his room and collapsed the camera tripod to make it easier to carry. He waited in the living room for me.

"Can I help you carry that down?" he asked, reaching for it as I approached the door.

"So you can spend a little extra time calling me a crook?"

"I'm not calling you anything yet. I just don't personally believe in, you know, horoscopes, or palm reading..." He took the tripod from me and followed me down the steps. Let the accusations fly. I'd heard it all before.

"I wouldn't say I believe in those things, either."

"What about UFO's?" he asked. "Or reptilian Illuminati?"

"Oh, definitely not UFO's," I said. "That's just a conspiracy by the reptile people."

"I knew it."

"So now you know I'm legit." I glanced back at him as we rounded a landing.

"Alicia and her family have been through a lot," he said. "I just don't want them to get hurt. Or ripped off."

"They'll get more than their money's worth," I told him. "We have a sliding scale."

"And easy financing, I'm guessing."

"Zero percent interest for the first twelve months, actually. You should hire us. You're definitely living in a haunted house."

"Definitely, you said?"

"We have footage of two distinct entities," I said. "One in the basement, one in Alicia's apartment."

"Can I see it?"

"I'll show you later."

He laughed. "Sure."

"I mean it," I said. "This whole neighborhood has a history."

We reached the shared hallway, and he started for the basement door.

"Wait," I said. "We don't want to risk the neighbors seeing our gear and getting upset. We have to wait a couple of hours."

"I doubt anybody goes down there at night," Michael said. "It would have to be a pretty serious laundry emergency."

"You don't think it's too early?"

"It feels worse the later it gets," he said. "It's just going to be you and the other girl down there? You don't want it to be too late."

"We've been in worse places than this."

"That's right. I forgot you're a couple of hardened, kick-ass ghost hunters."

"We are. And I thought you didn't believe in ghosts, so what are you worried about?"

"I said I didn't believe in horoscopes."

"What's your sign?"

"Leo."

"Figures. Typical Leo."

"Really?"

"I have no idea." I did, though.

"Call me when you go down," he said. "I'll help you out."

"Oh, really? What will you do, squirt the ghosts with a fire hose?"

"Yes. Because that's all I know how to do, squirt things with hoses."

We circled around to Alicia's front door, and I heard a rusty metallic creak from the far end, under the shadows of the turret roof. In the light from the house windows, I saw a dark form on the porch swing, which moved slightly back and forth, its chains creaking in time.

"Hello?" I said.

"Ellie! Hi!" Stacey rose from the swing, followed quickly by Jacob. "Uh, Jacob's here."

"I'm picking up on that," I said. I turned to Michael. "You can just drop that in Alicia's place. Thanks for helping."

"Let me know if you need me," he said, glancing at Jacob and Stacey before he walked through the door.

"What were you two doing?" I asked.

"Nothing," Stacey said. "I mean nothing, uh, professionally speaking."

"Good. How are you, Jacob?"

"Considering how these things usually go for me, I'm guessing I'm much better now than I'll be in a few hours," he said. "Just let me know in advance whether I should expect to get clawed, bitten, beaten, or burned this time. Then I'll be better prepared for the agony."

"There's a slight chance you could end up facing your own worst fear, whatever that might be," I told him.

"Great. I have so many, I can't wait to see which one is actually the worst." He looked over at the house. "So, did they *intend* to make this place look haunted when they built it, or did it somehow evolve to look more creepy over the years?"

"I'd guess both," I said. "Before we go in, though, I want to walk around the neighborhood..." I glanced inside, where Michael was talking to his sister. "Actually, I have another idea. Stacey, you take Jacob around the block, and record everything he says."

"I'll take video. What are you going to do?"

"Set up our gear in the basement," I said.

"No way. Not by yourself." Stacey crossed her arms. "Not after dark, Ellie."

"Michael volunteered to help me. He might as well pitch in, since we're de-haunting his house and Alicia's paying for it."

"Oh, I totally get it now. Ellie's into that hot firefighter guy," Stacey said.

"Really?" Jacob grinned and leaned to look in the window.

"I am *not*—that's not the point," I insisted. "This way, we won't be working down in the most haunted part of the house at midnight. And it'll be good to have Michael there in case another neighbor walks in on our set-up, since he lives here, too."

"So, to be clear, this has nothing to do with you being alone in the dark with that guy," Stacey said. "Am I getting that right?"

"Absolutely. He can help with the gear and he has emergency training..." I shrugged. "I can have it done by the time you've finished casing the neighborhood. Jacob, we're looking for the oldest thing you can find related to children disappearing—"

"Whoa, whoa," he said. "You're not supposed to give specific information or directions to the psychic, you know."

"I'm giving you some this time," I said. "We need to identify who this entity is. We don't need to hear about every ghost and every tragedy in every house on the street. Each one of these houses probably has its own ghosts."

"Yeah, true. So, missing kids." Jacob watched Stacey as she stepped inside to grab a camera.

"And *old*," I repeated.

"I'll see what I can do." Jacob took Stacey's arm, and the two of them walked down the porch steps. She smiled at him as they strolled away under the streetlamps and the mossy oak limbs, looking like a happy, sappy couple from some old black and white movie.

Michael was still hanging out in Alicia's apartment, talking with his sister and Kalil.

"Is your offer still good?" I asked him.

"Which offer?"

"Helping me downstairs," I said, while grabbing some of the gear.

"Sure."

"You're going to help her find the ghosts?" Melissa asked.

"I can help, too," Kalil said.

"Thanks, but I just need one person," I said. "We'll be back in a minute."

Michael picked up the rest of the gear in his arms.

"Careful, some of that's fragile," I told him.

"Just like when he brings in groceries," Melissa said. "He'll hang like a million bags on each arm to avoid a second trip to the car."

"It's worth it, too," Michael said. He was already to the door before I caught up with him.

Chapter Eleven

Though it was summer and the sun had recently set, the basement air was cold. Michael led the way down the steps, which I liked because it meant he wouldn't notice me peering down at the gaps between the stairs, watching for a shadowy hand to grab at my feet.

None of the washers or dryers were active, a good sign. I opened each of the washing machines, checking inside.

"I don't think that's a good place to hide a camera," Michael said. "Or did you bring something to wash?"

"Ha ha. I'm checking for wet clothes. Wet clothes would mean somebody might be coming back to dry them tonight."

"Are there any?"

"Nope." I closed the lid on the last machine.

"Nice detective work."

"Thank you." I took a spotlight from the assorted gear he'd laid out on the laundry-folding counter. I found a socket near the laundry machines, turning the gloomy basement into a bright day in the Sahara.

"I didn't expect to need sunglasses in the basement," he said, squinting and turning away from it.

"Sorry. I just want to see what I'm doing, and discourage any nasties from bugging me while I do it." The air felt cold and thick, like refrigerated molasses, as I moved through it setting up night vision, thermal, a remote EMF meter, and a motion detector. Michael asked me about each item of equipment and let me explain it. He had a smile on his face, but I couldn't tell if he enjoyed my company or was sort of inwardly laughing at me.

Finally, I set up the laser grid projector on its stand near the middle of the room, and I pointed it right at the door in the rock wall.

"Can you kill the lights?" I asked.

"Is this when we see the ghosts?" he asked. He turned off my searing spotlight, then moved to the light switch on the wall and flicked off the overheads.

"I hope so." I watched thousands of green laser dots become visible on the wall, and I adjusted the projector slightly, centering the grid around the Door to Evil.

"What does that do?" Michael asked, whispering as though the darkness required it.

"If something moves through here, it will black out some of those dots," I said. "It might detect something too insubstantial to see with your eyes, or even a sensitive camera."

"And it really works?"

"Sometimes. We can't count on any of our gear to help one hundred percent of the time. That's why we threw the kitchen sink at this basement. It's very active down here, and we don't want to miss anything."

"Very active, huh?" He was rubbing his stubbled chin, looking at the grid of green dots.

"Come on, I'll show you." I led him through the dark room toward the night vision camera. "Watch the display screen."

"I'm watching."

After a minute, a circular orb floated past. Something flickered in the corner of the screen, the shape of a small human arm, but melted away as quickly as it appeared.

"Are you seeing that?" I whispered.

"Those are ghosts? I expected something a little more...obvious.

Couldn't that just be dust in the air or something? There's definitely tons of that down here."

"These aren't the big entity we want," I said. "They're probably his retinue. Little spirits, fragments of the souls he's taken over the years. Let me try something." I took a deep breath and spoke in a much louder, commanding-you-around kind of voice, stating the name of one girl the boogeyman had taken. "Bonnie McAllister! Bonnie McAllister! Are you here?" I said the name a third time, thinking of Michael's sister and her Bloody Mary game. "Bonnie McAllister! Can you show yourself to us? We're here to help you."

Michael and I watched the screen. I held my breath.

There was a sound like whispering in the air. A young girl.

Suddenly the shape of a greenish, hollow-eyed face filled the display screen on the night vision camera, as if someone were peering right into the lens. My heart doubled its beating, and Michael took a sharp breath and stepped back. The face vanished as quickly as it appeared, and it was gone when he looked again.

"Wow. Did that really happen?" he whispered.

"We're recording, so we can check."

He shook his head. "I've never believed in ghosts. What was that?"

"A ghost," I said. "You might say you don't believe in them, but you also said you don't like to come down to the basement at night."

"That's because it's creepy."

"So what? Why were you worried about me coming down here?"

"I don't know. It doesn't make a lot of sense, does it? It just feels like a...bad place."

"It makes perfect sense," I said. "You want to be a rational, sane person, and you don't think that fits with a belief in ghosts. On the other hand, you can feel something's not right when you're down here. One part of you wants to believe there are no ghosts—but another, deeper part of you knows they're around."

"So I'm crazy."

"No, you're just like most people I meet. People can believe contradictory things, especially about complicated subjects like death. Think of how many people profess a belief in a heavenly afterlife but are still afraid to die. You have kind of the opposite thing going on."

"I don't believe in ghosts, but I'm afraid of them." He laughed a little. "It would be nice, though, wouldn't it? Knowing that people you care about still exist out there. Knowing that we all go on..." He glanced around the dark basement. "Although if the afterlife is just being stuck in a laundry room in an old house forever, that's going to disappoint a lot of people."

"If we can get rid of the fearfeeder, these other souls should get unstuck," I said. "If they're really his victims, and not other accumulated hauntings—"

Door hinges squealed, and electric light spilled out across the ceiling.

A large, dark form filled the doorway at the top. It shuffled down a step toward us, and the step groaned under its weight.

"Falcon?" I asked, squinting my eyes. "Falcon Fielding?"

"Falcon *Williams*," the boy said, his voice high and nasal. "Hoss is my stepdad."

"Sorry," I said.

"What are you doing?" He looked from me to Michael, then toward the green laser dots on the wall, his faced shrouded in the dark gloom.

"We're just checking for any unusual problems down here," I said.

"I heard you talking to my mom," Falcon said, as if I might not have noticed him standing there the whole time I spoke with Lulinda. "She didn't tell you everything, though."

She didn't tell us anything, I thought. "Have you seen anything unusual around the house, Falcon?"

"Yeah. In my fireplace. It's not a real fireplace anymore, it's bricked up inside. So nothing can climb down into it. But I see it there anyway."

"What do you see?" I asked.

I heard him gulp. "My mom gets mad if I talk about it. Hoss slapped me one time and told me to stop. But it won't go away."

"What is it?"

He hesitated. "You won't laugh?" He looked from me to Michael again, as if more concerned about Michael's opinion of him.

"We won't, I promise," Michael said. "We've all seen scary

things. That's why Ellie's here. She's a...what do you call it?"

"I'm a ghost removal specialist," I said. "I've dealt with ghosts all over the city."

"It's not really a ghost," he said. "It's more like a...dinosaur." The boy cringed as he said it. "It sounds stupid but it's real."

"Tell me more about it," I said.

"It's a skeleton, like at the museum. Skull and ribs and bone claws."

"What does it do?"

"It stands in the fireplace and watches me in bed. I wake up and it's there. Usually it doesn't move, it just looks at me." The boy shuddered—I could see it even in the dark room. "Then last week, I woke up and it was by my bed. Its skull was looking down at me. It's like a T. Rex. It barely fit in my room, it was all bent over..." His voice cracked, and I realized he was crying.

"It's okay." I walked over and put a hand on his shoulder. He was still a couple of steps from the bottom, so it was an awkward reach. "We're working to get rid of it. In the meantime..." I told him the same information I'd given to Alicia's kids—that it wasn't really a dinosaur, that it preyed on his fear, that standing up to it would weaken it. "Do you have a strong flashlight in your apartment?"

"I think Hoss has a couple in his tool drawer." He sniffed, wiping his face all along his arm, which I took as a cue to drop my hand from his shoulder.

"Get the brightest one and sleep with it in your bed," I said. "Fire it at the monster if it bothers you again. Imagine it's a powerful weapon. But the real weapon is your courage, the real attack is your choice to stand up to it."

"I'll try." He sniffed again. "Don't tell Mom I told you about it. And don't tell Hoss or he'll get mad."

"We won't," I said. "And...maybe you won't mention what we're doing down here, okay?"

"They'll find out," he said. "They find out everything." Falcon turned and ascended the stairs, huffing and out of breath by the time he reached the top. He looked back at us. "I hope you can get rid of it. It's evil."

Then he closed the door and left us in the dark.

"He doesn't seem like the happiest kid," I said.

"I've never seen him smiling," Michael told me. "He always looks miserable."

"We can't make him happy, but we can make his life easier." I drew my flashlight and pointed it at the door, the bright white beam drowning most of the tiny green dots. "We have to close this case quickly, before the boogeyman tries to take one of these kids. We need to get to the heart of it."

"You want to go in there?" Michael grabbed the doorknob and rattled it. "It's locked. I could call the management company in the morning, try to get Hernando out here. That's the maintenance guy, he'll have a key, but it usually takes a few days before they send him —"

"I don't even want to wait until the morning." I grabbed my toolbox from the counter and handed him my flashlight. "Keep shining that on the door."

"Okay..." He looked puzzled, but held it for me.

I knelt in the bright light by the door, opened my toolbox, and took out a slim leather pack. I unfolded it, selected a couple of slender steel bypass tools, and slid them into the lock.

"Do you bring your own lock picks everywhere?" he asked.

"Tools of the trade." There was nothing particularly complicated about the lock, and within thirty seconds, I was pushing open the door into a dark cavity behind the rock wall.

The intense cold hit us first. The air erupting from the darkness was so dense and cold I could feel it pushing against me. It smelled old and stagnant, the smell of things that have lain too long in their own filth. It was like prying open a coffin that's been buried for years—something I had to do once, unfortunately. I hope to never do it again.

Michael let out an "ugh" sound, and I gagged pretty badly myself. I pushed away from the door and rose to my feet. Then I snagged my flashlight back from him and pointed it inside.

There was, as expected, a furnace, a pot-bellied metal monster squatting in the corner, its copper tentacles snaking away into the ceiling. Its pilot light glowed red behind a small steel cage, the device letting off a low hiss. The thing looked ancient and clunky—no wonder the landlord kept it locked away from the tenants.

For a moment, I thought of Gehenna in the Bible, the place near Jerusalem where children were burned alive in sacrifice to

Moloch and other nasty gods. Vanishing children.

Despite the red glare of the bestial furnace, the air was ice-cold, as if something were greedily sucking up every drop of heat produced.

I advanced into the dark space, my flashlight barely denting the gloom. Michael stayed close beside me, protectively, which was much better than leaving me to go alone, and far better than turning and running away. The atmosphere was dark enough to panic most people. I felt almost sick with dread, my muscles tensing up, cold sweat rising all over my back.

The old walls were built from a combination of bricks and irregular rocks cemented together—it didn't look like the soundest foundation for the three-story mansion above.

Spiderwebs matted the walls, and I saw a couple of black widows lowering themselves on threads like floating teardrops of poison.

"Watch for spiders," I whispered.

My flashlight found a heap of old hand tools piled in a rusted-out wheelbarrow. Shovels and shears, also flaking with rust, were propped against one wall. I doubted these were the tools used by Hernando the maintenance guy. They looked like they hadn't been touched in decades.

The loose bricks of the floor sloped gradually downward as we approached the back wall of the room, and the smell of death was stronger. My instincts told me to run away.

"What's that?" Michael squatted on the bricks—I noticed they reflected a little sheen, and the dirt between them looked like it was verging on mud.

He reached out toward a slab of plywood that lay over some kind of hole in the floor, blocking most of it from view. Michael slid it aside. The hole, lined with dark, mossy stones, stretched away into solid darkness below. Cold, rotten air rose from it.

"What is it?" Michael whispered. "A tunnel? A sewer?"

"It could be an old well," I said. "Some old houses had them in the cellar so you wouldn't have to go outside in the winter. It's more common up north, though."

He rose and stood beside me while I shone my light into the

well, but the beam barely scratched the darkness. I rotated the iris on my flashlight lens, making the beam as dense and concentrated as possible, but it only showed us an extra foot or so of mossy stones. The darkness beyond seemed impenetrable. Not a good sign, not at all.

A sigh echoed within the well, so low and soft that I leaned my head closer to hear it. I couldn't tell if it was male or female, human or just an ill wind blowing through a dark cave.

I gazed down into the depths, trying to see anything at all. My skin crawled, my guts clenched in unease. The animal part of me wanted to flee, to close the door and never look back...but I couldn't help trying to see deeper into the subterranean world below. It felt like a place full of secrets and horrors.

Eleanor.

The voice echoed upward from the darkness. My complete first name, which almost nobody had called me since my parents died.

I recognized this voice, too. My mother. Just the way she'd said it the last time we'd spoken. We'd been fighting—I was fifteen, bucking for independence, wanting to ride with some older kids to an OutKast concert on a school night. I had a crush on one particular boy in that group. My mom wouldn't let me go.

"You'll understand when you're older, Eleanor," she'd said. Her last words to me, ever.

"I hate you!" My last words to her. Then I'd slammed the door to my room and never saw either of my parents alive again.

Her voice stabbed into me like a hook through the heart, drawing me toward the deep darkness below.

I bumped into Michael, which jostled me out of my rapt stupor a bit. He was stepping toward the well, too, his eyes fixed on the endless cold black inside. We were both moving that way.

He didn't seem to notice our collision at all—he just kept staring and easing forward. The toe of his shoe slipped over the edge of the well as if he expected to simply step inside. His face was blank, his eyes wide.

"Michael!" I shouted, snapping my fingers in front of his face. No response. He slid his other foot to the edge of the well while he stared down into it. I planted my hands on his stomach and pushed, feeling the ridges of his abdominal muscles through his shirt. He inched back, then started again, as if I were a minor obstacle to be nudged aside or run over.

Whatever evil lay in the well seemed to have captured his mind. It had almost done the same to me, but seemed to have a stronger hold on Michael. Maybe it was because he hadn't faced as many ghosts as I had, or because he'd been the one who'd uncovered the well.

Hoping for the latter, I knelt on the cold, damp bricks and shoved the slab of wood back into place, covering most of the hole, except where the wood bumped into his shoes.

Michael jumped as though something had bitten his toes. He finally looked at me, his eyes still wide open, his face chalk-white. He looked like he'd seen a ghost, or at least heard one.

"Are you okay?" I stood next to him, touching his arm to try to calm him. He was shaking.

"We have to get out of here," he said. Without waiting for me to reply, he grabbed my arm and hurried us both through the door, slamming it behind us. I don't really like other people hustling me around like that, but again I appreciated that he'd tried to pull me out of danger with him rather than run off and leave me there.

"What did you see in there?" I asked.

"Nothing. But I heard..." He shook his head.

"You can tell me." I stayed close to him in the dark basement, partly because he was still holding my arm and I wasn't in a rush to escape his strong grip. I was close enough to smell his scent, a woody oaky cologne mingled with the warm smell of his sweat. My blood was racing from more than fear.

"It was my mom," he said, his voice so quiet I moved in closer to hear him. "She called for me."

"I heard mine, too," I told him. "She died when I was fifteen."

"My mom died three years ago," he said. "Pancreatic cancer. She died less than a month after they found it."

"I'm sorry." I reached out my other hand to comfort him, but wasn't sure where to put it. It landed on his chest, where I could feel his heart thumping against my fingers.

"Melissa was just fourteen. It was hard on everybody..." He looked at the closed door.

"You took care of your sister after that?"

"Yeah. My mom's cousin wanted her to go live with them in

Tennessee, but we wanted to stay together."

"What about your...father? Can I ask about that?"

"That's easy." He managed a smile. "That loser left when I was eleven. Melissa was two. She was throwing one of her tantrums, and he said he couldn't take it anymore. That's exactly what he said before he left: 'I can't take this anymore.' Then he walked out on us. I've barely heard from him since."

"I'm sorry. Melissa was lucky to have you around, though."

"I might have gone crazy without her," Michael said.

"A lot of guys wouldn't have done that—young, single, and choosing to take care of your younger sister? You're a good brother. You're a good person. Aren't you?"

His bright green eyes looked into me, and I could feel so much in the small space between us. Fear. Sadness. An attraction like a live wire, drawing us ever closer together. At least, I know I felt that on my end.

I looked up at him, my eyes adjusting to the darkness enough that I could discern the features of his face, his nose and lips. It was an intense moment, and my toes actually curled in anticipation of what might happen next.

My phone beeped several times, and the ring told me it was Stacey calling.

I couldn't help a small sigh before I answered. Michael and I were still looking at each other, but the sudden, sharp feeling of intimacy and need was already starting to fade, broken up by the outside world's interference. I retreated back into my more familiar, less exciting professional shell.

"What's up?" I asked.

"You should probably get over here," Stacey told me. "Jacob found something. Early eighteenth century, he says. And he's kind of acting weird."

"Like violent weird?"

"No, no, like he climbed the fence and he's pacing somebody's front lawn, and I'm pretty sure they're home...Jacob! Get back here! They'll call the cops!"

"I'll be right there." I hung up after she told me the address. It was the big, brooding Tudor house where the Larsen family had lived, where seven-year-old Kris had vanished about twenty years earlier.

I looked back at Michael.

"Bad news?" he asked, probably because of the disappointed look on my face.

"Just the usual weirdness. I have to get to work, though. Maybe we should talk later?"

"Sure. You're all done here?" He glanced around at the cameras and microphones I'd set up around the room. "You don't need five or six more cameras?"

"I think it's enough." I hurried out of there, stuffing all my confusing feelings back inside, the psychological equivalent of getting dressed on the run.

Chapter Twelve

I caught up with Stacey at the old Larsen house, which sat on the corner lot two doors down. Stacey stood on the sidewalk, softly calling for Jacob, who'd jumped the fence and was currently making himself at home among the shrubs and flower beds, pacing back and forth.

"She's here!" Stacey called as soon as she caught sight of me.

"Finally." Jacob tromped up to the fence, standing between two huge azaleas. "This guy was crazed. Seriously crazed."

"I'm guessing you found something," I said.

"He did it right here." Jacob backed up several steps, until he stood in a crushed-gravel path that wound through the flower beds and tree islands of the house where he was trespassing. A balding, gray-haired man stood in a window of the house, glaring at Jacob, clearly able to see him in the light of the streetlamps.

"Uh, Jacob, there's a guy watching," Stacey told him. "He looks like the type who'd come out waving a baseball bat. Or, you know, a twelve-gauge."

"He lured the kids out here one at a time," Jacob said, looking at me. His arms were stretched out, his fingers splayed open as if catching information from the air. "It was all screened by trees then, an arbor with big shrubs around it. The house was different, too, completely different. He did the boy first, waking him up in the middle of the night with a made-up story about...buried treasure." Jacob nodded, as if double-confirming that in his mind. "He took him out to the trees where nobody could see them. There was a lot of moonlight. When he pulled the knife and stabbed the boy in the gut, he could see the anguish in the boy's face. Not just the physical pain. The boy trusted the man, and the man betrayed him." Jacob took off his glasses and rubbed his eyes. "That made the man feel something. Glee. Power. He reduced the boy to nothing but pain and hurt. Then he killed him. And he enjoyed it. It surprised him how much he enjoyed it."

"How did he know the boy?" I asked.

Jacob concentrated, his eyes closed. "Family member."

"His father?"

"Not exactly. But almost."

"How is 'almost' an option?" Stacey asked. "His uncle?"

"Maybe. But not just...they were twins. He and the little boy's father were twin brothers. They all lived in this house." Jacob pointed toward the heavy, dark house where the homeowner stood at the window, glaring at us while talking on a phone. "So, for the boy, it was *almost* like being murdered by his own father."

"What were their names?" I asked.

Jacob shook his head. "I'm not good with that. Names, dates, numbers..."

"Give me a time period," I said. Stacey had already mentioned one, but it's always good to ask again. And again. Calvin had taught me that.

"Eighteen...twenties? Thirties? He's wearing an old patched-up frock coat. I think he has money, though. They'd have to, with that house. Well, not *that* house, but the one that used to stand here, with full wraparound porches on both levels, an antebellum place."

I started jotting details on my pocket notepad. Though Stacey was recording him with a handheld video camera, I didn't want to comb back through that footage for key details. He was giving us some fairly good, specific information. Hopefully it was relevant to our case.

"So he kills the boy and leaves him here," Jacob said. "He goes back in for the little girl, the sister. Tells her something about magical creatures or fairies in the woods. He brings her out here, shows her the brutalized body of her dead brother. The little girl screams in terror, and he *relishes* it. She starts to run, he grabs her hair. She's crying and shrieking like a little pig. That's how he thinks of it when he snaps her head back and draws the blade across her little throat. It's just like killing a pig. He always thought the kids sounded that way when they whined and cried."

"That's awful!" Stacey said.

"Why is he killing them?" I asked. It was weird how Jacob would slip into the present tense when picking up psychic information, as if the tragic events were somehow still happening, again and again, centuries later.

Jacob shook his head. "His mind is a black cloud. He's crazed. I'm mainly picking it up from the kids' perspectives. It's really a place-memory, not a ghost."

"What's the difference again?" Stacey asked.

"A ghost is a lost soul, or a lost piece of a soul," Jacob said. "Place-memory is like an emotional scar. Trauma can leave a permanent mark on a place. And there was definitely some trauma here. He took the bodies through the woods..." Jacob almost walked into a very obvious seven-foot-high brick wall, stopping himself at the last second by reaching out both hands to stop the collision, as though the wall had walked into *him*. "Where did that come from?"

"You mean the giant wall?" Stacey asked.

"I didn't see it a second ago. Lost in the past." He shook his head.

"You should probably consider climbing back over the fence." I nodded at the gray-haired house owner, stepping out onto his porch with a scowl on his face and a rifle in his hand.

Jacob turned and waved at the guy. "Sorry. Lost our...Frisbee. I mean our cat. Whose name is Frisbee."

The guy didn't reply. Maybe he figured he'd let his glare and his gun speak for him. A real Ted Nugent type.

We helped Jacob scramble back over the fence, and he immediately walked past the wall and scrambled over the next iron fence, into another neighbor's yard. At least we were getting closer to our client's house. Soon, he might not be recklessly trespassing at all.

"He carried the bodies through here, through trees and scrub," Jacob said. "He felt *alive*, like he'd...turned from a shadow into a real person." Jacob shook his head. "That's the best I can understand. He felt more real because he'd killed those kids."

"Cuckoo, cuckoo," Stacey whispered to me. I wasn't a hundred percent sure whether she meant the 19th-century child murderer or Jacob himself, who plunged heedlessly through a small hedge, following the path of his vision with little regard for present-day obstacles.

"He took them down to the old well—"

"Look out!" Stacey called, just before Jacob could crack his knee on one support of an iron fence. He glared at the fence as though annoyed by its existence, then heaved himself over into the front garden of Alicia's house. There wasn't much actual garden left, because much of the area had been paved to provide a small parking area for the tenants.

"Right past this tree..." Jacob said, appearing to walk around a large invisible object. He pointed at the towering, irregular Queen Anne house where Alicia and Michael lived. "Through the brambles, into the old well. Hardly anyone used that well, anyway. The water tasted sour." He looked up at the conical turrets and shadowy recessed balconies. "This house wasn't here yet. It was just the woods and the old well. I guess there's no well anymore."

"That's not exactly true," I said. "Michael and I just discovered one in the basement." I didn't add any more information, didn't mention how it had drawn us toward it with whispered voices and a kind of morbid but irresistible fascination—I wanted to see what Jacob would learn on his own.

"Seriously?" Stacey asked. "I wouldn't drink from that basement."

"I'd better go check it out," Jacob said, starting for the porch.

"Can you do a quick walk-through of our client's apartment, too?" I asked. "I'd be much obliged."

"You and your fancy talk," Jacob replied.

"Since there hasn't been any activity in Alicia's bedroom, I was going to have the family wait there while he checks the apartment," Stacey told me. "Less interference with his Spidey senses."

"Good idea," I said, thinking back to Michael and I discussing the activity in his bedroom, or the lack thereof.

We climbed the steps to the front porch.

"Looks like Alicia's home," I said, glancing in through one of the windows. "Go ahead and quarantine the family, Stacey."

"And should I set up a perimeter?" Stacey asked.

"What do you mean?"

"I don't know, it just sounds good. Like from a zombie action movie." She covered her mouth with one hand and imitated a crackling radio. "Quarantine the area and set up a perimeter."

"Just *go*," I said, and she huffed a bit as she walked inside.

"I'm getting a really dark feeling from this place," Jacob said. "From all the houses I've passed on this block."

"Then you're on the right track," I told him.

He looked worried, a deep frown etched on his face.

"That was a grisly murder I just saw," he said. "I'm guessing I won't enjoy the rest of this, either."

"I heard you and Stacey had fun the other night," I said, by way of trying to lighten the mood.

He just gave me a puzzled look, like he couldn't figure out why I'd bring that up at this exact moment.

"Just making conversation," I said, then Stacey returned from inside and opened the door for us.

"Come on in, y'all," she said. "The family's sequestered."

"Hey, nice word choice," Jacob told her as he stepped inside. "Much nicer than 'quarantined.'"

"Thanks." Stacey took his hand and looked up at him with a kind of mock awe, as though his joke compliment had swept her off her feet. "I worked on it all night. I hoped you would say something."

"Are you recording, Stacey?" I asked. She could flirt on her own time.

"Oh, yep." Stacey raised her camera and pointed it at Jacob. "Action!"

Jacob walked in a slow circle around the living room, nodding to himself as he took in the vaulted space, the grand staircase, the row of archways across both the first and second floor, giving cutaway views of the hallways on both levels.

He glanced at the door near the foot of the stairs, which led to Alicia's room.

"We're avoiding that room," Stacey said. "Unless you feel, you know, drawn there or something."

"So far, it's the same general darkness of the whole neighborhood," he said. "Imagine a black cloud, or a fog of evil that's settled over these houses and just sits there like L.A. smog."

"The Smog of Evil," Stacey said in a deep, highly dramatized voice. "Next week on SyFy."

"Exactly." Jacob wandered into the kitchen, both of us following him, but he just gave it a glance and a shrug before moving on.

An interesting thing about kitchens: while ghosts are most drawn to the dark, deserted areas of the house, typically the attic or basement—or closets, in the case of our current boogeyman—the kitchen, in my experience, tends to be the least haunted area. Maybe it's the fact that kitchens are well-lit, but they're also the center of activity for the living, the emotional energy constantly churned and refreshed. They're the heart of the home, and I think something about that keeps the restless spirits at bay, hiding in the shadows. There are plenty of exceptions, of course.

We followed Jacob to the other end of the first-floor hall, where there was a door on every side, all of them closed. He glanced at the door to Alicia's master bathroom, then looked a bit longer at the door to the shared hallway, but finally opened the one under the stairs. He held out his hands and took a deep breath as he looked down the dim, dead-end stairs cluttered with cardboard storage boxes.

"It likes to come up through here," he said. "This doorway. It's obsessed with doorways. Where do these stairs lead?"

"Nowhere. Bricked up," I said. "They used to go to the basement."

"It comes up here regularly, doesn't it? This is like a well-worn trail. It usually keeps to itself. It watches. It's here a lot more than anyone realizes."

"Comforting thought," Stacey said.

"This is your problem ghost, isn't it?" Jacob walked down the first couple of steps, trailing his fingers on the walls. "Nasty thing."

"What can you tell me about it?" I asked.

"It's malevolent. And secretive, always hiding...I see it wearing masks all the time, hiding itself."

"Can you tell me who it is? Anything about its identity? Was it a person?"

"If it was, it's been a long time," he said. "It's twisted into something else over the years. I guess we have to go down to the basement." He said it reluctantly, like he'd stepped on a rusty nail and was resigning himself to going for a tetanus shot.

"We'll do that when we're done upstairs," I said. "The basement isn't connected to this apartment."

"Let's go upstairs, then." Jacob closed the door.

As he ascended the main stairs, he traced his fingers along the railing for a little bit, then scowled at them as if they'd come away with some kind of sticky residue. He didn't say anything about it.

He was drawn right to the closet in Kalil's room.

"This is another door," Jacob said, opening the closet door.

"I knew we called in a psychic for a reason," Stacey said.

"A doorway that it uses to step into our world," Jacob said. "It can kind of take over certain doors, and certain small spaces, and use them as a crossing-point. It's powerful. And it likes to terrorize living people. It...drinks fear like a bat sucking blood. The fear makes it stronger, but also corrupts it. The stronger it grows, the more evil it becomes. If it ever was human, I'm not sure it even remembers that. It's hard for me to get into its mind at all."

He had similar observations in Mia's room. "It loves to scare this girl. She's the youngest, and she has the most potent and concentrated fear of any of them."

"What are its intentions toward her?" I asked.

"Feeding," Jacob said. "Feeding and feeding until she's just an empty husk."

"How do we stop it?" Stacey asked.

"I'm not sure, but I don't think asking it nicely will work," Jacob replied.

We walked out in the hallway again, where he approached the decorative archway of the door to nowhere. He swung it open.

"Interesting design here," he said. "This is another one of the possessed doors—it's like the thing can manipulate doors all over the house. It comes...wait." He blinked and held up a finger as if to quiet me, though I hadn't actually been talking. He turned his head just a little, listening to something I couldn't hear.

"It's cute when he does that," Stacey whispered to me. "Like a puppy hearing its name."

"There's something else here," Jacob said. "He paces up and down this hall. Watching."

"Watching what?" I asked.

"He's worried about the family here, the woman and the kids," Jacob said. "He's a protective presence. Well, he wants to be, but he's not that strong. He knows he's supposed to move on, and all the natural forces are trying to move him on from this world, but he fights them. It's like pulling against gravity. He won't leave until they're safe."

"Who is he?"

"He's showing me his face. And a cross. A little gold cross hanging from his neck." Jacob pointed to his own collarbone.

"What's his name?" I asked.

Jacob gave a rueful little smile and shook his head. "I'm better with faces than names. Sorry. That's why he's here, anyway. He doesn't have a lot of power, and he's not native to this spot. He's doing what he can, trying to keep the thing in the basement away from those kids, but he's much less powerful than it is."

I glanced at Stacey, expecting her to make a B-movie joke about The Thing in the Basement, but she was listening quietly and intently.

"What else?" I asked.

"He's trying to be an angelic presence and failing," Jacob said. "That's how he sees it, in those terms. He wants to be the strong protector, but he's stuck as more of a passive observer. He's struggling to do more. To be more." Jacob paused.

"He's here now?" I asked.

"He doesn't leave if he can help it. Sometimes he fades and feels the pull of the other side trying to draw him away. It takes constant focus for him to stay here at all. He's fading more and more now, and that panics him because the job isn't done, the family's still in danger and he has to leave soon."

"What can he tell us about the thing from the basement?" I asked.

"It was already here when he arrived. He came here because of it, because of the danger." Jacob paused for a long time, more than a minute. Floorboards creaked overhead. It was probably just Michael or Melissa, going about their lives above us. "He's telling me how it always disguises itself, wearing masks to scare people. How it's feeding on all the kids in the house."

"Can he give us any advice for stopping it?" I asked.

"He doesn't even know what it is. He's seen what it does, though. He says it likes to get you when you're alone. He's scared for the living people in this house, but especially the family in this apartment." Jacob frowned. "He's fading. Like there's a tide pulling him away into the distance." He looked at me. "I don't think that guy's going to be much help."

"Doesn't sound like a threat, either," I said. "I'll take the good news with the bad. Though he might be trying to deceive us."

"Always possible," Jacob said. "Everyone lies eventually."

"Aw, I should embroider that on a pillow," Stacey said, following him back downstairs.

We'd finished showing Jacob the apartment, but the ghost-infested basement still waited for us below. I was not eager to go near that old well again, but clearly he was sensing some information about it, and I needed whatever he could find.

I just hoped that reaching his psychic powers into the horrible darkness of the old well, which had bewitched both Michael and myself, wouldn't be like throwing a lit match into a lake of gasoline, causing some kind of paranormal eruption of evil spirits. I was not remotely in the mood for something like that.

Chapter Thirteen

Jacob stepped onto the first stair into the basement and hesitated. Stacey reached around him to flip the light switch, and the hanging fluorescents buzzed to life.

"I obviously don't have to tell you this is the worst part of the house," Jacob said. "You've got it wired up like a TV studio."

"So much for not giving the psychic advance information," I said.

"It doesn't matter." Jacob continued down the stairs, pausing on the last one. This put me in the unfortunate position of pausing a couple of steps behind him, where something could snatch my ankles through the gaps. I shined my flashlight down between the stairs while I waited, but saw nothing except rusty junk, mostly the guts of an old washing machine that looked like it had been stripped for parts.

"Okay, Jacob," Stacey said after a while. "This is me poking you to get moving."

"Sorry. This place is...full." Jacob grimaced as he left the final stair for the brick floor.

"Which means?" Stacey asked.

"There's a lot of, I don't know, broken ghosts. Fractures, lost chunks of souls. They're clumped together. Imagine, as you're walking through here, that it's flooded with dark water, like a swamp, and there are body parts floating everywhere. They're mostly submerged. Here and there, you see them twitching, a finger curling, an eyeball in half a face turning to watch you pass. That's what I see."

"Gross," Stacey said, while we followed him toward the laundry machines. "I'm going to imagine unicorns floating in cotton candy instead."

"Dismembered unicorns," Jacob said. "Their hoof-stumps kicking, turning the cotton candy dark with blood..."

"That's almost worse. Why would you say that?" Stacey asked.

"Your suggestion made me see it that way for half a second," Jacob replied.

"Oh, weird. So if I said—"

"Don't, it's distracting," he told her. He turned to face the door in the rock wall, the one that led to the furnace and the well and whatever evil chthonic force dwelled below the house. I thought it was clearly the boogeyman's lair, but something told me it might be more than that.

"Stacey." I raised my flashlight, signaling her to raise hers. We approached the door, and I motioned for Jacob to wait while I opened it. There was a good chance something nasty and powerful lurked just on the other side, waiting to shapeshift into whatever we feared and kill us all.

So we entered cautiously.

Our ultra-bright tactical flashlights pushed back the shadows but didn't exactly cut through them or chase them away. The small red flame glowed in the belly of the old beast of a furnace, like a single angry, badly misplaced eye.

Jacob reluctantly entered the room with us.

I heard a sound that hadn't been there the last time, like crashing ocean waves as heard from within an underground cave, sloshing and echoing.

"I already feel sick," Jacob said. "Like drop dead, burn my corpse so it doesn't infect the village sick." His skin looked like bleached chalk.

"Should we get out of here?" Stacey stood close to him,

embracing him with one arm. "You okay?"

"We should get what we came for first," I said, and Stacey scowled at me. I felt bad saying it, but everyone upstairs was depending on us.

"She's right." Jacob cleared his throat and walked toward the slab of plywood covering the well. Stacey kept close by him, and I tracked along on the other side. A psychic medium like Jacob is a much more interesting target to supernatural types than a couple of regular girls like us. "What's under there?"

"That's exactly what I need you to tell me." I squatted beside the covered well. The slow, liquid sound was louder the closer I got to it.

I grabbed one edge of the plywood and slid it back, exposing the cold darkness below. The sloshing sound echoed from somewhere deep within, like the heartbeat of some massive primordial creature dwelling far below the earth.

Now Stacey was pale white, too, looking into the old well. I reached over and nudged her arm.

"Don't look inside it," I told her. "Keep your eyes on Jacob."

She nodded, looking rattled, but did as I said.

Jacob leaned forward just a little, but wisely kept a few feet between himself and the hole.

"Oh, no," he said. "That's...awful. Don't show me that."

"What do you see?" I asked.

"Not that!" He closed his eyes and covered his ears, as if protecting himself from some deafening shockwave.

When I'd been here just a little earlier, Michael had been drawn toward the well, mesmerized by the darkness, stepping slowly toward it as though in a trance.

Now, Jacob *slid* toward it as though dragged by an invisible chain, the soles of his shoes skimming right over the bricks. The liquid noises inside the well grew louder, making me imagine a slobbering, ravenous wolf.

Stacey and I jumped forward, seizing him by the arms. The unseen force pulled at him with incredible strength, and we had to fight to keep him from falling inside. The pull stopped after a few more seconds.

Jacob's eyes opened, staring down into the well with a thousand-miles-away look. His jaw was slack.

"Hey, Jacob?" I said.

No response.

"Wake up!" Stacey snapped her fingers in front of his eyes, but he was catatonic on his feet, as if his mind were lost somewhere in the darkness below.

He started to lean forward again, and we tightened our grips on him. Stacey shouted his name again.

"Kiss him," I told Stacey.

"Seriously?"

"Worked for Sleeping Beauty, didn't it?" That didn't really seem relevant, but it was the best idea I could think of in half a second.

"Um...if you say so." Stacey rose up on her toes and turned his blank face toward him. She hesitated, then gave him a good, hard kiss on the mouth, which lasted a few seconds longer than strictly necessary.

The invisible force pulling him forward stopped all at once, as did the strange ocean-crashing sound from deep inside the well.

Jacob turned and gazed at Stacey, blinking.

"What just happened?" he asked.

"Which thing, exactly, are you asking about?" She gave him a coy little smile, and she was actually blushing, which was pretty abnormal for her. Not for me, though. I'm always blushing like an idiot, especially when I trip over things or say something awkward in a conversation...which is itself way too common. I'm not great at small talk. I'd rather pick one interesting topic and stick with it for a while.

"We need to get out of here." Jacob glanced at the well again. He was back with us mentally, but he was still sickly pale, the darkness of the place bothering him at a deep physical level.

I knelt to push the wooden slab back over the dark hole, but Jacob hurried and beat me to it. Then he took Stacey's arm and waved for me to follow as he hustled her out of there. If it ever happened that he could only save *one* of us from, let's say, drowning or being trapped in a burning building, it was clear who he would pick. I couldn't blame him, though. I wasn't the one who'd just placed myself over a small gateway to Hell to save him with a reverse Prince Charming kiss.

I didn't risk looking into the well again, but kept my back to it as I followed them out of the furnace room and shut the door tightly behind me. Stacey and Jacob were embracing, both of them shaking. The laundry room itself wasn't a pleasant spot—the dark shadows seemed to drape everything like heavy curtains, and there was the oddly cold air and the undeniable feeling of being watched by things you couldn't see.

"What can you tell us, Jacob?" I asked him.

Jacob turned his head to look at me, still clasping Stacey close in his arms. There's nothing more romantic than sharing a brief encounter with nameless underground horrors, apparently.

"First I saw..." He took a deep breath. "Some of the people from the plane crash. The most mangled bodies. That's how some of them appeared to me when I awoke in that airliner wreckage; they were ripped to shreds but still walking around, too dazed and shocked to realize they were dead.

"When I looked into that old well, the first thing I saw was those people, climbing up the walls, looking at me. Coming to get me, furious that I'd survived when so many of them died. They wanted to drag me down with them."

"It wasn't really them," Stacey said. "This thing just feeds on your fears. It can look inside you and find what scares you."

"Stacey," I said.

"I know, feeding the psychic. Sorry." Stacey didn't look that sorry. She wanted to comfort him more than she wanted to follow our investigative protocol.

"Is that the same well you mentioned outside?" I asked Jacob. "Where the man carried the bodies of his niece and nephew after he killed them?"

"That's the well, but those two bodies are the least of it." Jacob looked around the room, narrowing his eyes, listening. "I can see them all more clearly now. These are the remnants of the dead over the years...that girl and boy are probably in here somewhere, if I could search long enough. But there are older dead. *Much* older than I usually find. They're so ancient that they don't even present themselves with faces or bodies anymore, or speak with voices, but I can feel them..." Jacob stepped away from Stacey and closed his eyes. "People who died thousands of years ago. Just ghosts of ghosts now, but still here."

"Why are they here?" I asked.

"This spot has been known as evil ground for a long, long time. The place of bad water, they called it. But people would forget, or new people would move in, and someone would discover or dig out the water. It would taste sweet at first, but then it went bad. Some very twisted, evil things have happened here, a lot of them so long ago that the specific memories have faded, but the atmosphere still remains..."

"Well, that's all much worse than what I was hoping to hear," Stacey said. "I was leaning toward a 'solve the old murder, crack the case quick' scenario, myself."

"What can you tell us about what's happening now?" I asked. "With the fearfeeder?"

"That well is definitely where he comes and goes," Jacob said. "It needs to be sealed tight. Physically and ritually."

"Do you know how to do that?" Stacey asked.

"You need somebody more experienced than me," Jacob said. "I'm not trained for it. You need a shaman, a priest, somebody who can bring some power into it. Some of these ancient spirits are hanging around just to keep this place in check, to make the dark things stay down below, but they're old and fading. Their protection is cracking."

"I think I know somebody," I said. "Will that stop the entity we're dealing with?"

"I don't think so," he said. "It's turned some of the closets in this house into possessed doors—computer programmers would call them back doors, secret ways to gain access. So I don't think it would stop the crawling dark thing at this point. Once you deal with your fearfeeder, though, you need to take care of this well so nothing else comes out, nothing else goes in. When Uncle Murderer from the early nineteenth century killed those children and put their bodies into the well, he made a connection with the darkness inside. One thing all evil spirits understand is blood sacrifice."

"What kind of connection are we talking about, exactly?" I asked.

"He mingled his soul with an old, old darkness," he said. "It's hard to say, only that he grew even more twisted than he already was...and probably a lot less sane."

"Is there any connection between him and the fearfeeder we've been chasing?"

"Possibly. The entity you're dealing with now keeps its identity hidden. It only wants to make itself visible when it's pretending to be something it isn't."

"Could they be the same entity?" I asked, getting right to the point of my question. "That's what I need to know."

"They could be."

"I know they *could* be," I said, feeling myself grow impatient, my calm professional veneer starting to crack. "I'm trying to get a definite answer."

"I don't have one," Jacob said. "It's possible that his murders tied him here, and he returned as a ghost, but the darkness in the well changed him into something else over time." He looked around at the laundry room—empty to my eyes, crowded with damaged and mangled spirits to his. "Something has to be done about this."

"We're open to suggestions," I said.

"I'll tell you if I think of any." Jacob stared at the closed door to the furnace room.

Stacey and I took the opportunity to double-check our gear, and then all of us left up the stairs, turning out the light behind us.

As I stepped out of the basement door, I could feel the nameless things in the darkness watching, like predatory eyes boring into us from the shadows.

Chapter Fourteen

"Be very careful," Jacob told Stacey as they stood on the front porch, embracing closely and gazing into each other's eyes. I was third-wheeling it a few feet away, waiting to go back inside. "There's a lot of danger in this house."

"Don't worry about me, I'm staying out in the van." She nodded at our cargo van, parked on the street not far away. "Ellie might be in trouble, though."

"I'll be fine," I said when they both looked my way. "Observation only tonight. I promise."

"Maybe I should stick around, just for a while," he said. "In case you need me."

"You can help me keep an eye on all the monitors again," she said. "You're good at that."

"I have spent years sharpening my TV-watching skills," he replied, and she gave it more laughs than the joke was really worth.

Stacey gave me a questioning look, and I shrugged.

"As long as you keep your eyes on the monitor, not on each other," I said.

I grabbed my headset from the van and returned inside alone. My first stop was to knock on Alicia's bedroom door. "All clear," I said.

Alicia stepped out, telling her kids to wait in her room, and closed the door behind her.

"Well?" she asked. It was a normal enough thing to say at the moment, but the word immediately made me think of the dark, stone-lined shaft in the basement, from which evil things bubbled to the surface.

I had her follow me to the kitchen so the kids couldn't listen through the door, and then I gave her what information I had. It certainly sounded bleak and hopeless coming out. Her facial expression alternated between skeptical and horrified.

"For now, we think we have some leads on who this entity really is," I said. "Identifying a ghost is key to removing it, so our odds are now much better. I'll stay here again tonight and keep watch. By tomorrow night, we should have some hard historical facts to help us trap the ghost."

"I need you to take care of this right away." She glanced at the clock on the microwave. It was later than I'd realized, approaching eleven p.m. I didn't know where the time had gone. "Is it safe for the kids to sleep in their rooms?"

"I'll stay close to them again," I said. "Stacey and I will both be watching all night, so you can rest. There was one thing I didn't mention."

"Does it get worse?"

"Not this part. The psychic encountered what he called a positive male spirit, here to protect your family specifically. He was not someone who had a connection to this house in life."

"Gerard," she whispered. Her husband's name.

"We didn't get a name—he rarely picks up on names, unfortunately. Jacob said this male ghost knew he had to move on, the next world was calling for him, but he was stalling and won't go until he sees you're safe."

"What else?" Alicia stared intently at me, leaning closer for any news of her lost husband.

"Did Gerard ever wear any jewelry?"

"Jewelry?" She laughed. "No, he wasn't that type. All he ever wore was a little cross his grandmother gave him, and he kept that under his shirt."

"What color?"

"Gold. Why?"

"The psychic saw that," I said. "He was still wearing the cross. A memory of it, anyway. Do you have a digital picture of your husband you can send me?"

"I absolutely do." Alicia flipped through pictures on her phone, looking wistful.

I grabbed my digital tablet from our gear-heap in the corner of the room, and I confirmed I'd received it. Her husband stood on a beach, tall and handsome, looking out towards swollen thunderheads above the ocean.

"Okay, this will take a minute," I told her. "You might as well put your kids to bed, if you want."

She nodded and went to retrieve the sleepy children from her room.

Using Google image search, I quickly assembled a photographic line-up of men who vaguely resembled Gerard—late twenties to early thirties, very dark skin. I combined these in a single document, a dozen images with Gerard tucked unassumingly in the lower right corner of the collage.

I put on my headset.

"Stacey, do you read?" I asked.

"Not as much as I should," she said. "You know, my mom keeps telling me those Janet Evanovich novels are really fun—"

"Never mind," I said, sighing. "I'm sending you a photo line-up. Ask Jacob if he recognizes anyone."

"Roger, Wilco," she replied.

"You totally knew what I meant before, didn't you?" I asked. "You knew I wasn't trying to start a conversation about Stephanie Plum."

"Sorry, transmission's getting fuzzy. Stand by." Stacey turned down the volume on her headset, but I could still hear her explaining it to Jacob.

"That one," Jacob said. "He's the one in the house, watching over the family."

"Please note subject has identified the man in the third column, three pictures down," Stacey said, really overdoing it now. "Is that our suspect?"

"That's Alicia's husband," I said. "So we've identified one ghost. Too bad it's not the one we need to catch. Gotta go." I stood as Alicia returned down the stairs, staring at me like she was starving and I had a platter of hot, fresh cornbread.

"Don't you mean 'over and out' or 'signing off' or 'good night and good luck'?" Stacey asked. I turned down the volume without answering her.

"We have as much confirmation as we can get," I said. "The psychic did pick Gerard out of these pictures." I showed her the collage I'd slapped together.

"So it's him," Alicia said.

"As far as the psychic can tell. Some entities, and particularly the one we're dealing with now, can disguise their identity. I have to mention that for accuracy. But I don't see why it would pretend to be Gerard in front of Jacob, who doesn't even know Gerard. Jacob had a very strong sense of this dark entity's energy, and I don't *think* he would have been fooled, but it's always possible."

"What are you saying?"

"I'm more than ninety percent sure this is your husband, but not a hundred percent," I said. "I try to be scientific, but this is one area where you'll want to check your own feelings, if you encounter him. You knew him better than anyone."

"I sure did." Alicia looked at me a long moment. "Do you think...?"

"What is it?"

"Could your psychic friend help me speak to Gerard?" She was whispering, glancing up at the closed doors to her kids' rooms. "I wish I could talk to him just one last time."

"Probably not tonight—Jacob's done a lot already, he's probably drained," I said. "I'll ask him about it another time. I can tell you, though, that if his spirit is here, you can talk to him anytime. He's paying close attention to you and your kids. He'll hear you."

Alicia's eyes shone.

"I've spoken to him a lot," she whispered. "Since he passed. Sometimes I felt like he was hearing me, somehow..."

"He heard you," I said.

The tears erupted and tumbled down her cheeks. I patted her on the back. She embraced me, and I hugged her while she sobbed a little. I could feel the weight of her life, raising two kids alone while working a demanding job with long hours, and I suppose nobody had held her in a long time. That's one thing about this job—dealing with a lot of death means we run into some high emotions.

"I'm sorry," Alicia said, looking embarrassed as she drew back and wiped her eyes. "I guess I've been wanting someone to say that for a long time."

"I understand, believe me. My parents both died in a fire when I was fifteen." I didn't want to talk about myself, but I wanted her to know that I was familiar with those extreme feelings of loss and isolation.

"That's awful," she said, touching my arm.

"I'm used to it. But the pain still comes back sometimes."

"I'm so sorry." She gave me a little smile through her tears. "Maybe that's why you like Michael so much. A firefighter."

My first instinct was to deny liking him yet again, but that would have been a lie, and lies didn't belong in this conversation.

"Is it that obvious?" I asked, and she laughed.

"I should get to sleep myself," she said. "Thank you for being here, Ellie."

"I'll do my best to help your family," I said. "I promise."

As she walked away and closed her bedroom door, I felt an even stronger sense of purpose about resolving the case.

"Stacey, copy?" I said, turning up my headset again.

"I'm reading you," she replied.

"I'm getting into position," I told her while I climbed the stairs. I'd turned off all the downstairs lights. "How are we looking?"

"Basement's a ghost aquarium again," she said. "And the laser grid has dark spots passing through it, blotting out the dots, about once a minute."

"And the rest of the house?"

"Total snorefest so far."

"Keep me posted." I flicked off the upstairs lights, leaving the house enshrouded in ghost-inviting darkness, and sat on my air mattress.

The first order of business was emailing Grant Patterson, our friend at the Historical Association, with all the details about the house on the corner. We needed to know who had lived there in the first half of the nineteenth century, and I told him about the twin brothers and the two children who would have been reported missing or dead. I added a couple of family names we'd turned up for that lot during our research at the city archives.

The subject line of my email: URGENT. We needed to make some swift progress. I told him that inside the email, too, with copious thanks.

Then I used my tablet to check through the cameras around the house. Just as Stacey said: weird, irregular shapes fading in and out of view on the night vision in the basement. The thermal showed small, drifting cold spots forming and dissolving with no apparent physical cause, all over the room.

Looking up and down the dark hallway, I took in the closed doors, the stairs, the cutaway arches behind me giving a view of the living room below. My eyes adjusted to the gloom, able to see in the pale streetlamp light drifting in through the balcony doors at one end of the hall. The house had fallen quiet.

I wanted to call Michael, but it was much too late to call anyone that I didn't know to be a confirmed night owl. What would I say? *Hi, sorry to wake you, want to chat some more about how you live in a house of horrors built on cursed ground?*

There had to be better conversation-starters than that.

Alicia was right—I was interested in Hot Firefighter Guy, but I wasn't altogether sure how I felt about those feelings. I like to keep people at a slight distance. Like behind a wall topped with barbed wire and surrounded by a moat full of piranhas. I'd always been that way.

Not always. Not before Mom and Dad died, a little voice in my head felt obliged to point out.

So what? That was another life. There was no reason to think about Antonio Torres, the boy who'd invited me to the OutKast concert I'd never attended, how open and fearless my crush on him had been.

It hadn't been that way with anyone else since then. Not since I'd raised the barriers around myself and installed catapults full of flaming arrows on top.

Since my parents died, I'd resisted being close to anyone, even being unfairly cold to my cousins when I'd gone to live with my Aunt Clarice in Virginia. She already had three kids, but she'd made room for me, anyway. Not that teenage me had appreciated it.

Then I thought of Alicia. She and her husband had clearly shared a deep, strong connection. Then she'd lost him, and it had torn her in half. I'd already lost the people I cared about most in a flash of fire. The flames hadn't consumed me, but they'd burned me to my core. If I let myself care too much about anyone else, or get too close, I would just be preparing myself to get burned all over again.

My place was with the dead.

I watched the house through my tablet for a while, then I stood and paced the dark hall, moving as lightly as I could so my boots wouldn't send out resounding clicks from the hardwood.

Stacey had turned down her microphone so I wouldn't have to hear her chatting with Jacob, or whatever they were doing out in the back of the van together.

I looked out through the glass doors onto the dark cavity of the recessed balcony. Past the wrought-iron railing at the front, the narrow old Wilson house stood in its blind-watchtower fashion in the moonlight. I finally let myself remember that night, but my memories were just terrified flashes.

I'd been in the van, watching Calvin in green night vision on one of the monitors. He'd run into the booth-sized trap, and I couldn't see what happened inside because the walls were built of that colorful, heavily leaded glass.

The fearfeeder had dropped from the ceiling like a cockroach, landing on top of the trap while Calvin was within it, baiting the monster with his life.

It crawled down one side of the booth—just a black mass of darkness shaped like a man—and scurried around inside, pursuing Calvin, just as Calvin had intended.

I'd warned him it was coming. Maybe I shouldn't have done that. Maybe that had caused Calvin to pause, to look back rather than running straight on through and out of the trap.

I had not heard any gunshots, nor seen the scummy-looking guy who Calvin had seen, the boogeyman of cops everywhere, the unknown person waiting just around the corner, or maybe in a pulled-over car late at night, ready to blast out the brains of anyone wearing a badge.

That illusion—sight, sound, and all—had been for Calvin, and the cameras and microphones had picked up none of it. All I heard

was Calvin grunting in pain over my headset, and all I saw was him
falling halfway out of the trap, collapsing, blocking the door so I
couldn't close it.

Then I'd gone running inside and found him on the floor
surrounded by his own blood.

I turned away from the house and its painful memories, walking
now to the dead-end door in the ornate archway.

"Come on," I whispered. I touched the flashlight holstered on
my utility belt, which I'd strapped on in case tonight turned into
more than a simple observation. "Come on, boogeyman, Closet
Man. Tell me who you are."

Something cold passed me, an unseasonably chilly draft. It was
over as quickly as it began.

"Who's there?" I asked. I clicked on my flashlight, but it didn't
reveal anything. I walked over to my toolbox to grab the thermal
goggles.

While I fished them out, I heard a tiny creak behind me.

By the time I had the goggles in place, the cold spot was gone.
The dead-end door was ajar by just a crack, as though somebody
had walked past and opened it.

I walked to the door, feeling my heartbeat kick up a little.
Intellectually, I knew there could be nothing behind the door—there
wasn't *room* for anything behind it—but at that moment, in that dark
and silent haunted house, I could believe that it would open onto
something else entirely, some scene of horror and death...but I
opened it anyway.

And found myself staring at a blank wall.

I let out a slow sigh, feeling a mixture of relief and
disappointment. It's my job to find, observe, and remove the ghosts,
but that doesn't mean I enjoy encountering them face to face, not at
all. It's just a necessary part of the work.

Something had passed through here, either Gerard or the
boogeyman, but it was gone now.

I walked up and down the hall, listening and watching. I would
usually make rounds of the house, checking in person for any
activity, but I didn't want to stray too far from the kids tonight.
Protecting them was my main concern.

Time passed. Slowly. I mostly checked the basement cameras to watch the activity there. Stacey mentioned over my headset that Jacob had gone home for the night, to catch some sleep before he woke up to count other people's money at the firm where he worked.

By about three in the morning, I was feeling drowsy, and fairly certain that nothing would happen that night. It happens a lot. Ghosts don't always follow a set schedule, unless they're obsessed with a certain time—the time of their death, usually. I once dealt with a ghost who appeared like clockwork at 1:11 each morning, the exact moment she'd been murdered by a jealous lover. That one was easy to find. Unfortunately, this fearfeeder was not so predictable.

Just as I was ready to give up for the night, Stacey whispered urgently through my headset.

"Ellie, I've lost both cameras in Mia's room," she said. "They blacked out."

"I'll take a look." I drew my flashlight without clicking it on, then took Mia's doorknob in my hand. It was like grabbing a ball of ice. "Stacey, I might need back-up. Get ready."

I turned the handle, which wasn't easy—the tumbler and latch assembly inside the doorknob let out cracking sounds as though they had been frozen into place.

Pushing the door open, I stepped into Mia's room with my flashlight out in front of me like a firearm.

The room was cold, as I'd expected from the doorknob, so cold my breath turned solid white in the air. Something growled soft and low in the darkness.

Mia lay in her bed, rigid as a corpse with her eyes wide open. She was staring at her closet, but I had to step deeper into the room before I could see it.

The two cameras remained in place on their tripods, undisturbed, pointing at the closet door. The door itself was open a few inches.

Something dark stood in her closet. The low growling sound rumbled from there, too soft to be heard by anyone outside the room.

"Stacey, hit the floodlight," I whispered, looking at the remote-controlled light she'd installed. Nothing happened. "Stacey!"

"I'm trying!"

I ran to Mia's bedside table and pressed the floodlight button

Stacey had installed there, but the light still wouldn't come on. I tried the lamp—dead. The wall switch for the overhead light—no response.

Mia looked at me, too terrified to speak, then looked back at the closet.

I clicked on my flashlight, narrowing and concentrating the beam with the little iris, and jabbed it at the closet. The dark figure slipped out of sight, but the room remained painfully cold, and I could still hear the growling. It was a mechanical sound, I realized, more like an engine than an animal.

"Stacey, get in here now," I whispered, approaching the closet door.

"I'm already on my way."

"Mia, run." I looked at the girl in the bed, but she shook her head very slightly, too scared to budge from under her covers.

The mechanical roaring grew louder as I reached for the cold closet handle and slid the door aside.

It sprang out at me, ignoring the high-powered tactical light in my hand. Behind me, Mia screamed.

Fleshface, the supernatural stalker-killer who'd risen from the grave in sequel after cheesy, low-budget sequel, swung his chainsaw at my head as he leaped up from the sunken closet.

My only defense was to dodge back, leaning back as far as I could while the chainsaw sliced through the space where my head had been. I'm not Matrix Girl, so this was not done elegantly, and led to me crashing backwards and sprawling on the carpet, in a fashion that might have been horribly embarrassing if I hadn't been preoccupied with feeling terror for my life.

I did escape the chainsaw, though. It passed over me and lodged into the door frame around the closet.

The apparition seemed dangerously solid. I could feel the displaced air when it leaped at me, smell the motor oil and exhaust from the chainsaw. It looked just like the movie monster, its head wrapped like a mummy's but with strips of human skin (or the Hollywood effect-shop equivalent) instead of ancient cotton. His enormous, heavily patched overcoat rustled as he pulled the chainsaw free.

"Mia, run!" I shouted again as I scrambled to my feet, backing away from Fleshface. It's not a good idea to fight chainsaw-wielding ghosts in the same room as a small child, if you can avoid it. Not that I've ever seen a ghost wield a chainsaw before.

Mia pulled her thick quilt over her head, hiding in her bed. It was frustrating, but I understood where she was coming from. Only the bed was safe. Leaving the bed, even reaching a finger or toe over the edge, or leaving any part of yourself exposed from beneath the covers, meant opening yourself to attack. Every kid who's ever seen a monster in the closet knows that.

Fleshface regarded me for a moment, his dark eyes glittering in their sunken sockets as I shined my flashlight at his head. I suddenly wished I'd seen at least one of his movies.

"Mia," I said. "How did they kill Fleshface at the end?"

"With his chainsaw," she whispered. I could barely hear her, but I was pretty sure that was what she'd said.

"Of course."

"He's powerful but slow," Stacey said over my headset. "The girl who kills him in the second movie is a gymnast."

"Sounds like a job for you," I replied.

Fleshface came at me again, the chainsaw raised above his head in a way that, I'm pretty sure, violates the standard chainsaw safety manuals. He looked ready to bring it down and split me in half. The smart, self-preservation thing would have been to run, but no matter how scared I was, I couldn't leave Mia alone with this monster.

I dodged to one side and let him charge past me. As Stacey had promised, he lumbered onward, not nimble at all. His chainsaw swung toward the floor, and he started to twist around, belatedly trying to follow me.

The only option I really had was to swing my tactical flashlight, its anodized shell of aircraft-grade aluminum designed to double as a blunt weapon when cops needed one in a pinch.

I swung it with both hands like a baseball bat, right at the fleshy strips on the back of his cranium.

This was a big risk. Most of these entities aren't very solid when you try to fight back—you find yourself wrestling with a cloud of energy that lashes at you with psychokinetic energy but has no real mass itself, no stomach or groin where you can plant your boot. There was a good chance I'd stumble right through the movie monster only to get hacked apart by its chainsaw. The chainsaw, of course, wasn't actually real, either, but represented a dense, sharp, rapidly moving center of the ghost's psychokinetic power.

The flashlight whipped toward his head...and slammed into the back of it with a satisfying crack.

Fleshface let out an awful moan, like a high wind through a graveyard just before a storm. He staggered forward, the tip of his chainsaw dragging through the carpet and shredding it into a cloud of lint.

I drew my flashlight back for another strike, but he was already turning toward me, his chainsaw swinging in an upward arc toward my ribcage.

I changed the trajectory of my flashlight in time to bring it clanging down on the chainsaw before it reached me, as if we were suddenly in a medieval sword fight.

A storm of electrical sparks erupted, briefly lighting up the room before he sliced my flashlight in half. I stumbled backward as he raised the spinning blade yet again, the tip pointed at my heart.

I was moving in the only direction open to me...right into the closet, a dead end where he'd have me cornered in one of his favorite spots in the house.

Another light flooded the room. Stacey stood in the doorway, her tactical flashlight in one hand.

"Buddy slaughter!" she shouted.

I couldn't make any sense of those words, but Fleshface stopped and turned toward her.

"Guess what I'm about to do," Stacey said. "I'm on my way to a party, where I'll drink beer and maybe sneak off with a guy. And if I hear any strange, creepy noises while I'm there, I'll be sure to go and investigate them all by myself, without telling anyone where I'm going."

I knew just what Stacey was doing, describing behaviors that would mark a character for certain death in any teen horror movie. Only the virtuous virgins survive.

Fleshface let out a roar and charged at her.

I went after him, raising a leg and landing my boot in the center of his back. My foot sank in a little—his body felt spongy, as if I'd just stomped on a Jell-O mold covered in a dirty napkin.

He went down, and I fell after him, since I'd put all the power I could summon into that kick. Three years of kickboxing class finally paid off.

The monster crashed on top of his chainsaw, and the blade ruptured out the back of his overcoat, directly in the path of my fall.

I managed to fling out my arms and catch myself, landing on my hands and knees, the buzzing chainsaw blade only an inch from my chest.

He squirmed under me, and I pushed back into a squatting position.

Though the chainsaw jutted out through his midsection, there was no blood or gore. His limbs twitched and flopped, as boneless as a scarecrow's.

Something poured out of his flailing form. At first I took it for some strange black liquid, thick and viscous, flowing from his crumpling overcoat and deflating mask.

Then they crawled up my leg, and I realized I was looking at a flood of spiders. Black widows, thousands of them, pouring out while the coat and mask shriveled to the carpet like empty rags.

I stood and staggered back, screaming as I pulled my sleeve over my hand and swept at the spiders crawling up both legs of my jeans. People rarely die from a single black widow bite, but just one can make you extremely ill. I didn't want to find out what a hundred of them might do.

Mia screamed along with me.

"Calm down, Ellie," Stacey said, looking at me like I was crazy while she turned on the room lights. "It's over."

"Do you not see—" I began to shout at her, but then I looked down. I was smacking at my legs for no apparent reason. All the spiders were gone. So were all traces of Fleshface.

"Did we kill him?" Stacey asked.

"I wouldn't bet on it." I drew my thermal goggles down over my eyes to check the room. "Probably just chased him away. Mia, are you okay?"

"Yeah," the girl breathed. "Is he gone?"

"Gone for now," I said. "Stacey, what did you yell at him when you ran into the room? Buddy something?"

"Buddy Slaughter."

"That's Fleshface's real name," Mia said. "In the movie."

"Gotcha."

Alicia arrived in a panic, wearing frayed blue satin pajamas, clearly drawn by her daughter's scream. While she sat on the bed to embrace and soothe Mia, the three of us told her what had happened. The room rapidly grew warmer, shifting from a bitter winter feeling into humid, warm summer air. Kalil appeared in the doorway as we spoke, watching and listening but saying nothing.

"Did you see anything, Kalil?" I asked him.

"No," he said. He was trying to sound nonchalant, but his voice trembled, hinting at fear underneath the surface. "I just heard screams. Is it gone?"

"We think so," I said.

"Can I stay in your room, Mommy?" Mia asked.

"Of course you can, baby. You too, Kalil."

"I'm okay," he said. "I'm not scared."

"I don't think I'll sleep again tonight," Alicia said. "It's almost four, anyway. I'll just go clean the kitchen."

"I'll help you, Mommy," Mia said.

"Kalil? Cleaning or sleeping?" she asked.

"Cleaning," he said with a sigh, but he looked relieved at having a third way out, not having to sleep alone or with his mom.

Alicia and the kids left, off to clean and organize an apartment that was already pretty neat and spotless as far as I could see. It was a relatively healthy reaction under the circumstances, I guess, getting busy with something that would both distract them from their thoughts and help them reclaim some feeling of control over their home.

Stacey and I remained in Mia's room. While Stacey took snapshots of the scene, I studied the gash in the closet door frame.

"Look at this," I said, and Stacey came over. I ran my finger across the shallow, diagonal cut. "This seemed much deeper to me at first. There's no chips, no splinters...like he cut it with a scalpel instead of a chainsaw."

"Maybe we should really insist on the family leaving the house for a few days," Stacey said.

"We know this entity can leave the house, though," I said. "If it follows them somewhere else while we're here, we won't be with them to protect them. When Calvin and I investigated the Wilson house, we urged the family to leave, and they did. But I'm trying *not* to repeat our choices from that investigation."

"Because it turned out badly."

"The entity disappeared after that. I couldn't find it on my own. It needed the family there to draw it out."

"So we're kind of using our clients as bait." Stacey frowned.

"We're keeping the entity predictable," I said. "If we change their routine, we change what it does."

"However you want to say it." Stacey took pictures of the distinctly non-chainsaw-like cut.

"It's shocking how precisely it wields its PK energy." I picked up the sliced halves of my flashlight. "It's usually blunt force, like knocking on a wall or slamming a door. Or it's up close and personal, biting and scratching. What this thing just did is off the charts."

"Great," Stacey said softly, in a tone that made it clear she wasn't feeling that great about it at all. She checked the night vision and thermal cameras. "The batteries are drained dry, but these aren't damaged otherwise. I'll go get replacements."

Stacey left, and I stood alone in the room. The interior of the closet was shadowy and still gave me a sinister feeling, like something was there, watching me. My thermal goggles revealed nothing, but the EMF meter registered the same high readings we'd found on our first walk-through. The closet was itself a doorway, somehow leading down into the soulless depths where the monstrous shapeshifting entity dwelled, hungry to terrorize the living.

Chapter Fifteen

Stacey and I left at sunrise, after breaking down our gear from the laundry room and stashing it in Alicia's apartment. The moment we stepped out of the house into the pale morning light, it was like a heavy, oppressive weight lifting from our shoulders.

"You know what I wish?" Stacey said, while I pulled the van out onto the street. "I wish, just once, that we'd run into a *nice* haunting, you know, a *nice* ghost who just plays the piano or tidies up the house at night. One who kind of says, hey, being dead isn't so bad."

"A lot of ghosts have some kind of psychological disorder, or else they wouldn't be here," I said. "A ghost who understands his situation feels compelled to move on. Like Gerard. He's got one foot in the next world already, so I guess he's not so powerful here."

"What do you think that next world is like?" Stacey asked. "Is there a heaven and hell? Or is it like the near-death experiences people have?"

"I don't know. Maybe there's nothing."

"How could there be nothing? You talk all the time about

ghosts moving on to the 'other side.'"

"Maybe that's just a term we have, and not a real place," I said. "Maybe a ghost is just a tangle of unresolved emotion and longing. Untangle the knot, and there's nothing left but emptiness." I thought of my parents, gone forever, my whole life defined and shaped by their absence.

"That sounds bleak," Stacey said. "What does Calvin say about it?"

"Calvin says we must embrace uncertainty or we aren't being honest with ourselves."

"Sounds like something he read in a fortune cookie."

"Probably," I said. I didn't feel like having this conversation with Stacey at the moment, or thinking about whether there was more to life after death than restless ghosts making life miserable for the living.

After dropping her off, I went home for a bit of sleep. I had nightmares about a dark masked figure hunting me with a chainsaw. I was glad to wake up surrounded by daylight, rather than awake from those nightmares in the deepest hours of the night. I'm sure I would have seen monsters in my closet, too. In this line of work, you never run out of fresh nightmare material.

I saw I'd missed a call from Calvin, so I called him back while I brewed coffee. My cat Bandit meowed at my feet, clearly remembering the day I'd accidentally spilled cream on the floor.

"Bad news on the Carson kid," he said.

"Which one was that?"

"Twelve years old, disappeared in '85," Calvin said. "Turns out when they found him, he was catatonic, wandering down River Street. Dirty from head to toe, wearing shredded pajamas. He didn't say a word. Kid lived to be twenty-three years old, but he never spoke again. Went persistent vegetative, then died. Shut down. Like something sucked the soul out of him."

"Great. Another possible bad fate for our client and her kids." I filled him in on the events of the previous night.

"This is getting worse, Ellie," he said, the worry plain in his voice. "I think you and Stacey should stay inside together from now on."

"But then who will—"

"I'll sit in the van," he said. "I'll keep watch."

"We can handle this."

"I thought I could handle it alone, too, Ellie," he said. "I was wrong. Learn from my mistakes. And to be honest, I want to see this thing beaten and caught."

"You're the boss," I replied, but I wasn't happy about it. This same entity had hurt Calvin before. I didn't want to see him get hurt again. Saying that aloud would just rile him up, though.

As we spoke, I grabbed my tablet and walked out onto what my landlord would call my "balcony," which was more like a brick ledge with rails. It was a nice place to sit and have coffee, soaking up the green sunlight filtered through the oak canopy above.

"What else?" Calvin asked.

"I have an email from Grant." I skimmed it quickly. "He's found something for us. Hopefully it's better news than you had about that poor kid."

"Couldn't be much worse," Calvin said. He was right about that.

After an exciting lunch of apples and celery, I met up with Stacey and drove over to the Historical Association mansion, a beautiful gray-brick place trimmed with black wrought-iron railing, a feature ubiquitous around the city.

"Sorry to meet you at the servants' entrance," Grant whispered, opening the side door for us. "The Docents Committee is having tea in the front parlor. Come, come, you both look lovely."

"So do you, Grant," I said. He was impeccably garbed as usual, in a white summer suit over a mint green shirt, the entire ensemble seeming to cool and sweeten the air around him. That was probably his cologne, though. I noticed an unfamiliar row of salt-and-pepper bristles on his upper lip. "Are you growing a mustache?"

"Simply an experiment, nothing more." He led us toward the polished rosewood back staircase, the railing made of elegantly sculpted black iron columns.

"You look like Clark Gable," Stacey offered as we followed him up.

"Then I shall never shave it off."

"Is that what the Docents Committee is meeting about?" I asked in a hushed, conspiratorial whisper. "Your new mustache?"

"Much larger issues." Grant rounded the landing, leading us up to the second floor. "They're deciding on the flower arrangements for next season *and* what to serve at the Society dinner in two weeks. There was some discussion of buying a new carpet for the first-floor reading room. The meeting might come to blows."

The upstairs hall was brightly lit and hung with paintings of Savannah and the nearby islands drawn from across the past two centuries. At one point, we crossed a cutaway balcony and glanced down at the front parlor, where a cluster of well-dressed silver-haired ladies, ranging in age from sixty to ninety, sat ramrod-straight in the antique wing chairs, having a serious discussion in low voices. I imagined the argument growing heated as Grant had mentioned, the elderly ladies shouting, flinging their cups and cookies at one other, finally descending into all-out brawl, pearls and purses flying.

I doubted it would happen.

"This way..." Grant turned an ornate little curved handle on one door. He brought us into his office, where everything screamed *antique*, from the polished walnut rolltop desk against the back wall to the chairs engraved with little grape-and-leaf shapes. Tall rectangular windows looked out on the grassy park across the street, framed by light, gauzy floor-length curtains. Bookshelves crowded the walls, densely packed but neatly organized.

Grant sat at a more modern desk at the center of the room, with a sleek black computer and stacks of documents. More documents, folders, and leather-bound books sat on a rolling cart parked beside his desk.

"I apologize for the mess," he said. "Have a seat. Should I smuggle up tea and cookies from downstairs?"

"We don't want to trigger an international nuclear incident," I said.

"Very true. The reading-room carpet might never be replaced. Well, let's begin with the Bible." Grant lifted a heavy leather volume the size of an unabridged dictionary and placed it before us.

"Are we going to get religious here?" I asked.

"Not at the moment. We'll skip to the end." He gingerly opened the old Bible, revealing rows of names and dates written in faded ink on two blank pages by the back cover. I nodded. Lots of families used to note births, marriages, and deaths in the old family Bible.

"The Barrington family occupied the land you're studying," Grant said. "This may look like a dry collection of names and dates, but see how much we can learn from it." He pointed to a pair of names with his pen, not touching the fragile old paper. "Two brothers, Joseph and Edgar Barrington, born on the same date in 1795. We know right away they're twins, but we can't say whether they're identical or fraternal.

"In 1820, Joseph marries Rebecca Moore, born in 1803," Grant continued. "In 1821, she gives birth to a boy, Joshua. Two years later, a girl, Sarah. Then the dates tell a darker story. Joseph dies in 1825 at the age of thirty, leaving a young widow and two small children behind. Both children died about two years later, on the same day."

"This is exactly what we're looking for," I said. "Grant, you're a genius."

"You can thank the Association's endless appetite for acquiring every stray piece of paper in the city," Grant said.

"It looks like the wife lived to be sixty—" I began, leaning forward and reading the handwritten dates upside down.

"Ahem. I've spent all day cobbling together this information, so *I* will be the one telling the story," Grant said.

"Sorry," I said, sinking back into my chair. "Please continue, sir."

"Thank you. As I was about to say, Rebecca lived until 1863, dying amid war and deprivation. She did not re-marry. And, as we can also see, Edgar lived until 1856 and never married."

"Sounds like Edgar could be our boogeyman," Stacey said.

"Boogeyman?" Grant's neatly groomed white eyebrows perked up in interest.

"That's what we're hunting this time," I said. "It hides in closets, it makes you see things and feeds on your fear."

"I've heard this before," Grant said. "Is it similar to the ghost that put Calvin in that wheelchair?"

"We think it's the same one," I told him.

"Oh, dear. Be careful, both of you." Grant looked deeply worried, lines crinkling his forehead as he frowned at me.

"We will," I said.

"Promise me."

"I'll even make a note of it." I took out my pocket notepad and jotted down the two words. "Be...careful." I turned the notepad around to show him.

"I'm satisfied that you're taking the threat seriously," he said. "Where were we?"

"Edgar Barrington," I said.

"Yes, thank you." Grant opened a binder filled with faded old documents in the blocky type of nineteenth-century printing presses. "As far I can determine from tax records and assorted correspondence, Edgar lived in the house with his brother Joseph. Joseph was the one who built the house. He prospered in the trade of agricultural commodities, mainly timber for shipbuilding and export. An American tale, truly—Joseph made his fortune, built himself a mansion, and found a well-bred young lady to install inside it."

"What did Edgar do?" I asked.

"Edgar worked for Joseph in a subordinate capacity...an errand boy, more or less. He never made a mark on his own. After Joseph died, the business foundered badly under Edgar's management...until Edgar was placed in a mental asylum in 1829, where he lived until his death. I have the commitment papers around here somewhere..." Grant reached for an old folder. "In any case, it fell to young Rebecca, a woman who'd lost her husband and both children, to manage the business. Which she did well, finally selling it at quite a profit. All of which evaporated in the war."

"Sounds like a tough chick," Stacey said.

"Indeed. Here are Edgar Barrington's commitment papers...According to his sister-in-law, he was often found crawling the floors of the house at night like an animal, or standing for hours in the garden, staring at nothing, laughing to himself or drooling. At other times, he would pretend to be his dead brother and insisted that people call him 'Joseph.'"

"Weird-o-rama," Stacey said.

"He was witnessed in public, disheveled, what the paperwork calls 'a state of utter disarray.' He would skulk around school buildings, churches, and parks, staring at children as they played."

"I'd like to change my vote from 'weird' to 'creepy,'" Stacey said.

"Several witnesses offered statements, including neighbors and business associates, but it seems clear to me that Rebecca, Edgar's widowed sister-in-law, spearheaded the effort to have him committed."

"Leaving her with the house and the business," I said.

"The man killed her children," Stacey said, sounding defensive. "And he was clearly a bag of nuts, stalking other kids..."

"How did his brother Joseph die?" I asked Grant.

"A horseback riding accident," Grant said. "Interestingly, Edgar was the only witness to Joseph's death." He said that with an air of a person casually unloading juicy gossip, knowing it will bring a big response.

"So Edgar might have killed his brother, as well as his brother's children," I said. I was scribbling on my notepad like a madwoman.

"Good thing he got locked up," Stacey said.

"Truly. He died in that asylum, too," Grant said.

"Uh." Stacey sat up in her chair, looking at me with wide, worried eyes. "This isn't going to lead to us digging around in another haunted old insane asylum, is it? Because I'd rather go snorkeling with sharks. With a big tuna steak dangling around my neck."

"Then you'll be happy to learn that is not an option," Grant said. "This particular hospital was demolished long ago. As was the Barrington house itself."

"The big Tudor place that's there now was built in 1905," I said. "That's where a boy named Kris Larsen disappeared in the nineties. Do we have any pictures of this Barrington family?"

"We have a photograph of Edgar Barrington, apparently taken at the asylum." Grant produced an old brownish photograph protected by plastic.

The man lay on his back, his mouth slightly open, his eyes glazed. His face looked pinched and thin, his nose and cheekbones so sharp they looked like they could cut paper. His hair had gone gray. His fingers were long and thin, like a pianist's.

"He looks dead," Stacey commented.

"He is," Grant said. "I found this along with his death certificate. He died of tuberculosis in 1856, probably acquired inside the asylum, which helps explain his bony condition."

I gazed at the picture for a moment, trying to connect this thin corpse to the robust dark figure who scurried along ceilings and walls, tormenting children in the night.

"I've also found a few items of correspondence written by Edgar, as well as some by Rebecca," Grant said. "You may find the Edgar one particularly interesting. It is dated 1828, and he seems to have written it to Rebecca while he was out of town surveying a timber purchase. Here."

Grant brought out the old hand-written letters. Edgar's handwriting was a jabbing, spidery crawl.

"*All I see makes me think of you,*" I read aloud from the section Grant had indicated. "*The mating creatures in their rut, the great trees fallen and bleeding, their sap like blood returning to engorge the earth with life.*"

"A real poet," Stacey mumbled.

"*It torments me to share our home yet not our flesh—* Wow, that's pretty blunt. *You are the wife of my lost brother. Biblical law makes it clear you should be mine,*" I read.

"He's wrong on that point," Grant said. "Deuteronomy requires it only if the first brother dies childless. Joseph had left a son and a daughter."

"Who both died two years later," I said.

"That makes me think of this Serengeti documentary I saw," Stacey said. "When a new male lion takes over a pride, after defeating the old alpha male, he also kills all the previous alpha's cubs. Makes all the females go into heat so they can have the new leader's cubs instead."

"I don't believe it made our dear Rebecca go into heat," Grant said. "The letter shows Edgar's unfulfilled desires for her."

"*You have shown me a colder face, and resisted me, and you call me mad. My madness is for you, Rebecca. We are bonded each to the other, by chains stronger than simple vows, stronger than blood itself. You are cruel, your presence stirs me to arousal, leaves me in torment and pain—*" I read.

"That poor woman, living with that creep," Stacey said. "I wonder if she suspected him."

"Did they ever find the two kids' bodies?" I asked Grant.

"I've read nothing about that," Grant said. "The children were reported missing and never recovered. The date of their disappearance was later recorded as their date of death."

"We know where the bodies went," I said.

"Then perhaps you will lay them to rest," Grant replied.

"No way. I'm not going down into that well," Stacey said.

"So, here's the scenario I'm seeing," I said. "Edgar lives in his twin brother's house, watching Joseph and his family every day. Edgar's not successful on his own, he's unmarried, he's basically living in his brother's shadow. Maybe he's already mentally disturbed and can't get his own life together. So he's jealous. Jealous and crazy. He kills his brother to try and take his place. Then, a couple years later, decides to kill the two kids. Maybe he wants to have his own with Rebecca. He clearly wanted her to marry him, and she clearly resisted, and finally had him committed. How does that sound?"

"Sounds like he was a total whack-a-doodle," Stacey said. "But yeah, that's the picture I'm getting so far."

We read through more correspondence, including the letters by others who'd observed Edgar's increasingly bizarre behavior. These seemed to have been written in support of Rebecca's bid to lock Edgar away in the asylum, providing evidence that he was off his rocker. Rebecca struck me as a strong and resourceful woman, weathering the worst tragedies, using lawyers and doctors to remove Edgar from her life for her own safety, though she'd been too late to save her children.

From a letter from Rebecca to her sister, written early in Joseph and Rebecca's marriage: "*I thank you for your kind comments about the house, but I must tell you, the house demands so much it seems to own me. Even with five household servants I cannot keep up. And the children! Two overwhelm me—I do not see how you manage five, dear sister. I remember believing marriage would free me from Father and his cruelty, giving me freedom and power at last—how foolish I was.*

"*I prattle about the burdens every woman must share in this life, but I face another in this home. I beg you repeat none of this. Joseph's brother Edgar continues to dwell with us, and his presence unsettles me. He has none of Joseph's loud and boastful manner, but is a creature of shadows and whispers. Strange that two men so identically crafted on the surface could be so different. Edgar sulks and slumps, and appears shorter than Joseph.*

"*It is unfortunate to say, but I must confess it somewhere to unburden myself. When, by ill chance, Edgar and I find ourselves unaccompanied, alone in a room with no witnesses, he looks on me in a manner that puts me in mind of a starving dog, eager to gnaw upon my bones. It is all the stranger that he wears the form of my husband. These encounters disturb me. There is no other proper word for it.*"

After more reading, we came across this passage, in a letter to a friend a year after her husband died: *"Edgar craves me in marriage. He drools like a hound. He makes no secret of his desire. But I have been married once, and have no wish to bind myself to a low creature who wears the face of Joseph yet is an inferior soul to my dear lost husband. My children place sufficient burdens upon me, as do the men from the office who come to me for advice, knowing that I understand my late husband's affairs and investments, and am not an irresponsible fool like Edgar. They let him make pronouncements, then ignore him and follow my advice instead.*

"Edgar grows stranger by the day and year. I must lock my bedroom door at night, for I have opened my eyes more than once to see him standing over me, his form rigid as a corpse seasoned two days in the ground, his breath panting as he watches me sleep."

There was a long gap in her letters after the day in 1827 when her children disappeared, as if she could not bring herself to write after losing her children, followed by a flurry of correspondence dated 1828 and 1829, most of it about having Edgar committed to the asylum.

"I'd be interested in finding anything she wrote after Edgar died," I said. "Did he start haunting the place right away?"

"I suggest we divide up the remaining papers and read through them separately," Grant said.

Stacey sighed as Grant placed a few inches of folders and unsorted documents in front of her.

It took us a lot of reading, hours of it, shuffling through old bank records and squinting at the faded handwritten letters. Stacey was the one who found it.

"Here," Stacey said. "1859, four years after Edgar died. Letter to her cousin. Sandwiched in between her fears about the rising division in the country, her belief that Lincoln's election was a sign of troubled times to come...listen to this. *I cannot release myself of agitation. By night, I find myself tormented by visions of Joseph and the children, and these visitations are far from happy. In my mind, my poor lost children stare at me with hate and loathing. I wish only for an end to this torment, as I wish for peace in our nation...'* And then back to blah blah here comes the Civil War," Stacey concluded. "That sounds like our boogeyman."

"Her husband and children, hating her from beyond the grave," I said. "That must have been her fear."

"Survivor's guilt. I'm pretty sure Jacob has that from the plane crash," Stacey said.

"So we've learned all about our boogeyman," I said. "Now we just have to trap him."

"How?" Stacey asked. "His house was torn down, and that old asylum was torn down, so we can't go there, which is a total shame. Where are we going to search for ghost bait?"

I thought about it for a minute. "Grant, where is Edgar Barrington buried?"

"I believe I ran across..." He shuffled through papers for a few minutes. Stacey stared at me with a very disturbed look on her face. I tried not to laugh at her reaction. "It would be Laurel Grove North."

"Can we track down his exact plot?"

"I have the bill of sale for it here," Grant said.

"Um..." Stacey cleared her throat. "Just to be clear, so I don't feel like I'm going crazy. We're not talking about robbing this guy's grave, are we?"

"Do you have a problem with that?" I asked her, keeping my face stoic.

"Well...there could be jail time involved. Among many, *many* other considerations," she said.

"That's why it's best to wait until after nightfall," I told her. "We're less likely to get caught that way."

Stacey gaped at me. All the color had drained from her face.

"It sounds like an adventurous evening," Grant said. "I would volunteer to wield a shovel and help to excavate your evil friend, but honestly, I'd rather be doing...just about anything else tonight."

Stacey remained speechless, a rare thing for her.

Chapter Sixteen

Laurel Park Cemetery lies on the west side of Savannah, over a hundred and fifty acres of huge old trees, statues, crypts, and gravestones mostly dating from the middle to late nineteenth century. Roads and paths curve out of sight under the shady canopy.

It was gloomy when Stacey and I arrived, the evening approaching us quickly under a dark and overcast sky. Great conditions for grave robbing.

We walked up one of the foot paths, past massive granite markers and dark marble obelisks, toward the oldest area of the cemetery. I carried a ridiculously oversized purse, more like a small suitcase, with a few flowers sticking out the top.

"Hey, I didn't really want to mention it, but we totally forgot to bring any shovels," Stacey said. She scanned the footpaths and the shadows under the trees, as if looking for someone, but the graveyard appeared deserted. We were the only living people in sight.

"We don't need them."

"So we aren't digging up the boogeyman's bones," Stacey said, looking relieved. "Right?"

"It would be nice if we could, but like you said, there could be jail time involved."

"Yeah. It would be...nice." Stacey shook her head.

We found the Barrington family plot, enclosed by stone and wrought iron. I opened the little gate and let myself in.

"My skin's already crawling," Stacey whispered.

"You're not helping the mood by saying that," I whispered back. I felt a little nervous, too. A monster lay under these stones.

We found Joseph Barrington's grave. *1795-1825. Beloved husband and father. I rejoice in thy salvation -1 Samuel 2:1.*

His brother Edgar lay nearby. *1795-1856.* No plaudits or Bible verses for him.

Rebecca Barrington lay directly in between the brothers, her headstone a little more ornate. A granite cherub perched on top of it, one hand extended downward as if to help Rebecca up out of her grave, the other pointing skyward as if to indicate their destination.

Nothing commemorated the two missing children. As far as we'd been able to determine, their bodies had never been found.

"Edgar's buried right in the middle of the family he destroyed," Stacey said. "Makes you think."

"What does it make you think?"

"Uh...it's just an expression. So what's the plan, ma'am?"

I knelt in front of Edgar's grave and brought an empty ghost trap out of my silly-sized giant purse, scattering the handful of flowers that I'd thrown on top of it.

"You really think we can trap him here?" Stacey asked. "With no stamper or anything? Are we just going to ask him nicely to step inside it for us?"

"Nope." It was a standard trap, a two-foot plastic cylinder with a leaded-glass jar inside. A layer of copper mesh was fitted between the glass and the plastic to create an electromagnetic barrier when the battery pack was activated.

I took a little steel trowel from the purse and scooped up a heap of dark earth and a few weeds from in front of Edgar's headstone. I dumped it all into the trap.

"Interesting..." Stacey said, watching me closely.

"Earth from the ghost's grave," I said. "It automatically reminds them of their true condition, and offers rest and peace. A ghost looking to escape its miserable existence can find it very attractive and sink right in."

"So that's our bait? Edgar's grave dirt?"

"Best bait we can manage."

"What if he's not looking to escape or move on or whatever?" she asked.

"Then he'll avoid this soil like the plague, making it completely useless as bait."

"Great. So...fifty-fifty chance, right?" she asked.

"I don't get the sense that Edgar is really trying to give up his role as boogeyman," I said. "So I'd put the odds at closer to ninety-ten. Not in our favor."

"That's comforting." Stacey looked up at the dark clouds ahead. "Is it about to rain?"

"Just watch out for other people," I said, shoveling more dirt, rocks, and small weeds into the trap. "I don't want to try explaining this to a judge."

Stacey paced around, looking nervous, watching the growing shadows while I filled up on nice, fresh grave dirt.

"Someone's coming," she whispered.

I glanced up, hoping to see an elderly pedestrian type taking an evening stroll and visiting the ancestors. Instead, I saw headlights cutting through the gloom. It was a golf cart, probably a maintenance or security person, and it was turning toward us.

I capped the trap and stashed it into my giant purse before standing up.

"Just wait for him to pass," I whispered.

The cart didn't pass, though. It slowed to a halt as it reached the portion of the path closest to us. A man stepped out—white beard, tan coveralls. I could see a dirty shovel and hoe propped upright on the back of the cart.

"Cemetery's closed," he said, walking toward us. He wore a hard, suspicious look on his wrinkled face.

"Already?" Stacey gave her best innocent, rapidly-blinking girl look. "I thought it closed at sunset."

"Naw, we close at five each day. It's posted right up front."

"Oh, I am so sorry, sir!" she said, covering her mouth as if horrified while doing the most honeyed Alabama accent I'd ever heard. "My aunt told me this cemetery had the most beautiful angel statues she'd ever seen, and I just had to go and see them for myself.

And she's right, but she didn't tell me how lovely the gardens were. We'll just skedaddle on out of here, I am so embarrassed."

The gruff-looking maintenance man had slowly begun to smile as the words gushed out of Stacey's cute blond head. She was doing a good job charming him, which meant I didn't have to deal with the situation. I appreciated that.

"Looks like rain," the man said, pointing his thumb at the dark, overcast sky. "You might get caught out in the weather. I'd better give you ladies a ride back to your car."

"Oh, goodness, you don't need to do all that, sir," Stacey replied. "I'm sure we'll be fine."

"I insist," he said. "You'll look like a couple of wet cats if you walk all the way back."

"Well, if you *insist...*" Stacey started toward the golf cart, and I trailed behind, feeling mildly annoyed. I'd wanted to get away from the guy as soon as possible, but I suppose we'd have looked more suspicious if we'd actually turned down a free ride so we could walk in the rain.

I rode on the back, facing backwards next to a dirty shovel, my now-heavy purse in my lap.

Stacey sat up front while the man told her all about the history of the cemetery, soaking up her attention while he puttered us forward at about five miles an hour.

A light, misty rain was drizzling by the time we reached the van.

We got ahead of the slow-moving rainclouds, which obscured the setting sun and brought an early nightfall as we drove downtown. After parking at the curb in front of our client's house, I led Stacey around back. I wanted to try again to speak with Mr. Gray.

I knocked on the slanted door marked with the brass *D*. The little windows near the ground were dark, so I didn't have much hope. Raindrops splatted my hair and face. I knocked again.

"I think he's out," Stacey said.

"Or he's doing a great job of avoiding us." I sighed. "Let's get inside."

Melissa was babysitting Kalil and Mia again. The kids were in the kitchen, eating peanut butter and jelly.

"My brother said you can call him if you need help again," Melissa told me, while Stacey and I started on the heap of gear that we needed to lug down and set up in the basement all over again.

"I think we'll be okay," I said. I didn't want Michael thinking I needed help and protection all the time. I was a ghost-hunting private detective, after all, who'd just recently kicked a boogeyman until it bled spiders.

"Are you serious?" Stacey asked. "You're not going to let that guy carry the heavy stuff for us, Ellie?"

"We can manage," I told her.

It took a few trips to move everything down, and we set up with the portable floodlight on again, since the overhead fluorescents were so poor. The room was already cold, and we could feel hidden eyes watching us from every corner.

We ran into problems—the thermal was stubborn about booting up, the microphone battery kept dying.

We were working on sorting those out when more problems arrived.

The basement door opened, and a tall man, easily six-four or six-five, charged down the steps. He had a square jaw and a comb-over that generally failed to hide his bald spot, and he wore a big brown-striped tie with a short-sleeve shirt.

"There they are!" he said, pointing at us.

He was followed by a shorter man, hefty with a black Elvis-esque pompadour and sideburns to match, his sizable stomach draped in a bowling shirt. The man squinted in confusion through his purple-rimmed glasses.

Then Lulinda Fielding followed right behind them, and the picture snapped into place. I wondered which of the two men were her husband, the elusive Hoss.

"I told you! My boy saw them down here yesterday," Lulinda said.

Falcon. The little turncoat.

"Just what is going on in here? Who are you people?" asked the Elvis wannabe. His voice was unexpectedly high and nasal.

"We're private investigators," I replied.

"They're rip-off artists," Lulinda said. "Talking about ghosts. They told my boy the monster in his closet is *real!*"

"Kid just whines and cries all the time," said the man with the combover. "Scared of dinosaurs. What kind of kid is scared of dinosaurs?"

"I'm gonna have to call the police," Elvis Guy said as he reached the basement floor. "What is all this mess?"

"We're studying paranormal disturbances on behalf of several of your tenants," I told him. "I'm Ellie Jordan, from Eckhart Investigations—" I reached for a business card.

"Well, I'm the property manager for this here house," Elvis Guy said. "Zayne Plunket. And I need all this mess taken out right now."

"Your own tenants wanted us here," I said.

"The only tenants I see are Hoss and Lulinda Fielding, and they want you *gone*."

"Just give me a second." Since Alicia hadn't been home the last time I was upstairs, I called Michael.

"Did you find any ghosts?" he asked when he answered.

"I found some of your neighbors. They called in your property manager," I said. "Want to come vouch for us?"

"Sure. Just tell Zayne to sing 'Hunka Hunka Burning Love' until I get there."

I snickered as I hung up the phone. "Michael's coming down," I told them.

Hoss, of the combover and ugly tie, snorted and shook his head.

"You still need permission from the property owner to do...whatever this is." Zayne adjusted his purple glasses as he leaned over to inspect the thermal camera on its tripod.

"Careful, that's expensive," Stacey said, moving closer to him. "And fragile."

"What does it do?" Zayne asked.

"It's a thermal imaging camera. It shows us cold spots indicative of active revenants or other noncorporeal entities," I said.

"What's that, now?" Zayne asked. The words rushed together to sound like *Whussat, nah?* I couldn't quite place his accent. Maybe it was Late Pilled-Out Elvis.

"Ghosts," Stacey said. "We're looking for ghosts."

"They're crazy! Call the police already!" Lulinda said.

"Leave them alone," Michael said, walking in through the door.

He'd arrived so fast that he must have run the whole way, but he didn't show any sign of being winded or anything less than calm and relaxed. "They're supposed to be here."

"Says who? You?" Hoss asked, glaring while Michael descended the steps.

"Alicia and I want her here," Michael said. He walked over to stand beside me, a nice show of solidarity. He glared at Zayne while he spoke. "This house is haunted. I've seen it, my sister's seen it, Alicia and her kids have seen it."

"And your child has seen it," I said, looking at Lulinda. She gave me an oversized pink-lipstick clown-frown and looked at the floor. I turned to Zayne. "We tried to speak with Mr. Gray, too, but he never answered his door."

Zayne looked from us to the Fieldings as if puzzled, scratching his big King of Rock and Roll belly.

"Who's Mr. Gray?" he finally asked.

"Over in apartment D." Hoss pointed to the door to Mr. Gray's apartment, his forehead bunching up over his eyes as he studied Zayne like he was the world's biggest idiot, maybe on display at the circus freak show. "Scrawny old guy. Always dressed sharp, wearing that same old-fashioned gray suit and bowtie. Pays you rent every month. You might have heard of him."

"Nobody's lived in apartment D for years," Zayne said, returning Hoss's scrutiny with his own you're-an-idiot look.

"We see Mr. Gray all the time," Michael said.

"You might want to go collect some back rent," Hoss said, pointing to the door. "I hate freeloaders."

"No, there's no tenant," Zayne said.

"You're out of your mind, Elvis," Hoss said, striding on his long, bird-stalk legs toward the closed door at the far end of the laundry room. He knocked on it.

Zayne looked around at the rest of us, an expression of disbelief on his face. Then he walked over to the door, took out a thick wad of keys on a keyring, and shuffled through them...slowly, as if he had hours to kill. Hoss watched him impatiently, arms crossed, toe tapping.

"Put some fire under that mule!" Hoss finally snapped.

Zayne didn't reply. He finally found the right key, slid it into the lock, and turned it.

The door to apartment D creaked open.

I walked over to see it, along with everybody else.

We looked into a small room with eggshell-bland walls, the floor made of cheap, warped hardwood. Cardboard boxes, paint cans, and a small pile of old lumber sat along one wall.

I flipped on my flashlight and walked inside. No furniture, just assorted old junk. It was all one room, except for a bathroom in the corner. I saw the short flight of concrete stairs leading up to the slanted doors where I'd knocked earlier.

"Nobody's lived here in a while," Stacey said, following me in.

"I don't get it. Where did Mr. Gray go?" Hoss asked, standing in the doorway.

"How many times do I have to say it? There's nobody named Mr. Gray, nor Miss Scarlet or any other color, living down here." Zayne stepped into the apartment. "There was trouble with water leakage, and people kept breaking their leases, saying the place was..." He closed his mouth.

"The place was what?" Michael stepped close to Zayne, who looked at the floor, scratching his stomach. "Haunted?"

"Well..." Zayne shrugged. "People will say anything, I guess."

"You know about this!" Michael said. "You and everybody at your company. That's why the rent's so low but the lease is expensive to break. *You* should be paying for the ghostbusters."

"Doesn't make any sense..." Hoss grumbled, kicking a piece of crumpled waste paper across the floor.

"We're not paying for anything!" Zayne snapped. "Y'all need to get out of here." He waved his arm as if directing traffic back to the laundry room. "Come on, now."

"You're all messing with me," Hoss said, with a glare for Zayne especially. "This is some kind of joke. Come on, Lu." He stomped out of the room, and Lulinda followed, with a dismissive glance at the lot of us.

Michael was still glaring at Zayne, who seemed to slump under the weight of Michael's look.

"I guess that settles that," Zayne mumbled, shifting his weight uncomfortably.

"And you're not going to give these investigators any more trouble?" Michael asked. He was certainly thorough about standing up for us.

Zayne mumbled something and wandered out of the apartment. I gave Michael a smile as we left. His return smile was warm and inviting.

Chapter Seventeen

Upstairs, Calvin had arrived and was waiting for us outside. The drizzling rain had passed, leaving the night smelling fresh and new. Michael walked over there with Stacey and me, since he'd agreed to help lug the big stamper into the basement, thankfully.

We gave Calvin the summary of what had happened and helped him into the van, where he would be watching the monitors all night.

"So you're the fireman," Calvin said, appraising Michael over his glasses. Calvin wore a coat and tie for the occasion, though he'd neglected to shave or untangle his salt-and-pepper hair, which had grown longer year by year since he'd left the police force.

"Yes, sir."

"Decent manners, too," Calvin said. "Not like these young people who don't bother with proper introductions."

"Oh, sorry," I said, feeling embarrassed. "Michael the fireman, this is Calvin the ghost detective."

"Good to meet you, boy," Calvin said, shaking his hand. "Heard you've been a big help."

"I just carry stuff to the basement."

"With a basement haunted as bad as yours, that's a big help."

"Thanks," Michael said.

"I need to ask you something, Michael," I said, opening a briefcase I'd stored in the back of the van. It was crammed full of folders holding photocopied pictures and documents from the library and the Historical Association. I flipped through them and found the picture of Edgar Barrington from the asylum morgue. "Do you recognize this person?"

Michael's eyebrows shot up. "That's Mr. Gray."

"Whoa," Stacey said. "Seriously?"

"This man's name is Edgar Barrington," I said. "We think he's our boogeyman."

"Mr. Gray's the boogeyman?" Michael asked.

"It could be the twin brother," Calvin said.

"That's right. Edgar had a twin brother, Joseph," I explained to Michael. "Joseph died in a horseback riding accident, possibly arranged by Edgar. His ghost could be stuck here along with his twin."

"Twins can have a strong psychic connection," Calvin added. "If Edgar's stuck here, Joseph could be stuck with him."

"It's crazy to think that old man is a ghost," Michael said. "I figured he was just quiet and lonely, kept to himself. He never really replied when I spoke to him, but just kind of nodded and smiled and continued on his way. Sometimes he was heading toward his apartment, sometimes leaving the house and strolling up the sidewalk..."

"Why do you call him Mr. Gray?" I asked.

"That's what Terry and Alex called him," Michael said. "They lived in apartment B before the Fieldings did."

"Maybe it was just from his appearance," Stacey said. "He wears a gray suit, never speaks to anyone. Somebody started calling him Mr. Gray and it caught on among the tenants."

"He does have a gray tone to his skin, too, like he's sick," Michael said. "I always thought it was the perfect name for him. What's his real name again?"

"Joseph Barrington," I said. "Edgar's his brother."

"And you're hoping to catch Edgar tonight. With this." Michael tapped the trap, half-filled with grave dirt. I'd dumped the excess dirt into a mason jar to make room for candles inside the trap, and so the trap's internal sensors wouldn't be buried in earth.

"Standard ghost trap," I said. "A layer of leaded glass on the inside, surrounded by an electromagnetic field, the whole thing insulated with plastic. This dirt is from Edgar's grave."

"And that actually works?"

"Sometimes. Tonight will depend on whether he's attracted to his own grave dirt or repelled by it."

"Better get that trap ready," Calvin said, turning back to the array of glowing screens to watch the house. "We're into the ghosting hours."

We carried the gear down to the basement, where I slid the trap into the stamper. I lit a couple of candles to help draw the ghost's attention. On my advice, we stayed quiet throughout this process.

I programmed the trap to snap shut when it detected a temperature drop of five degrees or more, combined with an EMF spike of at least two milligaus. That was virtually a hair trigger. I would be watching the trap on video with the remote in hand, but it was good to set the trap to close automatically when it detected a ghost, just in case something went wrong.

We left quickly and closed the basement door behind us. Then we lingered in the short hallway, near the bottom of the steps to Michael's apartment. Michael and I just looked at each other.

"Okay, I'd better check on the clients..." Stacey excused herself, stepping through the door into Alicia's apartment.

I felt rooted there, looking up into Michael's bright green eyes, and there was again that feeling of something warm and magnetic drawing us together. I hoped he felt it, too, and that I wasn't going completely crazy.

"Do you think you'll catch him tonight?" Michael asked.

"If we don't, I'm not sure what we'll try tomorrow night."

"Anything else I can help with?"

I was tempted to ask him to sit with Stacey and me, monitoring the apartment from the inside, but I worried my personal feelings about having him around would distract me from the work. Also, it might be hours before anything happened—what if the conversation grew awkward or he started to think I was boring? There were all kinds of ways for things to go wrong, and all kinds of mistakes I could make if I wasn't totally focused on what I was doing.

"I think we're all set for the night," I told him. I glanced at his lips and imagined what they might feel like on my own. Yep. Distraction. "Thanks again."

"Call me if you need anything at all," Michael said. "I want to keep everybody safe."

"Of course you do."

The moment lingered, and I wondered if he might hug me, or something else...

"Good night," he said, turning away slowly and starting up the stairs. Was he not interested? Or did he *have* to be such a gentleman? I'm sure he could read the look on my face like an open book. He'd probably seen it plenty of times on other girls.

"Good night," I said. I walked to the door to Alicia's apartment, then looked back to see his denim-clad legs climbing up and out of sight.

When I walked through the door, the apartment was quiet, the lights low. Stacey sat on the couch in front of the secondary nerve center she'd set up on the coffee table, consisting of a laptop and a couple of tablets.

"Where's the family?" I asked.

"They all went to bed in Alicia's room," Stacey said, pointing at the closed door near the foot of the stairs.

"All right." I sank onto the couch beside her.

"What's up with you?" Stacey asked, looking me over.

"Nothing. What are you talking about?"

"You're grinning like the Joker and your face is all flushed. What did you two do out there? Jazz aerobics?"

"We didn't do anything," I said. "Just said good-night."

"But you were ready for more, weren't you?" Stacey waggled her eyebrows.

"Get serious. Any activity?" I leaned in toward the laptop, which showed the night vision view of the basement, with its usual suggestions of half-formed apparitions. I toggled it to the thermal and saw the scattered little cold spots.

"Just the usual downstairs stuff so far," Stacey said. "Nobody's gone near the trap. No spidery boogeymen crawling out of old wells. Here's the thermal we set up in the furnace room." She showed me on a tablet. The well was an obvious black hole, ringed with waves of dark purple, at the far end of the blue-hued room. Freezing cold.

"Come on, Edgar," I said. "I'm ready to finish this job."

Edgar made no hurry to appear.

"So, want to talk about Michael?" Stacey asked.

"Nope."

"Jacob?"

"Go ahead."

"We're going out on Friday," she said. "That new movie's coming out, the historical one about what's-her-name, that Russian queen lady?"

"Catherine the Great?"

"Is that it?"

"I don't know. I never see anything until it's on Netflix." I checked the time. "I'll make some quick rounds of the apartment."

"Should I come with you?"

"I'll be fine." I strapped on my utility belt and drew my flashlight, a replacement for the one that had been cut in half. I checked the door under the stairs first, then I went up to check the kids' closets, the door to nowhere, and the sunken porch at the end of the hall. The Mel Meter didn't show anything unusual—not for those doorways, anyway, where the readings had always spiked. I looked around with my thermal goggles, but there was no sign of Edgar the boogeyman or Gerard the friendly ghost.

"All clear up here," I said into my headset, and Calvin and Stacey both confirmed they heard me.

I returned downstairs, where Stacey was watching an Isaac Mizrahi-thon on QVC, the volume lowered to a whispering-gerbil level.

"We don't watch TV during investigations," I said. "It could discourage the ghosts from appearing."

"Then why don't we tell our clients to just leave the TV on all night?" she asked. "Besides, it's not observation night, it's trap night. And for once there's someone else to help watch the monitors. Don't you love that T-shirt dress?"

I made my rounds multiple times that night.

At quarter until four, I was upstairs yet again when Calvin's voice came over my headset.

"He's here," Calvin said. "He just came out of the well...now he's passing through the door into the laundry room..."

"Stacey, watch the door to the dead-end stairs," I said. "I'll cover the ones up here." I pointed the glowing beam of my flashlight at the archway door.

"Yes, ma'am," Stacey said. With Calvin on the radio with us, she was being entirely professional tonight.

"He's moving toward the trap," Calvin whispered. "He's very close to it, like he's looking at it..."

I held my breath.

"Just jumped away," Calvin said, and I sighed. The trap had failed. "He's moving across the ceiling, just like I remember. Crawling like a black spider. Now's he's above the stairs, moving to the door."

"Great. Stacey, get ready."

"I'm in position."

We tensed, waiting for the dark entity to emerge from one of the doors.

We waited and waited.

"Maybe he went into the Fieldings' apartment," Stacey whispered.

"Check Melissa's closet," I said.

"It's clear," Calvin replied. "I..." He took a sharp, sudden breath.

"Calvin?" I asked.

"The monitors just blacked out," he said. "The van's gone dark. Something's tapping on the roof. I think it's out here, Ellie. I'm firing up the ghost cannon."

"We're on our way," I said. My heart was instantly racing. Edgar had crippled Calvin last time—maybe he meant to finish the job tonight.

I raced down the stairs, watching Stacey run across the living room and out the front door, her flashlight ready.

I jumped over the last few steps and hurried toward the door.

The dim lights in the room went dark, and so did the television, bringing a sudden silence throughout the house.

A voice spoke from directly behind me, like a lover leaning over my shoulder to whisper a secret, his breath as hot as desert wind on my ear.

"Eleanor."

It wasn't my mother this time.

I stopped, and the front door closed itself, the lock clicking into place.

I turned to face him. It was like stepping toward an open oven, the heat pushing against me.

Anton Clay's face had haunted my nightmares for the past ten years. He was handsome, his blue eyes piercing and powerful, his long blond hair tied back with a black ribbon. As always, he wore his coat with tails, his silk cravat and vest. His golden cufflinks and buttons gleamed as though reflecting a great fire.

This ghost had killed my parents and tried to kill me, burning our house down around us. In life, he'd had an affair with a married woman who lived in the old antebellum mansion located where my parents' neighborhood now stood. The woman had broken it off, and he'd responded by burning down her house, killing her, her husband, and their whole family, as well as himself.

In death, he was a pyromaniac ghost, who burned down every house built on the site of his death. Including, most recently, mine.

He stood in the dark living room as a solid apparition, seeming to glow with a fiery light of his own, heat rippling the air around him.

Absolute fear froze me into place. It was my worst nightmare, being trapped in a house with him again, and it was coming true.

"My sweet girl," he said, his voice right out of the early nineteenth century—the accent more stiff and English, not yet softened into the modern Southern cadence by generations of slow cooking in the sun. "Are you at last ready to join me? I have waited so long. Hungering for you while you blossomed and grew." He moved closer, scorching the air around me, flash-drying the skin on my face. "We belong together, Eleanor. You are mine."

I wanted to tell Calvin and Stacey what was happening, but my lips wouldn't move to form the words. I couldn't hear either of them on my headset anymore. I wondered if Anton had sucked out the battery power from my headset, just as he'd done with the lights in Mia's room.

Not Anton, I reminded myself. *Edgar. He's taking the form of my fear.*

"Beautiful, beautiful Eleanor," he whispered, reaching a hand toward my cheek. I was a child again, sick with terror.

"Edgar." I barely managed to say it, barely managed to push the air across my lips. It took all the courage I had, and then some, to talk back to him. I forced myself to say it louder. "Edgar Barrington. That's your name."

The apparition of Anton Clay hesitated a moment, staring at me, withdrawing his hand. Then the blue irises of his eyes turned fiery red, and his skin seemed to redden, too.

"You misunderstand the situation entirely," he said, with an arrogant smile. "I am within you, Eleanor. Always. Our little spidery friend, the one who haunts the house, has merely opened an opportunity for us to visit again. I am here with you, just as I was with you that night. Be joined with me, Eleanor. Be consumed by me." He leaned close, his scorching lips approaching my mouth, and I realized he meant to kiss me. "Our destiny is sealed."

"No." It wasn't a tough *no*. It was definitely more of a helpless-squeak *no*. I backed up a few steps from him, but he kept up with me. He was not rushing. He moved almost languidly, as though he had no cares at all, as though he were completely in control of the situation and knew it.

I backed into the wall. *Stupid.* He didn't try kissing me again, though. This time, he leaned back just a little, satisfied that I was cornered, and opened his hand, palm up.

A gout of flame sprang up, more than a foot high, conjured at his fingertips. The air roasted around me. I felt my cheek blister and smelled crackling strands of my hair. He smiled, the manic smile of a deep thirst about to be quenched, an addiction about to be satisfied.

Thin runners of flame rose all over the room behind him, tracing along the edges of the furniture, the corners and baseboards, the frame of the front door, outlining the room in fire. A stream of fire raced up the staircase handrail toward the second story.

Someone pounded on the front door, shouting. Stacey, trying to get back in. It sounded like she was kicking the door pretty hard, but the solid old oak held firm. The entity was keeping her out.

Fire and smoke billowed from beneath the door to Alicia's room. I heard the woman and her children screaming inside.

I lunged toward that door, but Anton grabbed me, his

fingertips digging into my arm like sharp talons. I struggled to get free, but the apparition was very solid, as solid as a living person. He barely moved, just smiled and gripped my arm while I pulled and lashed at him. His eyes drooped to half-lidded as he relished the screams of the burning children beyond the door. Getting his fix. Anton Clay, psychotic dead aristocrat, loved to burn things, but he loved to burn people even more.

With my free arm, I drew my flashlight and smashed it into his stomach. No reaction, like hitting a brick wall. If anything, his eyes drooped even more, his blissed-out drugged-up smile spreading wider across his face.

The flashlight had done some damage to him when he was in the form of Fleshface, up in Mia's room, but it didn't bother him at all now. Maybe that was because Fleshface was someone else's fear, and Anton Clay was my own.

The fingers biting deep into my arm grew hotter and hotter, smoldering through the leather sleeve of my jacket, burning into the skin underneath. I screamed in pain.

The flames rose all around us, the thin streamers of fire expanding into irregular shapes as they ate into the furniture and the structure of the house.

Fists pounded against Alicia's burning door, and their screams grew louder. I could make out the individual voices, even in that chaos—Alicia's howls of pain, Kalil's boyish grunts and cries, Mia's horrified shrieks. The entity was trapping them in there, making sure they couldn't escape the blazing fire.

"Listen to them die," Anton Clay whispered. "You can't help them. Just as you could not help your parents. Or *chose* not to? You were quite angry with them, weren't you, Eleanor? I could feel it on you, the heat of a furious young girl. Maybe you wanted them to die. Wanted to be free. Some part of you wished for that."

Even as his fingers burned into my arm, his words held me entranced, conjuring all the horror, guilt, and grief from deep within me. It was my fault. I deserved to die—

"Ellie!" a voice screamed. Stacey? Not Stacey.

Alicia. She ran into the room, flanked by her kids. They must have come out through the master bathroom.

She stopped cold when she saw the fire, and held out her arms to both sides to stop Kalil and Mia, too.

The three of them watched in horror as flames engulfed their apartment. The banging and screaming at their bedroom door stopped abruptly.

Their dying voices had been part of the boogeyman's illusion. Thank God.

The flames around them whisked out like birthday candles, leaving black and smoldering baseboards and furniture behind. The effect spread out like a ripple from the family, snuffing out the runners of fire as quickly as Anton had made them appear.

A loud crack sounded from the front door. It swung open, and Stacey staggered in, off-balance and wielding the crowbar from the van. She stumbled toward me, gaping in surprise at the fires surrounding the door.

Then the rest of the flames blew out, leaving us all in darkness.

The sharp-fingered hand released my arm. As my eyes tried to adjust to the dim glow from a streetlight outside, I saw Anton shrivel into something black, with sharp, angular limbs.

It hissed as it leaped at me. Stacey had recovered her balance and now hit us with a flashlight.

The shadowy figure of the fearfeeder, of Edgar Barrington's ghost, landed on the wall high above me. It scrambled like a spider on amphetamines into the high shadows of the two-story room.

I pointed my flashlight at the ghost and clicked, but I only got a brief, weak puff of light before the battery died. Barrington had drained it along with my headset, and probably every device on my belt. The most annoying and difficult ghosts are the ones that suck all the power out of my ghost-hunting gear.

Stacey tried to follow it with her light, but it shot out of sight into the upstairs hall. If Jacob was right, it could use any of its favorite doors up there to escape and retreat into its lair below.

All of us stared after it, watching to see if it would return, possibly in some new and more horrible form. After a little while, we looked at each other instead.

"Is everybody okay?" I looked at Alicia and her kids. They nodded, still in shock from all they'd just seen. I was so glad to see them alive and unharmed that I could have hugged and kissed them. I refrained.

"Everybody's fine!" Stacey said, looking out the front door. I stepped forward and saw Calvin out there, parked in his chair at the bottom of the porch steps.

"Wow," I said, completely shaken. "Thanks for coming, everybody. Was there any fire in your room at all, Alicia?"

She shook her head, looking at the smoke curling up from every spot the flames had touched.

"I heard a voice calling me," Alicia whispered. She turned her eyes up to meet mine. "Gerard. I followed his voice out here."

"Thank you, Gerard," I said, speaking into the air.

Stacey shined her light over the blackened, smoldering furniture, then up the staircase handrail, which was in no better shape.

"Hey," she said, "Where's a fireman when you need one?"

Chapter Eighteen

Michael didn't answer his phone, probably asleep at four in the morning. I went upstairs myself to wake him, leaving Calvin and Stacey downstairs with the family. I'd grabbed a fresh flashlight from the van in case Edgar decided to make a return appearance.

I knocked on his door as loud and hard as I could. I wasn't feeling shy or nervous, because Alicia and her kids really needed him to look at her apartment and make sure it was safe. It was a strictly professional ghost-hunter-to-firefighter situation.

Eventually, he opened the door. Tousled bed hair, sleepy green eyes, thin t-shirt, red boxers. Oh, my. I was feeling less professional by the second.

"Oh, hey, it's you," he said, his voice drowsy and scratchy. His gaze landed on my burned sleeve and wounded arm, and his drooping eyelids raised. "What happened?"

"I played with fire, I got burned. Sorry to wake you up, but I need you to look at—"

"Come inside and take off your jacket," he said, reaching for my non-wounded arm as if to help me walk.

"Go inside and put on your pants," I replied, dodging back from him.

"That needs attention right away."

"My arm can wait. There was a fire in Alicia's apartment."

"Is anyone else hurt?" He started forward as if he intended to run downstairs that second. I stopped him with a hand on his stomach. His firm, warm stomach. I pulled my hand back quickly.

"No, but can you make sure the fire's not going to start up again? And the place isn't going to come crashing down? Those would be good things to know."

"Just a second." He left the door open and darted inside. I followed him into the dark apartment and waited in the living room while he got dressed.

Melissa emerged from her room, blinking, wearing a sleeping gown.

"What's up?" she asked.

"The ghost tried to set your house on fire," I said. "It was my fault. It was taking the form of my fears."

"You're afraid of fire?" she asked, looking confused.

"Yes." Well, true enough. I've never been one to burn candles or incense for "atmosphere." To me, the only atmosphere created by open flames is one of impending danger and death.

"We'd better get on top of it," Michael said, dashing out of his room fully dressed. He grabbed a fire extinguisher from the kitchen.

"You're fast," I said.

"Fire's faster." He sprinted out of the apartment without waiting for me.

"Are we safe up here?" Melissa asked, rubbing her eyes.

"I think so."

"Are Mia and Kalil safe?"

"Yep."

"Okay." She yawned. "I'll come, too."

She disappeared into her room, and I waited impatiently, not wanting to leave her to walk down the all the stairs alone. She finally returned wearing jeans under her sleeping gown.

We hurried downstairs, where Michael was inspecting the apartment. Alicia and her kids sat on their couch, charred at the top and armrests, listening to Calvin. Stacey was watching the basement on her tablet while they spoke.

"...at this point, we have to consider this place too dangerous for the kids, especially at night," Calvin said. "You'll want to make other arrangements for tomorrow night. Friends, relatives, hotel, anything."

Alicia nodded. "For how long?"

"We'll finish the job as quickly as we can," Calvin said. "Tomorrow—well, today, it's going to be sunrise soon—Ellie and I will work out a new plan of attack. If that doesn't work, we'll develop another one, until the entity is gone."

"I can't afford to stay in a hotel too long," Alicia said.

"This is strange," Michael said. He stood by the staircase, where he'd been inspecting the railing. "Ellie, come have a look."

I walked to stand beside him, trying not to picture him in his underwear again. "What is it?"

He ran his fingers along the top of the railing, revealing unburned wood beneath. He showed me his blackened fingertips.

"There's really not much fire damage," he said. "It's mostly smoke stains and soot."

"Because the fire was mostly an illusion," I told him. "So it's all still structurally sound? Nothing's going to fall apart on the kids?"

"It's fine," he said. "The furniture's singed, of course. But there's no other repairs to make. All the place really needs is a good washing."

I tried not to crack a smile, thinking of Alicia's obsessive cleaning and organizing. Here was a job she could really sink her teeth into.

"Now we have to take care of your arm," Michael told me.

"I'll be fine."

"Go!" Calvin insisted, turning to look at me.

"Yeah, your jacket is kind of gross and melted all over you," Stacey said. "Probably want to take care of that."

"Go on," Alicia said. "We're okay now."

I nodded and let Michael steer me back to the door to the shared hallway.

"I have a first aid kit in the van," I told him.

"Mine's better." He turned toward the staircase to his apartment.

"How do you know?"

"It's a full trauma kit." He held my arm as we started up the stairs. It wasn't strictly necessary, or even at all necessary—an injured forearm didn't interfere with my ability to walk. I didn't try to pull free of his hand, though. It was nice to let someone else be in charge for a minute. Maybe two minutes, even.

"Do you always treat burn injuries by making people walk up four flights of stairs?" I asked.

"I'm doing you a favor. Exercise stimulates endorphins. The body's natural painkillers."

"Funny thing, my arm still feels like it's on fire."

"Maybe we need to find a bigger staircase."

Inside his apartment, he had me stand by the sink, under a bright hanging light, and examined my arm. His kitchen was small but pleasant, lots of cheerful polished wood, a row of potted herbs on the window sill flavoring the air with sweet and spicy aromas.

"I like your apartment," I said.

"Really? All the weird-shaped rooms and attic roofs don't annoy you?" He opened the pantry and brought out a red backpack-sized first aid kit.

"Nope. Not as much as the gateway to hell in your basement."

"Is that what's down there? I was hoping for raccoons or squirrels." He heaved the kit onto the counter and propped it open. The interior was full of compartments holding everything from an oxygen mask to finger splints.

"You really are one prepared Boy Scout," I said.

"Seriously, what do you call the thing in my basement?" He brought out a pair of steel trauma shears and gently took the shoulder of my wounded arm. "Hold still."

"The closest term I know would be a 'dark vortex.'"

"That wasn't mentioned in the rental agreement." Michael said. I watched his face as he cut my jacket sleeve around my upper arm, half-worried that the hefty shears would slice my arm open. They looked like they could snap through bones.

He cut a slit all the way down the side and carefully removed the jacket from my wound. He was gentle, but I still hissed in pain.

"Darkness and suffering attract more darkness and suffering," I said. "It's like gravity. Start with something small and let it build over the years—thousands of years, in this case, and you get...bad things."

"Bad things? You're confusing me with all these technical

terms." Michael cut the sleeve of my cotton shirt into pieces and undressed my arm, revealing the red, partially blistered forearm.

"The science is pretty scarce in all of this," I said. "There's not a lot of hard established facts. Just folklore and superstition."

"I'm cleaning it off," he said, his voice shifting to something careful and soft, like he was talking to an injured child. It was like he'd snapped into character, into work-mode. I wondered if he spoke like that to every hurt person he helped on his job. I felt myself going a bit warm and glowy in the chest area. "This should help with the pain, too," he added.

He eased my arm under the faucet, into the running water.

"It's freezing!" I hissed.

"It isn't," he said. He moved the faucet handle slightly. "Now it's almost warm."

"I thought this was supposed to make it feel better."

"You don't feel better yet?" he asked.

I became less aware of the throbbing in my arm and more aware of him standing close to me, holding my arm, a welcome intrusion into my personal space.

"I'm better," I whispered after a while.

He turned off the water and patted my arm dry, while avoiding the burned area itself. Then he studied it again: four dark red patches, a couple of them with little flesh bubbles at the edges, burn blisters that made me think of hot pizza cheese.

"These marks almost look like fingers," he said. "Like somebody grabbed you."

"That's what happened. I told you this ghost takes the shape of your fears, right? I'm afraid of...fire. It's my fault the apartment burned."

"It didn't really burn, though. I've seen worse."

"I'm sure *you* have."

He smiled and gazed at me for a moment. I looked right back at him.

"We'd better wrap it up," he said.

"Oh," I said, off-guard by his sudden dismissal. "I guess I should get back to work."

"I meant with this." He tore open a package labeled Water-Jel Burn Dressing and carefully laid the cool, gel-soaked material across my arm. I could feel the pain seeping out while he bandaged me.

"What's in this?" I asked, poking at the wrapping.

"Mostly tea tree oil. Nature's antibiotic." My fully dressed arm continued to rest in his hand, the gel pulling out the heat and pain. "Don't be so hard on fire. It can be fun. I always wanted to build and light the fire. Back at my mom's house, I mean, when we were kids. We don't have a fireplace here." He said it like it was a sad, tragic situation, not having a place to burn things for pleasure. "I used to go camping with my friends, and we'd build these huge bonfires. Fire's alive, I think. It has a mind of its own. It's fascinating."

"My parents died in a fire," I said.

"I meant to say fire is the most evil force on the planet. That's why I'm devoted to putting them all out. Some people, they like fires, but I don't know what's wrong with them."

I laughed at his backpedaling. It made him seem awkward and vulnerable for once. Something about that made me feel comfortable leaning just a little closer to him, and pretty soon after that we were embracing each other, my head against his chest, listening to his heartbeat.

I happened to look up at him and found him looking down at me. He kissed me, and it was like a shock of energy, traveling down my spine and curling my toes.

"Cuckoo, cuckoo," announced the mechanical bird, emerging from its house on the wall. "Cuckoo, cuckoo, cuckoo," it elaborated. Five a.m. Boss and client waiting for me downstairs.

I backed away and looked up at him. "Does that go off every hour of the night?"

"When it's working right."

"How do you stand it? I think I would've smashed that bird a hundred times by now."

"My mom bought that clock at a yard sale. It never worked. After she died, I just started looking at it one night, and I opened it up. I researched how it was supposed to work and how to fix it. I kind of liked bringing it back to life." He shrugged.

Oops. My turn to backpedal. "I was just thinking that cuckoo clocks are the best kinds of clocks. Why doesn't everyone have one. They're much better than, like...grandfather clocks."

"Or digital clocks."

"That goes without saying. And then you moved on to gnome clocks?"

"Antique automatons," he said. "Some people will pay a lot for a fully restored one."

"The cuckoo's telling me I need to get back to work," I said, moving away towards the door.

"I have to get to work, too. I'm late."

"You go to work at five in the morning?"

"Some people have it lucky," he said. "I'm just one of them."

"Okay. Well have fun..putting out fires and rescuing cats from trees." I put my hand on the doorknob. I hadn't taken my eyes off him.

"Did you know most cats are actually able to climb down the tree by themselves?" he said. "They just don't *want* to."

"Oh. Maybe you could show me the statistics on that sometime." *What? Get out of here!* I was exhausted, not thinking clearly at all. "Thanks for the bandages and the...everything."

"I should check the progress of your burn tomorrow," he said.

"Okay. Good." I smiled at him. Had I not been smiling already?

"Just make an appointment with the nurse on your way out. And avoid walking into any open flames for the next twenty-four hours."

"Thanks for the advice, doc." I walked out of the apartment and hurried down the stairs, feeling a golden moment of pure elation and excitement before I reached Alicia's apartment and had to focus on stopping the monster again.

Chapter Nineteen

Any time a ghost tries to kill me, I get a free breakfast.

That's according to a deal I made with Calvin a few years ago. Since he was at our client's house that night, I held him to it: a blue-crab omelet at Narobia's Grits and Gravy. This is a gem of a place, a family business located in a small building over on Habersham. It's always crowded because the food is unbelievably good and the prices are crazy low. Calvin was able to buy breakfast for the three of us for about twenty bucks. So it's not like I was being *too* demanding. Working a lot of nocturnal hours around the city, you learn where the best breakfast spots are, though I'm usually eating supper at that time.

We talked about the case, just reviewing what we'd learned and where we were. We needed a new plan, but we were all too brain-dead to really put anything together. I was still badly shaken from seeing my most hated ghost and nearly dying at his hands—even if it wasn't really him, the boogeyman had done a pretty convincing imitation.

Anyway, the grits were buttery and amazing.

Then I went home to sleep, and my dreams were filled with fire, my parents, Alicia's kids, Anton Clay, and the spidery black boogeyman watching me from the ceiling. I think daytime nightmares are more vivid and intense, but that could be because I'm usually having them in the middle of an investigation, when I'm working vampire hours and dealing with unsettled and dangerous spirits.

I let myself sleep until early afternoon, and my arm was still burning in pain. I guessed I would need to cash in Michael's offer of a follow-up appointment—just thinking about it made me a little thrilled. I could still feel his unexpected but entirely welcome kiss on my lips. We'd only met a few days earlier, but it felt like I'd known him much longer than that. He made me feel safe and protected.

You're never truly safe, I reminded myself. *Especially when you let yourself care too much about other people.*

I tried to shake off that downer feeling as I took a long, hot shower, leaving my bandaged arm jutting out through the curtain. Bandit watched from the bathroom floor, giving a couple of inquisitive meows about this odd behavior on my part. He obviously wasn't too concerned, because the moment I turned it off, he hopped into the tub for his usual drink of warm water.

With my leather jacket cut to pieces, I picked a heavy denim one instead and pulled it over my black summer-weight turtleneck. I was in serious danger of getting physically attacked again that night, if things went well.

I met up with Calvin and Stacey at the office, and we hung around the long work table in the back. Files and pictures were spread out everywhere, including pictures of people and houses, Rebecca Barrington's letters detailing her brother-in-law's insanity, missing person reports from more recent decades, a few relevant articles from the *International Journal of Psychical Studies*, and lore and art describing the boogeyman in every culture—always the dark thing hiding in small places, menacing children by night, sometimes hauling them away in a sack. There was no consistency in appearance among these entities, only a common pattern of behavior.

"He never shows his real face," I said. "He's always wearing a mask."

"Isn't he really that black crawling shape that runs around on the ceiling?" Stacey asked.

"That's a kind of psychological costume itself," Calvin said. "It represents how dark and twisted the soul has become over the years."

"So what if we confront him with his real identity?" I asked. "That might weaken him, or at least confuse him. He's used to the living always perceiving him as their own worst fears...not as Edgar Barrington, a sick and twisted human being. We could send Stacey to the print shop to get blow-up pictures of Edgar, and we'd need a mirror, too. Maybe confronting him with his real identity, after all this time, would be enough to make him move on."

"It's possible, but it may not work," Calvin said. "We may still have to trap him."

"Didn't I see a design for a mirror trap in the *Journal* once?" I grabbed the nearest tablet to check the web archives of the paranormal periodical—we had a subscription enabling us to access all the back issues at any time.

"That was for catoptric ghosts," Calvin said.

"What are those?" Stacey asked. "They sound like cats who wear glasses. Instant internet meme."

"Spirits who use mirrors as doorways," I told her, my eyes and fingers still busy with the tablet.

"But Edgar uses *doorways* as doorways," Stacey said. "Closet doors. Right?"

"That's why I doubt this is a good approach," Calvin replied.

"Thanks for the encouragement," I said. "Here, I found it. Lead glass mirror, with the copper mesh installed over the pane. You capture the ghost's image in the mirror, then activate the mesh to keep it there."

"If you ever face a mirror ghost, it might be useful," Calvin replied. "I don't believe this is the best entity for testing out new prototypes."

"Okay, so maybe it's only part of the solution," I said. "Even if I can just steal some of its energy."

"I'm not feeling good about this plan," Stacey said. "Except the part where I go to the print shop and get giant Edgar pictures. I'm totally on top of that."

"I think we might have to use this." I walked over to open the supply-closet door. The big walk-in trap stood in its corner, like a dusty phone booth built out of old stained-glass church windows.

"The bear trap didn't pay off very well last time," Calvin said. "I'd like to see both of you walk away from this case alive and intact."

"I'm the only bait we have," I said. "Besides the kids, and we obviously aren't going to use one of them. Edgar wants me. I was afraid he would try to attack you, Calvin, but that was just a distraction to get Stacey out of the house, to isolate me."

"Maybe he figures he dinged me pretty bad already," Calvin said.

"And now it's my turn," I said. "Come on, Stacey. We have to dismantle this trap and reassemble it over at our client's house. It's going to take a while."

"Sounds like a good time to call Captain Fireman," Stacey said.

"He's at work. What about Jacob?"

"Work," Stacey said. "Unless you want to wait until tonight to set it up."

"I definitely don't. Come on." I grabbed a drill and began disassembling the big trap. We wrapped the glass panes with blankets and secured them in the back of the van so they wouldn't get scratched or broken.

"I'll continue studying all of this and hope a good idea leaps up and bites me in the nose," Calvin said after we were done. He gestured to the spread of documents on the table. "I'll come over this evening to monitor the mobile nerve center again." That meant *sit in the van.* "Good luck, kids."

"See you soon." Stacey climbed into the passenger seat, and I started around to the driver's side.

"Ellie," Calvin said. I turned back to see a hard, flinty look on his face. He usually kept his emotions below the surface, but I could see Calvin was ready for some revenge against this ghost. "Be careful. And if it chases you into the trap...don't look back."

"Okay," I said. "We'll see you tonight. Everything's going to be fine, Calvin."

He knew better than to believe me, though. We could all end up dead tonight.

I drove downtown. We stopped at the Speedi Sign, then had a quick dinner of vegetables and rice from a Chinese place while we waited for our print order.

With Michael and Alicia both away at work, along with many of their neighbors, we were able to park right in front of their house. I let Melissa know we were there, and she offered to help. I didn't see any reason to turn her down. It was the middle of the afternoon, the sun bright and golden with only a few clouds in the sky—exactly the kind of weather that sends many ghosts into hibernation, waiting for darker times.

To make life easier, I picked the lock on Apartment D so we could carry the heavy trap pieces down the short concrete steps and through the vacant apartment, rather than down the long stairway the tenants used to access the laundry room.

During one of my trips between the van and the basement stairs, the clouds momentarily blotted out the sun, turning the world storm-gray.

I rounded the back corner of the house, lugging a heavy, blanketed chunk of thick, colorful leaded glass in both arms. In that gloomy moment, I saw the man for the first time, though Michael, Alicia, and the others had reported seeing him regularly.

He stood next to the open cellar doors, gazing down at the steps as though confused, his long fingers slowly scratching at his temple. He stooped with the posture of an old man, and his hair was gray, and Michael was right about the gray pallor of his skin. His suit and his wide-necked tie appeared in lighter and dark shades of gray, too. The impression was of an old man broken down by worry and care, but if you looked more closely at his face, he didn't look elderly. He looked prematurely aged, maybe by stress or illness.

I could see how he'd acquired the nickname Mr. Gray at some point, long enough in the past that the tenants, moving in and out each year, had learned it from each other without realizing that some earlier tenant had coined the name, probably as a joke.

He turned his head slowly toward me. He was a conscious entity. He knew I was there.

He gave me a gentle smile, and if I hadn't known it was a ghost, I would have thought him some kindly, sickly, possibly heavily medicated man standing there in the garden. As it was, the smile chilled me. Just the sight of him chilled me.

"Joseph?" I said. "Joseph Barrington? That's your name, isn't it?"

His smile faltered, and his mouth dropped to a flat line. The kindly look gave way to a blank, cold mask.

"Your brother killed you, didn't he?" I asked. "Edgar. He killed you and your children."

The sunlight swelled again as the interfering cloud moved on, and the apparition melted into nothing amid the rising light.

"I hope you don't mind if we use your apartment for a minute," I said to the place where he'd just stood.

"You okay?" Melissa asked, rounding the corner with another chunk of the trap wrapped in a blanket.

"I was just talking to Mr. Gray," I said. "I guess he didn't feel like replying."

"He doesn't speak much," Melissa said. "He usually kind of smiles and nods and keeps walking. My brother told me Mr. Gray's a ghost. Is that true?"

"It's true." We walked down the steps and through the bare apartment to our growing array of trap pieces, laid out on blankets across the floor. "He's the twin brother of the ghost who's been menacing your house."

"He seems so nice," Melissa said. "I thought he was maybe kind of senile since he never spoke, but you know, he was always dressed nicely and well-groomed, so I figured he wasn't desperate for help."

"People are often dressed and groomed well for their funerals," I said. "He was probably buried in that suit."

"Stop! You're giving me chill bumps." She set her parcel on the floor, and a portion of the blanket fell back, revealing a colored-glass corner. "What are you building down here? A ghost blender?"

"A trap," I whispered. Then I glanced at the furnace-room door and held my finger to my lips.

Stacey came with the final pieces, and we considered different spots to set up the big booth trap. While we discussed it, the door creaked open at the top of the laundry room stairs.

Lulinda Fielding stood there with a basket full of laundry.

"Oh," she said, stopping on the top step to look down at us. "What are y'all doing?"

"Sorry for the mess, Mrs. Fielding," I said. "We'll have it straightened up soon."

"I can still get to that washing machine." She continued down the steps. "I ain't rearranging my whole day for y'all."

"We understand, ma'am," I told her.

She looked among the three of us suspiciously while she loaded up the laundry machine. The silence in the room was uneasy.

"You're helping them, Melissa?" she finally asked, when her clothes had begun washing. She leaned back against the machine and folded her arms, looking hostile.

"Yes, ma'am," Melissa said.

Lulinda looked at the open door to the ghostly Mr. Gray's apartment, and she sighed and her shoulders sagged. She brought out a pack of Eve cigarettes and packed them against the palm of her hand, but made no move to take one out and light it.

"I saw something once," Lulinda said. "After we moved in, before Falcon started seeing things. I never put it together with him seeing that dinosaur skeleton in his fireplace, because it was a different thing. But y'all coming around here got me thinking." She looked down at her cigarettes, looked up at us, and put them away.

"What was it?" Melissa asked her.

"In my closet one night, not two or three weeks after we moved here," Melissa said. "He was in there, looking out at me. My granddaddy. I was so scared that night, thinking he was back from the dead." Melissa hesitated, then seemed to make a decision and went on. "He used to be real bad to me in life. I got scars. I tried not to smile at his funeral. I was still a kid then, and I thought, if he knew how happy it makes me to see him dead, he'd come back and haunt me."

"How many times did you see him?" I asked.

"Just the once," she said. "But I could see him standing there as plain as I see you right now. He was staring at me the way he got when he was drunk, just before he slapped me around." She took a deep breath. "But he never came back. I thought it was just a nightmare."

"How often does Falcon see his monster?" I asked.

"Too much. Way too much."

"It targets children," I said, remembering that Michael had only glimpsed it once, too, right after moving in. "It'll check around on any new residents of the house, but it's looking to feed on children.

They have more energy to take."

"*Feeding* on them? It's feeding on my boy?"

"Exactly."

"And what can y'all do about it?" She looked around at the blanket-wrapped pieces spaced carefully around the floor.

"We going to remove it," I said. "I hope you and your husband don't have a problem with that."

"What is this thing, really?"

"The ghost of a man who used to live near here," I said. "Edgar Barrington. Ghosts sometimes find ways of feeding on the living. It makes them more powerful, but also distorts them from a lost human soul into...something else. In this case, a creature that feeds on fear."

"And you know what you're doing?" Lulinda asked me.

"I've removed ghosts many times before, all over the city," I said, speaking with a lot more confidence than I felt. Our plan was shaky, and I had nothing but doubts about it.

"I hope you get this one," she said. "I'll try to keep my husband from bothering you."

"We'd really appreciate it," I said.

"And stay out of my laundry." She pointed to the chugging machine and climbed back up the stairs. She wore cutoff denim shorts to showcase her long legs. The back of her shirt read SALTY DOG CAFE.

"Okay," I said when she was gone. "I think we should place the big trap in the back area of the room, between the furnace room door and the door to Apartment D. I want some room to maneuver in front of both doors. We set the cameras far back in the corners, out of the way..."

It took a long time to prepare the room, especially since we had to carry all our gear down from Alicia's apartment and set it up all over again. It was too much equipment to leave unguarded in the laundry room all day, especially when Hoss Fielding still didn't seem to want us there at all.

We also brought the big pneumatic stamper down to the laundry room again, and I loaded it with the trap filled with Edgar's grave dirt. Then I set the stamper to automatically slam the lid down onto the trap if it detected signs of a ghost inside. Hopefully, Edgar wanted to rest in peace and would be drawn to the earth of his own burial site, so that we could trap him and remove him from the house.

By nightfall, Stacey and I were sweaty and exhausted. I closed up the doors to Apartment D. We'd kept the cellar doors open all day to keep us fueled with fresh air.

Then I caught up with Alicia, who was home from work, and went upstairs to see Michael—strictly because of my burned arm, of course.

Chapter Twenty

"How are you feeling?" he asked. I sat on the small couch in his living room, with a view of the tree-lined street outside.

"Tired," I said. "Worried."

"About tonight?"

"There's plenty to worry about," I told him.

"How does your arm feel?" He finished undressing the wound, revealing the four dark red finger marks. They were long and thin, like those of Joseph Barrington when I'd seen his ghost in the back garden. Edgar's twin.

"Not great," I said.

"The blisters have shrunk," he said. "That's good. I'd say you're fine as long as you don't get grabbed by another burning hand in that same spot."

"I wish the odds of that were lower," I said. "I'm calling him out tonight. We're taking him down."

He brought me to the kitchen to rinse my arm in water again, then he applied a fresh burn dressing, which brought a welcome new dose of that cooling gel.

We were standing in the same place we'd been when he kissed me. I looked up at him, drawing my wounded arm close to my side.

"Listen," he said. "Sorry if I surprised you with that. I don't always think before I act. Sometimes I save the thinking for later."

"Do you go through this with everyone you treat?" I asked. "The kissing and apologizing?"

"It's not part of the standard procedures," he said.

"Really? You don't get kisses when you come sweeping through the window to rescue some pretty girl from a fire?"

"Make the pretty girl into a forty-year-old fat cigar smoker with a walrus mustache who got lodged behind his steering wheel in a fender-bender, and yes, that happens sometimes."

"I came back," I said. "I must not have been too upset."

"Maybe you came back for revenge."

"Definitely," I said, thinking of what Edgar Barrington's ghost had done to Calvin. "And I'm going to take it right now." I reached my hands on top of his shoulders, rested my fingers on his neck. "Wait. What about your girlfriend? Angelique?"

"Angelique?" He looked confused.

"Your sister mentioned her."

"I haven't talked to her in months. She said she was tired of worrying about my job, about me going into dangerous situations and getting hurt. I think she was seeing somebody else, though. What about you?"

"I spend a lot of time running into dangerous situations and getting hurt," I said. "We could share war stories."

"I'm asking if you're seeing anybody. But I have to warn you, if you're not married or dating a friend of mine, you're fair game."

"You make me sound like some wild animal you're hunting," I said.

"I like a girl who understands what I'm saying." His hands were on my hips now, drawing me closer to him.

"Right now, the closest thing I have to a boyfriend is the ghost of a nineteenth-century slaveowner who wants to set me on fire."

"You can do better," he said. Then he kissed me again, holding me close to him. It was longer and slower this time, and all around much more interesting. I was absorbed for a minute in the touch and taste of him.

"I should go," I pulled back from him. Just like last time. "We have some stuff to finalize downstairs. I'll call you before the action starts."

"You're always running away," he said.

"Oh." I laughed a little, but kept moving toward the door. "It's just bad timing."

"Okay. But—and I don't want to pressure you—I'm looking for something a little more long-term than thirty seconds. Maybe a five-minute relationship? Ten?"

"I can't be tied down like that," I told him. "I'm a wild animal, remember?"

I left his apartment, feeling unusually tall and very happy at the idea of seeing him again. Hopefully I would live long enough for that to happen.

Since I seemed to be Edgar's preferred bait, it fell to me to face him.

By midnight, I stood in the laundry room by myself, my utility belt fully loaded, all my gear stocked with fresh batteries. I kept in touch with Calvin and Stacey over my headset, but I still felt alone and vulnerable down there.

I'd switched off the lights, which left the basement in complete darkness. I watched the door to the furnace room on the display screen of a night vision camera. I had my thermal goggles on my head, ready to bring them down over my eyes.

The air felt heavy and cold, as the basement always did after sunset. On the screen, I could see hints and blurs of things drifting past, like pieces of deformed fish floating in a viscous green swamp.

"How does everything look upstairs?" I whispered.

"Dead," Stacey replied over the headset, also whispering. "I mean, uh, clear. Nothing's stirring. No dead people hanging out."

"Okay." I glanced at the two traps—the regular one half-filled with stolen grave dirt, the candles lit as a lure. The walk-in trap, walled with colored leaded glass, both doors closed for now. I didn't want to draw Edgar's attention to it too quickly.

I glanced at the closed door to apartment D, wondering if Edgar's brother Joseph might make another appearance. I assumed that ghost was more or less on my side, since Edgar had killed him, but you never really know. Blood runs thicker sometimes, even among the dead.

Finally, I turned my attention to the door to the furnace room, also closed. Edgar's favorite place to pop out in shadowy boogeyman form.

Aside from the open static of my headset, the room was silent for a long time, punctuated only by Stacey checking in.

The room grew colder and colder. Small footsteps approached me from the furnace doorway, but I didn't see anyone there.

I pulled down my thermal goggles. Specks of cold hung in the air in front of me. As I watched, they drew together and became larger. Individually they suggested nothing, but together they suggested the rough shape of a small child, not much larger than a toddler—a portion of a leg here, a couple of fingers there.

"Who is she?" a tiny voice whispered, so quiet I could easily have imagined it.

More cold spots gathered, and I felt the temperature drop. I could hear other voices in the shadows, their words too low and muffled to discern. It was sort of like being surrounded by people who speak a different language. You don't know what they're saying, but you suspect they're talking about you. Except, of course, these people were all dead.

These were fragments of ghosts absorbed by the well over the millennia, slowly merged into a cloud of lost souls, serving as the power source of the dark forces below.

The cold and the whispering moved closer. The ghosts were investigating me, a reversal of our usual roles.

"It's looking really active, Ellie," Stacey said.

"I can hear them," I said. "They're all around me. Should I do that thing we talked about?"

"Do it," Calvin said, cutting in.

"Okay." I took a breath, then straightened up, looking at the dark room all around me, dense with a blizzard of drifting deep blue spots. I spoke much louder now. "I know some of you here are old spirits," I said. "Seers and mystics who left pieces of yourselves here, thousands of years ago, to help guard the living against the darkness here. I hope you will understand my intent tonight, and give what aid you can."

There was no immediate response. Then the room became much, much colder, so fast I could hear the air crack. I was shivering hard—it was arctic.

The cold spots swelled around me, growing larger and darker, many of them phasing into purple. No friendly prehistoric Guale medicine man appeared to offer a hand, or anything remotely like that.

"I think I upset somebody," I said. I was shivering all the way to my bones, and I literally couldn't tell if it was cold or from fear.

This was the right thing to do, though. Just as I'd told the kids, the only way to fight a creature who feeds on fear is to resist it with courage. It took all the courage I could muster to stand there alone in front of the furnace door, waiting to face Anton Clay or whatever form the boogeyman decided to take. I felt like I didn't have nearly enough of that courage, though—all I wanted to do was run away, up the stairs, and out of that house, rather than face the thing on the other side of the door.

I took a deep breath and held my ground.

"Should we go ahead?" I whispered.

"Whenever you're ready," Calvin replied.

I took another deep breath, then I picked up the mason jar half-filled with Edgar's grave dirt and I unscrewed the lid.

"Hook up the relay to the speaker, Stacey," I said.

"Consider it hooked."

I turned on a small spotlight and pointed it away toward the wall, giving me enough light to see. Then I stepped closer to the door and knocked three times, pounding as hard as I could with my fist.

"Edgar," I said. "Edgar Barrington. I command you to come up. Come out and face me." There. That sounded like something out of a tough-guy movie, maybe a cowboy standing outside a saloon, challenging an old enemy to a duel.

My voice boomed beyond the door, on a slight delay. Stacey had installed a small but powerful speaker next to the well, which amplified my voice into a roar and sent it echoing down into the darkness below.

"Nothing so far," Stacey whispered.

"Edgar Barrington!" I repeated, hearing my amplified voice like rumbling thunder as it bounced around inside the well. I took a pinch of the grave earth in my fingers and cast it at the furnace room door. Little clumps of dirt and tiny pebbles rattled off its surface. I didn't know if the gesture would help me gain control over Edgar, but it was an idea. "Present yourself."

My voice seemed to echo for an unusually long time—or

maybe it was something down below, answering me.

"Ellie, I'm losing power," Stacey said. "The camera watching the well is dead. Everything's shutting—"

"Wait for me," I told her. Then my headset died, the power robbed by one ghost or another.

The floor shuddered, and then flames boiled out around the door to the furnace room, a billowing conflagration that swept around all the edges of the door and began to eat into it. The heat surged out into the frosty room.

I watched as the fire spread in streamers across the door, until I could see nothing but a rectangular doorway filled with flames. I heard the whoosh of the fire, felt the heat on my skin, smelled the crackling wood of the door itself.

Wild, uncontrolled fire. I loathed it.

A streamer of fire extended from the billowing flames and anchored itself to the brick floor. Then another, moving like a candle flame stepping from one wick to the next. The shape of a man emerged, standing on those flickering legs, the head like a floating torch.

It burned down quickly, showing me charred flesh, eyes with red-rimmed pupils, the stained teeth of a grinning skull. Tongues of flame still flickered here and there among his soot-encrusted coat and vest.

Anton Clay, in one of his less handsome forms.

Courage.

"That's a nice trick," I said, my voice shaking as I tilted the jar and drew a line of earth along the floor as a barrier between us. "You'd be a hit at Burning Man."

His jaws opened, and an *actual* tongue of flame moved in his mouth, flickering among his teeth, licking them and staining them black.

"Eleanor," spoke a voice from inside the flame. *"I knew you would return to me."*

While he chatted, I took the opportunity to move around one side of him, sprinkling a thick line of earth perpendicular to the first one. I poured it all the way to the wall, then snapped the jar forward, throwing a long dash of it between Anton and the furnace door, cutting off his main path of retreat.

"Do you really believe that will work?" he asked. He was back to the usual mask, the pretty face and spotless silk garments he'd worn in life.

"It's from your grave, Edgar," I said. In my mind, I'd imagined drawing a circle of earth around him, but what was emerging was more of a sloppy rhombus.

Now came the most dangerous part: I had to circle back around him, keeping my distance, so I could enclose him with earth from the other side.

"You don't understand who I am at all," he said. "I am myself, Anton Clay, merely using our friend here as a vessel to reach out to you—"

"I don't believe you." I eased around to the other side of him, ready to finish surrounding him with the ring of dirt.

Then he moved, faster than my eye could follow or my brain could react, suddenly standing less than an inch from me, his eyes burning into mine.

The jar of dirt exploded in my hands, slicing up my fingers. I barely had time to close my eyes before splinters of glass peppered my face. It felt like getting stung by a swarm of angry bees.

Something slammed into the center of my chest so hard my breastbone creaked. It knocked me backwards, sending me across the room until my spine slammed against the metal side of a laundry machine.

I crumpled to the floor, aching all over, unable to breathe, unable to see. A thick layer of dirt coated my face, and I was afraid to wipe it away from my eyes because of all the little glass pieces in my hands. I wasn't excited by the idea of scratching out my eyeballs.

Slowly, I eased up to a sitting position, still struggling to draw air. I didn't even want to open my mouth for fear of choking on dirt and glass. My nostrils and sinuses already felt coated in the gritty soil.

I pulled apart the snap buttons on my denim jacket, pawed my shirt tail loose, and used it to wipe my face. I opened my eyes as soon as I dared.

A cloud of dark earth floated in the room like a brown fog, dampening the floodlight, which was turned aside and on its lowest setting anyway.

He stood several feet away from me, not far from where I'd

been when he sent me flying. He was a dark shadow in the fog of dust, facing me, standing perfectly and unnaturally still, in the way that dead things can. Watching me. Waiting.

Sneezing and coughing out dust, I rolled to my hands and knees and crawled backward along the row of washing machines, away from him. He turned his head slightly, but made no obvious move to attack, like a cat letting its prey squirm before it moved in for the kill.

I placed my hands on the washing machine and slowly pulled myself to my feet. Pain flared all over my lower back, making it hard for me to stand straight up. My hands were wet with my leaking blood. I could feel it all over my face, too, warm and fresh. I wondered how many cuts I'd suffered. My arm with the burn injury was throbbing harder from getting knocked around.

"Come closer," he said, still looking and sounding like Anton Clay. "You belong with me, my lost lamb. We'll make a glorious fire together. Your ashes will mingle with mine. I have an eternity of sweet burning to share with you."

I could scream for help, but I still wasn't ready to do that yet. Not until I'd worn him down, at least.

"You forget who you really are, Edgar." I reached my fingers into the inch of space between the washing machines, hoping none of the black widows that thrived in the basement were waiting there, ready to bite my fingertips. The last thing I needed was a dose of painful venom on top of all my injuries.

I found the sheet and pulled it out. We'd had Speedi Sign print us a blown-up version of the picture of Edgar's corpse, and this was mounted on cheap corrugated plastic so it wouldn't roll up or flop around.

"Look at yourself," I said, swaying on my feet, barely keeping my balance. Spots of blood from my face dripped onto Edgar's picture, painting open red sores on his dead face. "You're dead, Edgar Barrington. You have to move on. This world belongs to the living."

A sneer twisted Anton's face, baring his teeth, his face like a snarling dog's.

"Such an ugly picture," he whispered.

Then my floodlight went out, plunging the basement back into darkness. I had my thermal goggles on my head, but their lenses were caked with dirt and I didn't exactly have time to stroll over to my toolbox and fish out the wipes.

I reached for my flashlight instead, but before my hand closed around it, the large picture in my other hand burst into flame. It went up all at once, as though it had been dipped in lighter fluid and ignited with a blowtorch. The fire seared my hand and my face, singeing my hair.

I shouted in pain, dropping the ball of fire to the floor. The plastic curled and melted in the heat, like a human body curling into the fetal position when the cremation fires hit. Noxious burnt-plastic fumes rose around me, making me cough, and I staggered closer to Anton.

"And now, an end to our story," Anton said. A gout of flame rose in his palm. With it rose thin trails of fire all over the basement, tracing the outlines of the walls and the laundry machines, similar to what had happened in Alicia's apartment.

He didn't have to be close to me to strike me with fire. The burning picture had made that clear.

I took a deep breath and shouted as loud as I could: "Now!"

At the far side of the room, well behind the glowing figure of Anton, the door to the vacant basement apartment swung open.

Stacey ran out, swinging a flashlight and glaring at Anton. A stethoscope hung around her neck, bouncing as she ran. She'd brought it to listen at the door in case our electronic equipment failed again, which it had.

Anton turned toward her, hissing as if he'd been stabbed in the back.

Then Anton was gone, but the flames still burned along the walls and machinery. I thought of the lint-encrusted dryer exhaust vents, usually one of the biggest fire hazards in the home. I wondered if Michael would be proud of me for knowing that.

A woman appeared in Anton's place, shrouded in a bridal veil that had withered and yellowed into something that looked like mats of old spiderwebs. I could just see the outline of her head and wide hoop dress within, impenetrable shadow-shapes the firelight couldn't seem to reach.

She turned toward Stacey. Where Anton had held a flame in his palm, the bride figure crushed a handful of dried flowers, their petals falling to the brick floor like flakes of skin. The bride matched Stacey's description of the ghost that had killed her brother.

"Anton!" I shouted, visualizing my lifelong tormentor. "Anton Clay!"

The dead bride turned back toward me—and once again, it was Anton in his fine coat and vest, his face distorted in a look of intense hatred, his irises glowing red. The scattered flower petals on the floor burst into flame, illuminating his polished black boots.

Stacey knocked on the closed door to the colored-glass booth, and Jacob stepped out. Our psychic friend removed his glasses and glared at Anton.

Anton's face ruptured open and his clothes erupted in flames. What remained of the clothes shifted to charred rags. One arm was broken in three places, and the other was missing. The figure became taller and wider, not resembling Anton at all by the time he turned to face Jacob.

I didn't recognize this new figure, but I could guess—one of the plane-crash victims who'd been on board with Jacob, one of the mangled spirits who'd approached him as he lay in the wreckage.

I'd told everyone to think of their deepest fear, then imagine flinging it at Edgar like a rock. He had the ability to take on our fears, but now we were *forcing* him to do it.

Changing its shape, shifting from one apparition to another, had to drain the entity's energy, making it weaker and easier to manage. Hopefully this would soften it up and prepare it to move on when confronted with its real identity.

On top of that, as I'd told the kids, the best way to fight a fearfeeder was with courage. What could be more courageous than intentionally facing your own deepest fears?

"You're terrifying," I said, approaching the monster, who now looked like some hunched, snarling Frankenstein mutation, trying to be three different things at once. "You can horrify anyone with their worst fears. Any*one*. Why does the boogeyman always disappear before your parents can look inside the closet? Why do you keep running away as soon as other people come to help? You did it upstairs in Mia's room. Then again last night."

The thing grunted and fell to its hands and knees. Its face stretched out like an animal's snout, and sharp rows of teeth grew along its upper and lower jaws, ripping their way out from its gums and emerging bloody.

It hugged the floor, its legs thick but stumpy, and it began to grow a thick, fleshy, reptilian tail.

"An alligator?" I said, backing up as the jaws snapped at my ankles. I looked over to see Michael emerging from the trap, staring hard at the shapeshifting entity on the floor.

"My dad," he said. "Before he left, he took me to one of those cheap alligator farms for tourists. Held me over the fence and said he'd feed me to them. Laughing." Michael hadn't taken his eyes off the beast. "Good old dad."

I'd hidden the other people carefully. The big booth trap had been activated, the mesh within creating a barrier for electromagnetic energy. Ghosts couldn't escape it. I was pretty sure they couldn't perceive anything inside it, either, so I'd hidden people there. Instead of using the booth as a trap for the ghost, I'd used it a hiding place *from* the ghost. I sort of got the idea from *Superman II.*

Since there hadn't been enough room in the trap for everyone, Stacey had taken the less secure position of waiting in the vacant apartment. Since that seemed to be the domain of Joseph's ghost, we were hoping that Edgar's ghost would tend to avoid it.

Now Alicia emerged from the booth, where she'd been crammed in with Jacob and Michael. She stared at the alligator-man writhing and snapping on the dirt-coated floor, and it changed again.

It turned into a large, shadowy mass and rose above us, folds of darkness spilling open like black cloth. It stood nine feet high, draped and hooded in black, its face a dirty white skull.

Death itself.

Alicia regarded it, shivering.

It reached out its skeletal hands, and the flames rose larger all over the basement, sweeping up the wooden stairs.

"You have all made a mistake." Its voice was a low hiss that seemed to whisper in both my ears. "You have given yourselves to me."

"I am afraid of you." That was Calvin, rolling into the room from apartment D, the last of our merry band. "Not any mask you wear. Not anything you pretend to be. Only *you*, the thing you really are behind all the disguises." He approached it, showing no fear. That motivated the rest of us to move in closer to the apparition.

The grim reaper shrank back to a normal human size, its skull and cloth vanishing. It stood there, not far from the furnace door, a faceless column of shadows and darkness.

"Show yourself!" Calvin demanded. "Show your true face."

I reached into the big canvas pocket on the back of Calvin's wheelchair and brought out something that looked like an oversized vinyl book with a battery compartment on the back. I opened the cover, revealing what Calvin had made for us back at the workshop. A mirror pane was inside, crisscrossed with copper wires, which could be powered at the touch of a button.

"Remember who you are, Edgar," I said, turning the mirror to face the darkness.

A woman appeared in the mirror—or the decayed corpse of one, the eye sockets empty, the face crumbling to reveal bone beneath, the hair like dried straw.

"Is that Bloody Mary?" Michael whispered. "What my sister saw in her mirror?"

The darkness took the form of the reflection.

"Edgar Barrington," I said, "We demand that you show yourself."

"I've been here all along," said a low voice. It raised the hair on the back of my neck, because it came from a place no voice should have been—directly behind me.

Keeping the mirror where it was, I turned back to see Mr. Gray in his crisp old-fashioned suit, regarding me with his dark eyes. He gave a gentle smile. I could feel the cold radiating from him, even as the fires in the basement grew.

"I would not miss this," he said, filling the air with frost as he walked past me, approaching the entity in its decayed-woman shape. He didn't go too far, I noted, hanging back from the grave dirt on the floor and the dust lingering in the air.

"You're Edgar?" I asked. "Not Joseph?" It looked like I'd identified the wrong twin.

"You should know," he said. "You've been calling my name."

"Wait a minute," Stacey said. "You're Edgar. The one who

killed the children?"

Edgar gave her an angry look, and a butcher knife appeared in his hand.

"Not that we have to talk about that now," Stacey added quickly. She pointed her flashlight at the decayed crone. "If Edgar is Mr. Gray, then who is...?"

"Rebecca Barrington," I said. "Is that right?"

The old crone straightened up, and in a blink she was a beautiful young woman in a light gray dress with puffy sleeves and a sash at the midsection. She appeared all in tones of gray, like Edgar.

Edgar tremored at the sight of her, seeming to grow younger, his frenetic energy palpable in the air.

"Rebecca was the boogeyman?" Stacey asked.

"It was you," I said to the apparition. "You had Edgar kill your husband and children. You wanted to be free of them."

"I killed my husband myself," she said, her voice the same low hiss I'd heard from the fearfeeder before, when it had run away from me the previous night.

"The black widow spiders," I said, suddenly understanding. "It's your energy that attracts them."

She looked at me, her pretty face proud and haughty.

"And you had Edgar kill your children," I said, looking at him. "He did it...because he loved you?"

"That one knows nothing about love," Rebecca said with a smirk, her eyes turning black again for a moment as she said *love*. "He only wanted to be his brother. Successful and popular like his brother, instead of deranged and useless like himself. He coveted his brother's house, his brother's wife—"

"You promised to marry me," Edgar said. "You betrayed me."

"And what will you do about it?" she asked.

Edgar looked down at the floor, covered with his own grave earth between himself and Rebecca.

She gave a hollow laugh. "I am protected against you, even if you wished to harm me. But you could never wish that, could you, Edgar?"

He still hesitated, the butcher knife in his hand.

"Kill *them*, Edgar." She pointed right at me. "Kill all of them for me. And then I may accept your affections."

The ghost of Edgar turned to me, a hard glint in his eye. Michael tried to grab him, but the apparition became insubstantial.

Michael stumbled through, then stood between me and the child-killer's ghost.

"*Now,*" Rebecca urged, her beautiful face flickering, revealing glimpses of her skull beneath her skin.

Edgar turned toward her...then advanced, placing one foot directly on the scattered earth, then the next.

She frowned, and it was a deeper frown than would be possible on a flesh-and-blood human face.

I noticed she stood in a clear spot, surrounded by the spilled earth, and hadn't moved much from there since she'd first appeared to me as Anton Clay. The dirt on the floor wasn't taken from her grave, but it was taken from the family plot where she was buried. I wondered if that made her want to avoid it, too.

Edgar took another step. His form decayed rapidly as he moved toward Rebecca's ghost. His flesh seemed to dry and crumble, and his clothes began to rot, revealing bone underneath.

Still he walked toward her across the dirt of his own grave. Halfway there, he fell to his knees, his apparition falling apart as if catching up to the actual condition of his body over in the old cemetery. The soles of his shoes split open, showing bony remnants of feet within.

Rebecca hissed, stepping back as Edgar's corpse-like ghost continued crawling toward her. He let out bone-shuddering grunts and groans, and moved slowly, as though it were causing him great pain but he was forcing himself to continue onward. His face was little more than blots of gray flesh clinging to his skull. Veins of rust spread across the butcher knife.

"Stop him." Rebecca looked around at us, all of us staring in a kind of shock as the ghostly drama unfolded. "Someone *must* stop him."

"I don't think we will," Stacey said.

Rebecca screamed, her form flickering as if she wanted to escape but couldn't.

Edgar collapsed to the soil, no longer able to support himself on his hands and knees. He dragged himself forward, his form no more than rags and crumbling bones now, his butcher knife turned entirely to rust. He gave one last groan and stopped cold, lying facedown in the dirt. Then only disconnected bone fragments remained, half-sunken into the soil.

Rebecca laughed, and she looked healthier somehow—less grayscale, a little more color, her cheeks flushed.

"Who else wants to try?" she asked, smiling around at the rest of us, her teeth just a tad sharper than before. "You think you know who I am, but you know nothing of *what* I am, of the old things below us, the gifts they have given me...the horrors they have shown me..."

"You don't belong here," I said. "You need to cross to the other side."

"This is my home," she said. "I belong nowhere else."

I'd chosen to confront the fearfeeder with its true identity in hopes of reaching the man inside the monster—or the woman inside, as it turned out—and encouraging the spirit to move on. It didn't sound like that was going to happen tonight.

I stepped closer to Rebecca, holding up the mirror so she would have to face her own reflection.

She hissed at me, the sound purely animal, making me think of hissing cockroaches I'd seen on TV once.

"Look at yourself," I said. "See who you really are."

Then I pressed the button to activate the electromagnetic grid. It gave off a slight hum, and I could feel the energy buzzing in the air around me.

"You wish me to admire my own beauty?" Rebecca asked with a sour smile.

I held the mirror a bit longer, but she did not react at all. Calvin had been right—this mirror trap was not effective against non-catoptric ghosts.

"Uh, never mind," I mumbled, putting it aside. "Stacey, grab the broom." I gestured to the row of washing machines. In a gap between the last machine and the wall sat a push broom, dust pan, and a yellow mop bucket, all of them dusty and hung with spider webs.

Stacey nodded and jogged past me to fetch it. I kept my eyes on Rebecca's ghost while Stacey handed me the broom.

Then I began to sweep the scattered earth toward Rebecca, banking it up one side and then the other, moving the barrier closer in around her. She backed toward the charred door behind her.

"Come a little closer," she said, holding out her hand as if to grab me. "Just one step."

Not being a total sucker, I held back. When I'd banked up the dirt as close to her as I dared, I raised the broom like a battering ram and charged at her.

Rebecca shrieked and dodged aside as best she could, but she wasn't my target.

The wide wooden head of the push broom slammed into the charred door behind her, knocking it open to reveal the darkness of the furnace room. She snarled and grabbed for my broom as I pulled it back, but she didn't move fast enough.

My idea was to keep sweeping the dirt toward her, driving her back into the well. Then I would surround the mouth of the well with her grave earth to keep her trapped inside until we could seal it tight. It wasn't a perfect or satisfying solution, but it was all I had. We'd failed to make her move on, and the experimental mirror trap had failed, too.

"Stay back," Rebecca hissed.

"You've been haunting this neighborhood for so many years," I said. "Terrorizing and killing children. Do you drag them down into the well with you? Is the bottom of the shaft littered with their bones?"

"Leave us alone," Rebecca said, and it was as though something else spoke through her, something plural, with many voices. "We will kill everything you love."

"That's sweet," I said, sweeping more earth toward her.

"Drop your broom, little witch," Rebecca said.

"Careful, Ellie," Calvin warned.

"I can handle her," I said. My words brought a sneer to her lips.

"Someone's coming," Jacob told us. His eyes were closed.

Above us, the door at the top of the stairs blew open, bringing in a flood of light from upstairs. A warm wind swept down the stairs, snuffing out fires as it swept through the room.

"You can't," Rebecca said, whispering to the wind as it approached her, blowing out the rest of the fires and churning up grave dust from the floor.

"Who's here, Jacob?" I asked.

"The man who guards the children," Jacob said, finally opening his eyes. I looked at Alicia.

"Gerard?" Alicia whispered, watching the swirling dust in the mysterious wind.

"No!" Rebecca screamed, holding up her arms and inching back toward the charred and broken door to the furnace room. "Make him go away!"

"I don't see anything," Stacey said.

The mysterious wind struck the low wall of earth I'd heaped up. I staggered back and out of the way as the dirt rose into a dark whirlwind, obscuring my view of Rebecca Barrington. I thought I could hear her screaming through the whooshing roar of the spinning air. My hair blew every which way across my face.

"What's happening?" Michael had to shout at me so the wind didn't swallow his voice. He pulled my close, protectively.

I just shook my head and shrugged in response: *I have no idea.*

The wind slowed, dropping into low eddies on the floor. As the churning dirt sank in the air, I saw Rebecca again, encrusted in earth but still standing. She even seemed taller, until I realized she stood on top of a mound of collected soil.

Rebecca grinned at me, a vicious look on her pretty face. I took that as a bad sign.

"That Negro ghost has been pestering me," Rebecca said. "Ever since that slave family moved into this house."

"Excuse me?" Alicia said.

"Yeah, hey, rude," Stacey added.

"You cannot kill me," Rebecca boasted.

"We don't have to," I said. "You're already dead."

Something groaned beneath the floor. A pair of skeletal arms, wrapped in black rags and the shriveled remnants of old flesh, emerged from the heap of soil and grabbed Rebecca by the legs, its sharp fingers hooking deep into her ephemeral clothes and skin.

She screamed as the arms pulled her down. She dropped waist-deep into the earth, as though the dirt were several feet deep instead of just a few inches.

The head and shoulders of a corpse emerged, staring up at her. Enough of his face remained that I could recognize Edgar, his face decayed in such a way that it had a permanent deep sneer on the left side.

His hands moved up to Rebecca's throat.

"No!" she screamed. "Not with you!"

"Now we shall be wed," Edgar's voice whispered between his crumbling jaws.

Then he sank back into the soil, pulling her down with him.

Rebecca shrieked and thrashed, sending up dust as she disappeared into the earth, but she was already growing pale and insubstantial. Her final scream sounded distant. As her fading head descended into the dirt, she gave me a final look of pure hatred.

Then she was gone. A low mist clung to the heap of earth, crawling among the pebbles and flakes of red dirt.

"Stacey, grab the trap," I whispered. "We need to sweep this up before one of them leaks out. I don't trust either of those ghosts."

Stacey hurried to remove the small trap from the stamper. It was still half-filled with earth, and three candles were mounted above them. She blew the candles out, removing them from the trap and dropping them to the basement floor as she walked over to me.

"I'll bandage you up," Michael told me. "After I spend an hour picking the glass out of your skin. Come on." He reached for me, but I pulled back.

"Not until we're squared away down here," I said.

Stacey and I knelt on the floor, collecting the dirt from Edgar's grave, which now held both Edgar and Rebecca, together at last, to remain that way for centuries or more if the trap lay undisturbed. Now it was the boogeywoman's turn to suffer her own worst nightmare, being trapped with her brother-in-law, the man whose advances she'd spurned with contempt, after he'd done the dirty work of murdering her poor children for her. The kids had spent their short lives unwanted and unloved.

I saw Calvin watching us silently, his face as expressionless as stone.

"How are you feeling?" I asked him.

He nodded slightly.

"We finally got him," I said. "I mean, her."

"*You* got her," Calvin said.

"We all did," I said. "We defeated her by standing together."

"You and Stacey did a fine job. You always do." He cleared his throat. "I don't think you need me anymore. This investigation proves it. You succeeded where I failed."

"Only because we learned from last time," I said, feeling concerned. He seemed melancholy, not a normal state for him.

"I've trained you as best I can, Ellie," he said. "Maybe it's about time for me to pack it in."

"And do what?" I asked. I noticed Alicia and Jacob speaking quietly to each other across the room.

"Retire. Move. Sit at the beach."

"We're *near* the beach. Get a place on one of the coastal islands. That would be healthy," I said. I tried to sound calm, but his words panicked me.

"I have family in Florida," he said.

I didn't know what to say to that, so I took the trap, now brimming with soil, over to the stamper. I placed the lid on the trap, then brought the pneumatic arm down for good measure, sealing the two murderous ghosts inside.

"Gerard?" Alicia gasped. She was staring upward at something I couldn't see. Or someone, I supposed, standing just in front of her. She raised one hand and seemed to caress the empty air. She nodded a little, as if listening, and tears crept out of her eyes and down her cheeks.

The rest of us fell silent. Michael was close to me, clearly impatient to do something about my injuries.

I wondered what Alicia was seeing and hearing. She looked entranced.

Finally, she whispered, "I love you, too, baby." Her hand fell back to her side, and she looked down at the floor, crying softly to herself.

I walked over to hug her, and she embraced me.

"He said he'll always watch over us," Alicia whispered, low enough that only I could hear her words. "He said he'll be waiting for me. He said...love is the only thing that lasts forever."

"You big sweetie," Stacey said, punching Jacob in the arm. "You helped her talk to her husband one last time."

"All I did was warn her that he was coming," Jacob said. "He asked me to do that."

"I can't believe Rebecca was the boogeyman the whole time," Stacey said. "And Edgar was just hanging around, waiting for his next chance with her."

"She would've gotten away with it, too, if it weren't for us meddling kids," Jacob said. Stacey snickered and leaned against him, and he placed an arm around her.

"Thank you," Alicia said, stepping back from me. "All of you. I have to...go sit down." She turned and started up the stairs, swaying uneasily on her feet as if she'd just suffered a major shock. I supposed she had.

"We still have to do something about that old well," Jacob said.

"I've called a specialist," Calvin said. He still had that sad look as he stared at the blackened remains of the furnace room door, clinging to the door frame by a couple of hinges. The doorknob lay on the floor amid charred bits of wood.

"Let's go," Michael said. "You don't want twenty infections all over your hands and face."

"Wait," I said. "Calvin—"

"Go with him," Calvin said, finally looking at me. He wore a small, almost sad smile. "You need someone to care for you."

I nodded. I think he was talking about more than my immediate injuries.

Michael led me upstairs to deal with my gory, bloody face, while the rest of my team got to work breaking down cameras and removing our gear from the scene.

Chapter Twenty-One

"Are we there yet?" Stacey asked as we trudged up the remnants of the steep trail, which I located mostly by memory. Behind us lay a steep, tree-lined cliff overlooking a steep drop to the valley below. We'd awoken before dawn and driven a long, long six hours, from Savannah on the eastern coast of the state to the nearly impassable ridges of the western Appalachians. We'd taken down the fearfeeder two nights earlier, and taken a day to rest before the journey to bury the two dangerous ghosts.

"I thought you'd enjoy a hike in the mountains," I said. Stacey was the outdoorsy type, but I was more the air-conditiony type.

"I'm just excited to see this graveyard for monsters." Since Stacey was such an experienced hiker, I was letting her carry the ghost trap full of soil and spirits in her backpack.

I led the way into the dense woods, remote from any settled area. Calvin had picked the site because it was likely to be remote forever, the geography of the ridge and valley region making the construction of roads and bridges difficult and expensive. Few people had ever lived in the area.

Geography wasn't the only reason, though.

Wielding a small machete, I hacked through thick, thorny brambles, slowly advancing until I reached an overgrown wall. It wasn't much higher than my hips, but it was solid, built of hard local rocks crudely cut to fit together. Poison oak and thorny vines hid most of it.

"So this is like your own private hell," Stacey said. "For ghosts who can't be trusted."

"Yep." I hacked a clear space along the top where we could climb over without getting our clothes tangled in thorns.

The other side looked, at first, like just another shady patch of mountain forest, but the trees were thinner here, and the place was littered with overgrown rocks and boulders, thick with moss and poison ivy.

The air was about twenty degrees colder on this side of the wall.

"Okay, this is different," Stacey whispered. "I'm guessing these overgrown rocks are grave markers?"

"They are," I said. "They're just rocks, not carved headstones. If you scrape the plants off any of them, you'll find names inscribed."

I led her deeper into the small old graveyard. Though it was around noon, it was so dark under the canopy that I pulled my flashlight and pointed it into the shadows ahead. "See the old church?"

"Oh, yeah." Stacey stared at the ruins ahead—the uneven rock foundation, the collapsing wooden walls.

"That was the church of Reverend Mordecai Blake about a hundred years ago," I said. "Raw mountain religion—snake handling, faith healing, speaking in tongues. The church was basically a cult that included several families. Blake took things to extremes. Anyone who questioned his teachings, disobeyed him, angered him, or tried to leave the church was put into the Judgment Box."

"That sounds pleasant," Stacey said, warily approaching the ruins.

"Imagine a coffin with air holes in the side and a padlock on top," I said. "Sinners were put inside with half a dozen venomous rattlesnakes. Supposedly this left it up to God's judgment whether the person should live or die. Several people didn't, including children."

"That's awful," Stacey whispered.

"State investigators finally came to arrest him, but he refused to go with them. The preacher locked himself in the church and let his snakes bite him to death rather than go to jail. His ghost is still here, and the ghosts of some of his loyal followers. You do not want to be in this graveyard after sunset."

"I don't really want to be here now," Stacey said. She crossed her arms, shivering a little. I felt the same way. An atmosphere of dread permeated the entire place.

"Well, let's get digging." I shrugged off my backpack and removed the short spade hung from a loop, then pulled on a pair of gardening gloves. Stacey did the same. I showed her a row of tiny rock-heaps near one wall of the old graveyard. "This is where we've buried the other nasties. We mark them with little cairns so we don't accidentally dig them up..." I picked a spot, hacked away some weeds and brambles, and plunged the head of the spade into the earth.

"So...what happens when the battery in the trap dies?" she asked.

"The lead glass should keep the ghosts inside. If they do escape, they'll still be stuck in this graveyard, prisoners of the dead preacher and his followers."

"So Reverend Blake is like our prison warden," Stacey said.

"Basically. We're using him. He doesn't know he's helping us— it's not like he signed up for it or we discussed it with him—but he's a strong ghost who rules this graveyard. It's not as pleasant as those places where we release non-violent ghosts, like the one over in Goodwell." Goodwell, several hours south of us, was a ghost town with a nice, strong brick wall around its cemetery. We use it as a kind of wildlife preserve for nuisance ghosts—they're able to wander free among the old trees there, instead of being buried inside their traps.

Strange sounds interrupted us while we dug, making us look around. Snapping twigs, as if someone were walking toward us. Rustling leaves, as though a wind were blowing on the calm day. Whenever we looked towards the sounds, they stopped. Once I heard a hiss, only to see a bobcat watching us from the shadows of the thick undergrowth with its big yellow eyes. It scurried out of sight.

Finally, we had dug down a few feet into the dark, rocky earth. I took the cylindrical trap from Stacey's backpack and dropped it into the hole.

"It feels like we should say something," Stacey said.

"Like a eulogy?" I asked. She nodded. "Okay. Dearly beloved, we are gathered here today to imprison the spirits of two awful human beings. Edgar Barrington killed his sister-in-law Rebecca's children because she asked him to do it. Rebecca murdered her own husband, and terrorized and killed children for a hundred and fifty years after she died, feeding on their fear and transforming into even more of a monster than she was in life. Dear Lord, please keep them trapped here so they can never harm anyone else again."

"Amen," Stacey said, and I threw the first heap of dirt onto the trap.

We buried it quickly, then heaped a few handfuls of stones on top to mark the spot. I could feel something watching me from the darkness of the collapsed church, but I saw nothing there.

"Let's get going," I said.

"How are your hands?" Stacey asked, watching me remove my gloves. Little beads of blood had welled up from the larger scratches.

"Michael took out the glass pieces from my face and hands with tweezers," I said. "I still checked with the doctor yesterday. I've just been rubbing calendula cream on all the scratches and hoping they don't scar."

"Jacob was happy that he finally got out of a case without having his face totally mangled," Stacey said, while we walked back toward the low rock wall. "I guess it was just your turn."

"Then it'll be your turn next time," I said.

A long, low groan echoed across the cemetery. We looked back and didn't see anyone. We looked at each other, and then we scrambled over the wall and down the steep trail as fast as we dared.

Chapter Twenty-Two

It was a couple of hours after sunset, and I was back in the unnaturally cold furnace room, looking into the dark well under the house.

I wasn't alone. Michael stood on the other side of the well from me, and in between us stood a friend of Calvin's, a man with thin gray hair and a Rudolph-red nose, dressed in jeans and a khaki shirt.

Michael had met us on the first floor—though fit and spry, Lachlan was seventy-one years old, and there had been no reason to make him climb all those stairs to Michael's apartment.

"Michael, this is Dr. James Lachlan," I'd said. "He's a Jesuit—"

"—*was* a Jesuit," Lachlan interrupted with a smile. "The Vatican had me removed years ago. I had trouble waiting for the long, bureaucratic chain of permission before performing major exorcisms. And a few other restricted rites."

"Sorry to hear that," Michael said, shaking his hand. Michael seemed surprised by Lachlan's thick Australian accent.

"It's well in the past. I didn't want you mistaking me for a priest and confessing your sins to me by accident."

Michael laughed and led us toward the basement door.

"Michael's a good name, then," Lachlan said. "We'll be calling on your namesake for assistance. Let's hope he doesn't grow confused and think I'm talking to you instead."

"My namesake?" Michael started down the steps, looking back at us. Lachlan followed, then me.

"The archangel." Lachlan sounded a little bemused. "You're unaware you were named for God's champion demon-smiter?"

"I didn't even know they had a championship for that," Michael said. The former priest gave him a chuckle.

"Let's see the trouble spot," Lachlan said. He held a black case in one hand, which looked like the sort of things doctors used to carry back when they made house calls. He'd refused to let Michael or me carry it for him. Michael and I both carried high-powered tactical flashlights instead. Michael had already brought a few things down here while waiting for our arrival.

We'd opened the charred remnants of the door and stepped inside. The room was freezing, and the sound of distant rushing wind echoed up from the well.

I watched Lachlan as he looked deep into the darkness below, and I wondered what he was thinking. In the Church, he'd been a teacher at Jesuit colleges as well as a demonologist and exorcist. Now defrocked, he drifted from one secular university to the next, teaching ancient Middle Eastern history and languages. He was currently at the University of Georgia, only a few hours away.

"Here's what happens next." Lachlan placed his doctor's bag into Michael's hands and unzipped it, letting Michael hold it like a butler or servant. "I will exorcise this to the best of my ability. It's important that you stay back, and do not look into the well while I work. The moment I tell you to seal it, do so." He looked at Michael, who nodded.

Lachlan directed me to light a few white candles he'd brought, as well as a brass censer loaded with frankincense. The smoke flavored the air with a citrusy, woody odor. I placed the candles around the floor, trying not to show my distaste for the presence of open flames.

The ex-priest waved the censor above the well, chanting in Latin.

When he was done, he handed that to me, and I set it aside while he sprinkled salt into the well, chanting louder, his voice echoing back from below. More voices seemed to accompany it.

Lachlan tossed more salt into the well, and I heard churning, hissing voices down inside it.

Suddenly we appeared to stand on a crumbling brick ledge sloping toward a black abyss. Thick, cold darkness stretched as far as I could see. The voices screamed, howled, shouted in languages I didn't understand.

I felt off-balance, and my feet slid down a few inches toward the bottomless dark. Michael grabbed my arm to steady me.

Lachlan continued the rite, and the voices grew into a deafening wall of howls and tortured cries. I couldn't understand the words, but I sensed curses and elaborate blasphemies in the voices. My mind filled with visions of rotten faces, their eyes dark and hollow, their jaws stretched wide with screams, their hands cold and grasping. I felt dizzy and sick to my stomach, and I wanted to collapse.

Then it was over, and we were in the basement again, Michael still steadying me. Lachlan nodded to him, and I told him to go ahead.

Michael picked up the things he'd already stashed here—a drill, a steel plate big enough to completely cover the well, and a handful of long steel screws. Lead coated the underside of the square.

He laid it on top of the dark opening, then he went to work. It took quite a while for him to drill through steel and brick to anchor the sheet of metal in place. He was absorbed into the task, saying nothing, his hands moving with strength and intelligence. Plastic goggles shielded his eyes, and Lachlan and I remained several feet away to avoid sparks and flying bits of brick.

"Is that it?" I asked Lachlan.

"We've completed the full rite," he said. "What were you expecting? Seven-headed dragons rising from the depths to bring on the apocalypse?"

"Something like that, yeah." I felt skeptical about whether this had really been effective, and how long it would hold. Jacob had mentioned holy men and seers from centuries and millennia past who had tried in their own ways to seal the well, and whose remnant ghosts worked, with limited success, to keep the darkness in the well contained and away from the living. Later generations had always found their way back to this place, when enough time had passed and the legend of its evil had been forgotten.

Perhaps a hundred years from now, my ghost would be here among those ancient ones, trying to do the same work. I wasn't a medicine woman or a psychic, but at least I was stubborn.

As we left, I took a final look at the square of steel and lead bolted to the floor. The room already felt warmer, and my Mel Meter showed lower readings than the basement ever had before. The black hole—call it a dark psychic vortex, a ghost portal, or a minor doorway to hell—seemed closed for now. My job was as done as it could be, but I was still unsettled about it.

Outside, Lachlan climbed into the passenger seat of the van, waving off my attempt to help him. Before I climbed inside, I turned back to Michael.

"So that takes care of it?" he asked, reaching for me.

"Let me know if it doesn't." I let him draw me closer.

He didn't reply, but gave me another long, fantastic kiss on the lips. I felt myself grow very warm against him.

"Careful, there's a priest watching," I whispered when we were done.

"An ex-priest. And he's not watching."

"He's an ex-priest who probably wants to get to his hotel right away," I said. I traced my fingers along Michael's upper arm. "Thanks for all your help."

"It was my house, too. So I should thank you."

I glanced at the van. "I'd better go."

"Running away again?"

"As usual." I eased back from him, starting for the van.

"Listen," he said. "Saturday. This friend of mine from high school is in this really bad Cheap Trick cover band—"

"I love Cheap Trick."

"No, no, the music will be terrible. I was wondering if you'd endure the show with me anyway."

"How could I say no to a terrible cover band?" I smiled.

Michael stood on the sidewalk and watched as I drove away.

"He seems like a nice young man," Lachlan said from the passenger seat.

"He does."

"Appearances can be deceiving, of course. But not always." He looked out the window as we drove past crumbling old mansions, some of which had been terrorized over the years by the ghost of Rebecca Barrington.

We drove on through moonlit streets under the moss-hung canopy of oak limbs. Savannah's ghosts hid in every corner, behind every wrought-iron gate and marble column, stalking the gardens and dark streets, most of them invisible unless you knew how to look for them.

I wondered whether they had their own kind of community, and what they thought of us, the ghost trappers who removed spirits from their haunts. I doubted their opinion would be favorable.

I wondered about the future. Was Calvin serious about retiring and leaving things in my hands? I couldn't possibly be ready for that. Stacey was still much too green. So was I.

We'd faced our fears and come through alive. The illusion of Anton Clay had been almost too real, too intelligent compared to the other forms taken by the boogeyman. Maybe my parents' murderer really was inside me somehow, connected to me, following the course of my life from where his spirit remained anchored, on the overgrown empty lot where my childhood home had once stood. Calvin had declared Anton too dangerous to attempt trapping.

I knew I would need to confront him one day, somehow remove him from that patch of ground and make sure he never harmed anyone again. But not tonight.

I dropped Lachlan at a bed and breakfast on State Street a few minutes later. Then I blasted the stereo, summoning music to chase the ghosts from my mind.

THE END

From the author

Thanks so much for taking the time to read *The Crawling Darkness*. If you enjoyed it, I hope you'll consider leaving a review of this book (or the first one!) at the retailer of your choice or recommend it to someone else. Good reviews and word of mouth are the most important factors in helping other readers discover a book.

Terminal, the fourth book in the Ellie Jordan series, is already in the works. I hope you'll continue the adventure when that book releases in May 2015!

Sign up for my newsletter to hear about my new books as they come out. You'll immediately get a free ebook of short stories just for signing up. The direct link is http://eepurl.com/mizJH, or you can find it on my website.

If you'd like to get in touch with me, here are my links:

Website (www.jlbryanbooks.com)
Facebook (J. L. Bryan's Books)
Twitter (@jlbryanbooks)
Email (info@jlbryanbooks.com)

Thanks for reading!

60405905R00133

Made in the USA
Lexington, KY
05 February 2017